THE
SECRETS
ACT

ALISON WEATHERBY

2 Palmer Street, Frome, Somerset BA11 1DS
www.chickenhousebooks.com

Text © Alison Weatherby 2022

First published in Great Britain in 2022
Chicken House
2 Palmer Street
Frome, Somerset BA11 1DS
United Kingdom
www.chickenhousebooks.com

Chicken House/Scholastic Ireland, 89E Lagan Road, Dublin Industrial Estate,
Glasnevin, Dublin D11 HP5F, Republic of Ireland

Cover and interior design by Helen Crawford-White
Cover photo (girl) by Dmitriy Bilous/Trevillion Images
Cover photo (girl with bike) by Mark Owen/Trevillion Images
Cover photo (note) by Peter Greenway/Arcangel
Typeset by Dorchester Typesetting Group Ltd
Printed and bound in Great Britain by CPI Group (UK) Ltd, Croydon, CR0 4YY

A MESSAGE FROM CHICKEN HOUSE

Young women have always had to be extra smart – to get ahead, to be taken seriously, and to receive the recognition they deserve. It was even worse in wartime, despite the freedoms granted to women; Ellen and Pearl, our two teenaged code-cracking heroines, have to be especially clever. Can they decipher a grave spy threat in a race against time – all while untangling romantic feelings, friendship and loss? Let's hope so: the tide of war is turning and only they can help stop it. Alison Weatherby's fine debut has a wonderful period atmosphere – and timeless importance.

BARRY CUNNINGHAM
Publisher
Chicken House

For my strong, clever girls –
Sabine and Delphine

1

ELLEN

This was not at all what the letter had said would happen.

Ellen had been told to go to Bletchley in Buckinghamshire, which was not as easy as it sounded since all location signs and station names had been removed at the start of the war. Thanks to the kindness of a woman on the crowded third-class carriage, Ellen had managed to make it to the platform at Bletchley train station, where she stood waiting for someone from her new job to collect her. After the small crowd dispersed, Ellen paused in the rather large and cavernous building, silent except for the flap of a wayward pigeon, and tried to steady her nerves. When no one appeared to escort her, Ellen made her way outside, where the road was empty under the dimmed street lamps. Ellen could barely see the shape of her arm when she raised it to check her wristwatch. She had foolishly hoped there would be a shiny, warm car waiting with special headlamps, hiding her from any German bombers flying overhead. Instead, there was nothing but the rustle of wind through trees and the disconcerting shriek of an owl.

Ellen was uneasy, exhausted, and out of sandwiches. She had never taken such a long journey alone – her mother had accompanied her to the interview in London – and although she was certain this was the right location, everything else about it seemed wrong. Adjusting her white reflective armband, she remembered the newspaper her mother had packed; it was as if her mother had known Ellen would need every tool possible from the pamphlet on blackout safety. She sighed, annoyed at both her mother's uncanny preparedness and the situation, and unfolded the reflective *Cardiff Times*, adding yet another layer of visibility for anyone looking for her. When one travels clear across the country to start a mysterious job, one expects to be collected at the train station.

The letter of employment had arrived at her home only weeks after her initial interview in London. Over break-fast the next morning, her parents agreed it was her duty to serve the King like her brother. Her mum, smiling wistfully, made a nostalgic comment about life back in Oxfordshire. She told Ellen to embrace the chance to get out of Wales for good. 'I never wanted my English child-ren to end up with a common Welsh accent. This is the chance to shake it,' she'd remarked. They'd moved to a village outside Cardiff when Ellen was quite young – Wales was home to her – and she never understood her mother's constant pining for England. It had been the source of arguments between her parents for as long as Ellen could remember but, to her knowledge, her father had no intention of ever leaving his job at the bank to move back.

Ellen had not been given a choice to return to the University of Wales in Cardiff for her second year. Her father made it clear that the interview and employment had resulted as much from his connections as her intelligence. Because of his efforts, there was to be no questioning of her opportunity with the Foreign Office. Ellen appreciated his endeavours – being proactive was very unlike him. Besides, Ellen loved her father's warm smiles and general selflessness (which was required around her strict, rigid mother) and wanted to do right by him. Plus, this was a chance to finally prove to her mother she could navigate the world on her own.

But now, staring into the empty street, Ellen already felt homesick for the silliest things – the heavy quilt on her bed, the smell of her father's evening cigarette, the tin of biscuits always available to squelch late-night hunger pangs. She tried not to think of her hollow stomach or the way her eyes kept filling. The sounds of the empty, dark town made her nervous – every snapped twig or distant crack of a door slamming made her flinch. It felt like she was somewhere she should not be, which was a bad way to begin the next chapter of her new life.

The breeze kicked up, raising the hairs on the back of her neck. A faint noise in the distance caught her attention. Footsteps. Thuds getting louder, closer together. Frantically, Ellen looked for a place to hide, but felt daft as soon as she did. She had seen enough safety fliers to know not to walk around in the dark. How many people had died falling into holes or walking on to train tracks? Instead, Ellen stood firm with her suitcase close to her chest, ready to hurl it at whomever was heading in her direction.

Down the road, she spotted a very faint sliver of light, perhaps a torch rigged for use during the blackout. Ellen made herself very still, though her eyes scanned the road for an escape route, just in case.

'Sorry, sorry, sorry!' the girl's voice shouted as she ran full bore down the lane. In spite of her speed, the girl came to a halt quickly and with more grace than Ellen had expected. She cleared her throat and said, 'You are waiting for an escort, correct?'

'I, uh, yes. Someone is to collect me for Ble—'

'Shh!' the girl interrupted, waving the torch like she was trying to fend off monsters. 'There are ears all around. I know where you are heading. Follow me. You have your bags?'

4

Ellen nodded dumbly, then mumbled 'yes' when she realized the girl might not be able to see her nodding in the dark.

The girl strode purposefully down the narrow road. She did not even look back to see if Ellen was keeping up. Ellen marvelled at the girl, maybe as tall as her own shoulder, walking with such force and determination. She had short hair and wore a knee-length dress of some sort under a plain, boxy coat. In the light of day, Ellen would be able to complete a thorough analysis of the girl and their surroundings. At that point, she would have an almost completely accurate assessment of who the girl was, whether she was both short and young, and what her intentions were – a satisfying and calming process. Tonight, however, she was forced to rely on gut feelings. She didn't like that. Feelings were squishy, emotional, unrepeatable things that never made sense, and for a girl with a head for maths there was nothing worse.

Finally, the girl turned, slowing her pace only slightly, and pointed the muted torch at Ellen. 'Out with it,' she instructed. 'You want to ask something. I know you do. They always do.'

Ellen stopped, adjusted the grip on her suitcase and rubbed the ankle of one stockinged leg against the other. *They?* thought Ellen. *Who is they? Have I been lumped with 'they'?* 'You work at, er, for the Foreign Office?'

'I do,' the girl declared decisively.

5

'What do you do?' Ellen prodded. The more the girl talked, the more her accent became defined. She dropped some of her consonants, but not regularly, which could have meant she was from London. The careful manner with which she spoke made it sound like an accent she was trying to lose.

'I deliver *things*, usually, not people. The person tasked with your retrieval was ill. I had to end my evening plans early to collect you instead,' she said, turning down a narrower pathway. 'My name is Pearl, by the way.'

'Ellen,' Ellen called after her. 'Ellen Davies.'

'Well, Ellen Davies, let me give you a piece of advice. Do not ask too many questions about what people do. It takes most new recruits a while to learn that, but it will be drilled into you soon enough. It is better if you approach your employment with caution.'

'All right,' Ellen stammered. Meeting new people was always hard for her and she relied on the data from what Mother often said was 'endless questioning' to feel more at ease. Ellen sorted through the questions in her mind, prioritizing them. *Only ask the essential questions, the burning ones that are also appropriate*, Ellen's mother would say, *or people will get exhausted with you before they get a chance to know you. That is not how to make a friend.*

Pearl gestured with the torch as she walked, using it more like a prop than an instrument for visibility. She appeared familiar with the route, not needing the light to identify the dips in the road.

Ellen cleared her throat. 'Can I ask how long you have been at . . . there?'

'I suppose. But that is your last question. I have been here nearly since the beginning. My mother started working here in 1938 and I left school and started shortly after. It seems like ages with how much things have changed around here.'

Ellen blinked a few times. Pearl had been there for more than two years? Perhaps she would appear older in daylight, but in the dark, she had the height and appearance of a thirteen-year-old. Ellen had been told in her interview that most employees had already finished university, and therefore was surprised Pearl had not even finished secondary school, and, she assumed, had not attended university. All Ellen's tutors and parents' friends had made such a fuss last year when she was the youngest at the University of Wales at sixteen, and she had always felt so strange about the attention. Praise about her exams and papers was different – the work deserved accolades. Being singled out for her age was another thing. Looking at Pearl's purposeful stride, though, Ellen realized this girl didn't have the same sort of problem with confidence, regardless of her age. Or if she did, she kept it well hidden.

'Well, I shall not ask anything else,' Ellen said. 'I wouldn't want to get anyone in trouble.'

7

'Appreciated. Plus, with an accent like that – Welsh, correct? – it's best to keep quiet for a while. People judge the silliest things here. I should know,' Pearl added a bit mysteriously. 'Besides, we should not dawdle. It is not smart to be out at night.'

Within only a few moments they were at a large gate. The guard waved Pearl through with a smile. He peppered Ellen with a dozen questions and she nervously produced her letter. The guard went inside his little brick house and they watched through the window as he flipped through a stack of papers for what seemed like ages. Finally, he emerged and welcomed Ellen to the Park. He told Pearl to deliver her to the mansion. Pearl took Ellen's elbow and steered her quickly down the path.

'Hold on,' Ellen said as a massive brick building with dozens of arches and bay windows came into view. The one lamp post outside the mansion was dark, but she could still make out several chimneys and contrasting rooflines against the eerily bright grey sky. Pearl kept walking towards the building, but Ellen could not budge from her spot.

It was not easy, making that first step. All the answers, all her hopes, were inside that building. An escape from the constant bickering of her parents over the uncomfortable roast dinners that had become mostly potatoes since David left; a chance to find people like her. If, as they said in her interview, the Foreign Office was truly recruiting the best of the best from the top universities, Ellen would find keen friendships with like-minded recruits. Also, this job would enable her to use her exceptional intelligence to directly help with the war effort. Of course, the interviewers did not say how exactly, but Ellen had ideas. She knew this was a big moment and in spite of the way her stomach sank when she saw that awful-looking building, Ellen wanted to take it all in. Someday, she told herself as she swallowed down her apprehension and excitement, she would remember this as the moment before she changed the world.

'Hurry up!' Pearl called. 'The war is not going to win itself.'

Reluctantly, Ellen followed her through the ornate wooden double doors of Bletchley Park, which contained all the secrets of what her life was going to become.

2

ELLEN

Pearl sighed 'Follow me,' and Ellen did, passing through heavy wooden doors into a richly panelled hall. Beyond the hall was a bustling room filled with a sea of women typing at side-by-side desks. The girls lurked in the doorway until a woman in a forest-green wool jacket showed them to a hard bench in the vestibule. In contrast to the room with the typewriters, the vestibule was empty, draughty and silent. Ellen's stomach rumbled loudly.

'Someone will attend to you shortly,' the woman assured her. Then she added, to Pearl, 'Wait with her until then.'

Pearl grumbled a bit in response and flopped on to the bench, her shoulders slumped in her ill-fitting wool coat. Ellen wondered if Pearl's lack of respect meant a major authority figure, her father perhaps, was no longer around.

In the dimly lit room, Ellen took a good look at Pearl and rounded out her assessment. She started from the top and worked her way down: hair, eyes, mouth, build, hands (far more important than most thought). Then she pulled together anything audible from an accent or word choice: birthplace, education, employment. It was a fairly reliable system for forming a person and usually was rather accurate. She had started doing this analysis her first year at university when forced to interact with new people almost every day. Having a system, made these interactions more tolerable, not to mention reliable and efficient.

Pearl's short, wavy hair was barely held under control by a limp navy slide. Her small, broad nose appeared to have been almost squashed on to her face between her wide brown eyes. Pearl appeared young at first, and not simply because she was short; her face and limbs were stocky, just on the verge of plump, like they needed a good stretch. But on balance, Ellen placed Pearl closer to her own age, seventeen. She wore no make-up or jewellery, and under the too-big coat wore a plain but smart green dress and bulky cardigan. The clothes were well-worn and mended, and seemed oddly fancy for work attire, but Ellen recalled Pearl's statement about interrupted evening plans.

'Sorry you have to stay with me and had to abandon your previous engagement,' Ellen said meekly, hoping that the girl did not resent her already. She was always messing things up, it seemed. People were never as orderly and direct as numbers.

'No need to apologize,' Pearl mumbled. 'It was over anyway. That bit is hardly your fault.'

Pearl sat back and pulled a folded paper and a pencil nub from under her wool cardigan. A dried spring of lavender fell from her pocket and she sniffed it absently before tucking it back in its place. She flattened the paper – a cryptogram from the *Daily Telegraph* – across her thighs. Ellen could not help but smile.

Every morning in Cardiff, her father would toss the day's puzzle her way with a glint in his eye and a silent challenge. Ellen would work through as many anagrams, riddles and linguistic acrobatics as she could before her mother pulled the cold teapot from the table and ordered everyone to leave so she could clean the dishes. Ellen could not help but look over Pearl's hunched shoulder. It was hard to sit next to a puzzle and not peek.

'Eight across is "cutter",' she said.

'Huh?'

'"*A boat that should suit anyone.*" It is called a cutter. A type of sailboat. But also a tailor cuts fabric, like for suits and such,' Ellen explained, proud. She loved explaining puzzles and, even more, she loved the grateful, thankful looks her father gave her when she told him how she got to an answer. Pearl, on the other hand, was not nearly as receptive.

'I did not ask for help,' she snapped.

Ellen nodded, shrinking back into the hard-backed bench, wishing she could disappear into the rich, ornate wood.

'I, uh . . .' Ellen started, knowing full well she had insulted Pearl. She remembered Mum's annoying coaching and her father's gentle guidance, telling her to be more understanding, more thoughtful, and to apologize when she made people bristle. 'I'm sorry. I did not mean anything by it. I adore a good puzzle.'

Pearl sighed and looked up. 'No, it's all right. Your answer's correct, you know.' She paused. 'Thank you, I suppose.'

Ellen fidgeted a bit, with a combination of pride and unease. Back home, she had known how to deal with the loneliness, her peers shunning her at university for being more cerebral than sociable. But here, well, she was not sure what to expect. In theory, these people would understand her. At least, that was the hope.

'How did you work it out?' Pearl asked, leaning closer to Ellen.

'I'm from Wales, and we know our boats there.' Ellen smiled in what she hoped was a welcoming manner. 'I used to help my father with the crosswords in the paper. Almost every morning.'

'Ah,' Pearl said, nodding. 'My father's dead. I'll look for you in the canteen if I need help with my crosswords again.'

As Ellen considered this, another woman in severe black glasses appeared.

'Ellen Davies, please come with me. There are some papers you'll need to attend to immediately. You can return in the morning to be orientated.'

'I guess this is goodnight,' Pearl said, giving her a little limp salute before turning and walking down the hall.

The woman took Ellen to an empty desk in the middle of the noisy typewriter room and handed her a document on stiff white paper.

'I will need you to sign this now, before anything else,' she said.

Ellen looked at the lengthy document: the Official Secrets Act. Skimming through it, Ellen felt her breath catch as she read:

```
s/he commits the act of spying if s/he
communicates to any other person any
secret, which is calculated to be or
might be or is intended to be directly
or indirectly useful to an enemy.
```

The woman tapped her fingers on the desk impatiently while Ellen read the line again. She swallowed down the fear in her chest and blinked at the words on the paper, which swam in front of her like fast-moving moths at a light bulb. Finally, Ellen signed, feeling like she'd missed a chance to have a monumental moment. As soon as the 'i' in her last name was dotted, the woman whisked the paper away.

'There is a driver waiting for you outside the front gate. He'll take you to your billet. You are expected back here by eight in the morning. Everything else will be sorted then.'

Ellen followed the burgundy carpet down the hall to a rather grand staircase she had somehow missed on the way in – the front entrance was directly opposite. She was relieved to see a black car waiting just outside. Once she settled into the warm car, she tried not to fall asleep as they drove. After they passed a sentry gate, they went by rows of houses that grew further apart the longer they travelled. When the road curved and hedges practically touched the side of the car as they barrelled down the road, Ellen realized she would never be able to navigate back in the morning.

After what seemed like both no time at all and for ever, they pulled up to a tall, narrow farmhouse with a falling-down garden fence and tiny windows. Stupidly, Ellen had assumed everyone lived under better conditions in England, but this was nearly identical to the old, worn farmhouses dotting the Welsh countryside like stony white sheep. A tired-looking woman, who introduced herself as Mrs Waverly, held a baby in her arms as she showed Ellen to a draughty attic bedroom. She spoke in hushed tones, with occasional glances towards the sleeping baby. Ellen did not have the energy to do a full evaluation.

Her initial assessment was that, aside from being tired, Mrs Waverly was young, but her face was etched with lines that indicated either great happiness or great sorrow. Or both. Ellen rubbed her eyes with the heel of her hand, exhausted enough to leave the rest of her ritual until tomorrow.

After hearing the long list of house rules and shutting the door to her grim, draughty room, Ellen thought, as she drifted off to sleep under the home-made quilt, that this would be the time when the heroine in the book cried from all the day's events. If, unlike Ellen, the heroine cried over such things.

Ellen woke to the sound of the baby crying. She was groggy and chilly, but optimistic. A chest of drawers was wedged under the sloped ceiling opposite the bed. There was a tiny window with what looked like tea towels for curtains and a rod in the eaves where she suspected she was meant to hang her clothing. Ellen dressed in her wool skirt and her soft, lemon-yellow jumper from Howells department store. She was lacing up her brown Oxfords when she heard a noise in the stairway. When she opened the door, Mr Waverly stood at the bottom of the stairs, leaning on a cane. His hair was bleached a pale blond by the sun and his face was a lovely bronze. Aside from the cane, Mrs Waverly's husband did not appear to be much older than the boys in Ellen's classes at university. Instead of

16

wishing her good morning, Mr Waverly held out a package wrapped in brown paper and motioned for her to follow.

'Breakfast,' he grunted once they were outside in the garden. 'Best be on our way and give those two a chance to sleep. Besides, I was told to deliver you to the front gate no later than half seven.'

Ellen nodded, not wanting to contradict him. She followed his lanky frame to the rusty red-and-black farming truck, noting how carefully mended his trousers were.

Ellen hopped on to the worn seat beside Mr Waverly, placing the salty-smelling, warm package on her lap. She was not entirely sure when she was meant to consume it but reckoned eating in his vehicle would be rude. Flipping around in the seat, she stared through the back window at the house, now partly obscured by trees. It was a simple stone cottage, two chimneys popping off either side, a few shuttered windows and one dormer at the top – her attic room. It was modest, but solid.

'Do you approve?' the farmer asked. His voice was gravelly and rough, but his accent was polished, as if at some point he had owned more than frayed linen shirts. She noted his long fingers, nails free of dirt, wrapped around the steering wheel. He had perhaps been thrust into the business by duty or familial obligation. Maybe because of the war. Ellen smiled, feeling the facts click together in her brain like gears in a machine. Everything was clearer in the daylight.

'The house is lovely,' she said. The Waverlys were not as financially well-to-do as her parents, but they had pride, so Ellen tried to be respectful. She knew her mother would've looked down her bony, sloping nose at the Waverlys because of their class.

Mr Waverly grunted and remained silent for the rest of the journey. Ellen watched fields of cattle and sheep, wheat and grain speed by and noted landmarks – trees, gates, crossroads – so she would be able to get herself back at the end of the day. More houses appeared – brick terraces and spacious semi-detached homes – indicating they were getting closer to town. Soon they were at the gate to Bletchley Park, tall and metal with barbed wire curling atop it. Mr Waverly stopped the vehicle, but did not turn it off, clearly wanting Ellen gone.

'Do you think you can make it back to the house on your own tonight?' he asked as Ellen slid down from the truck.

'Of course,' she lied, unsure what else to say. By his tone, it was clear he had no intention of collecting her and she didn't like to put him out. Mr Waverly drove away as soon as her door shut, not even bothering to reply.

3

PEARL

'**M**um,' Pearl pleaded, 'I cannot be late again.'

Pearl's mother was spreading a thin layer of her rhubarb preserve on toast. She sighed, her massive bosom heaving under a neatly pressed blouse. She put the toast on a delicate flowered plate and pushed it towards Pearl. 'Have a quick bite. You need your energy,' she declared with a nod firm enough to shake her greying curls.

'Mum,' Pearl whined, 'I have to check in with Miss Waincross at half seven.' This was only partly true. Her shift didn't start until eight, but if she got to Bletchley early, she'd have a chance to walk into the mansion with Richard. He and the rest of the dispatch riders used the back gate directly behind the garish house instead of the main entrance. On the days she 'happened upon him', Richard never queried why she was loitering by the back gate, just as she never asked who he was visiting inside the mansion. They had both signed the Official Secrets Act, after all. They knew better than to ask.

Pearl's mother turned around, hands on hips, scowling. 'Stop acting like a child. I managed to choke down my toast and I have to be at my desk in twenty minutes. If you don't dawdle, you'll have plenty of time to eat and walk. But if you leave this toast on the table, untouched, I will *know* and I will find you and force-feed it to you in front of everyone.'

Pearl grabbed the toast and took an exaggerated bite before closing the door behind her. She did not doubt her mother would do everything she said and perhaps more. After all, she was a high-ranking secretary and always seemed to have eyes on her daughter.

Pearl swallowed down the last of her toast as she stepped on to the main road outside their house, a short walk from the high street. The town of Bletchley was quiet these days. Pearl and her mum had moved to their bunga-low a few years before her mum was recruited to work at the small, hidden venture that was to become Bletchley Park. Since then, they had watched their neighbours go off to war, leaving the women home with the children and grandparents. It was only after the Park started adding more employees that men returned to the town. The blokes who worked at Bletchley Park, though, stuck to themselves and tended not to mix with the locals. Thankfully, Richard was different. He frequented the pub in town and told colourful, funny stories to anyone of any class or standing. He was open and chummy and Pearl adored that about him. She was lucky to have someone who asked her how she was getting on and truly cared about the answer. Also, he motivated her to get to work early most days.

As a messenger, Pearl's position was both the bottom rung on the ladder and the most critical. Although she aspired to work in the huts with the other girls, figuring out puzzles and working late into the night, she told herself daily that every job at the Park was important. Besides, her mother reminded her, other jobs were rarely as glamorous as you'd imagine and, from the snippets she'd picked up along the way, Pearl knew she was right. Information at the Park, because of its sensitive nature, was completely siloed. No one knew what anyone else was doing in each hut, by design. It was Pearl's job to take envelopes from the main office to the offices in the huts, then collect envelopes and bring them wherever they needed to go.

This morning, Pearl found Miss Waincross at the desk in her wood-panelled office and lightly tapped on the door frame. Her supervisor looked up from a pile of papers and welcomed her into the office with a weary smile. Miss Waincross was older than Pearl, in her early twenties, and carried herself with the poise of a movie star.

Today, Miss Waincross was wearing her tweed suit and

a scarf around her neck decorated with the Union Jack. Her lipstick was bright red and expertly applied, her light brown hair set in perfect, glossy curls. She never had a thread out of place, and her skin always seemed to glow with a recent application of powder no matter how many hours she was holed up in her office. She'd arrived at Bletchley after Pearl and her mum – in early 1939 – having been recruited directly from Cambridge. She appeared to be the product of good breeding, proper schooling and a lot of money, but like a true gentlewoman, Miss Waincross never talked of her past. Pearl admired and feared her equally, but mostly wanted to please her.

'Ah, good morning, Pearl,' Miss Waincross said when Pearl entered the room. She tucked the paper she'd been reading, folded like a letter, under a plain brown folder.

'Morning,' Pearl replied.

'Good that you're early. It's a welcome distraction from the nonsense I've been reading. Here, I have something for you to take over to Hut Four.'

Pearl extended her hand for the familiar standard-issue envelope. It felt a little different, somehow – the flap ever so slightly loose under her thumb.

'How are things?' her supervisor said as cheerfully as a primary school teacher. 'As they should be?'

'Of course,' said Pearl, turning the envelope over in her hands. Miss Waincross often said things like this;

pleasantries that clearly meant so much more.

'Brilliant. Now, off with you,' she said with a dismissive wave of her hand.

Pearl walked down the hall and around the corner. The long corridor in front of her was lined with doors, all of them shut. She looked down at the envelope in her hand. She'd been right, it wasn't quite as tightly closed as normal; the seal was slightly undone and the corners bent. As she walked, Pearl couldn't help but tease at the seal. She was used to them being new and crisp like they'd come straight from the storeroom shelves.

This envelope didn't feel right.

Pausing for a moment, she heard nothing but the sound of her own breath, measured and deep. The hallway was empty. Looking over her shoulder once more, Pearl stepped in against the wall. Turning the envelope over in her hands, she wondered why this one was so worn. While she had not meant for the seal to come undone more, it was extremely easy to peel, most of the flap coming off in one fluid strip before she'd fully registered what was happening.

Oh no! She felt her throat tighten. She had to seal it again, which she attempted to do against the wall, pressing the flap repeatedly with the heel of her hand. Only when she turned it upside down to see if her frantic repair job had worked, the pressure of the heavy hidden documents tore through it. The cascade was slow at first and then much too fast for Pearl to rescue the tidal wave of secrets. She watched in horror as papers spilt across the shiny polished hallway floors.

Her breath caught in her throat as she gaped at the puddle of white papers and the lightly bruised tinge of their carbon twins, their faulty container still held upright in her left hand. Her heart thudded as she thought of the consequences of what she'd done. Footsteps echoed – or was that her heartbeat? – and she dropped to her knees so quickly she was certain they'd be as purple as the carbon papers the next day. With fast, swooping motions, she collected the messages in a messy pile and tried in vain to stuff them back into the ragged envelope. Without really trying, she recognized names, locations, military terms – information she couldn't parse together into a cohesive message but knew was absolutely not meant for her eyes.

'Oh Pearl,' came a voice, dripping with disappointment. 'What happened?'

Although her heartbeat was drumming loudly, Pearl realized that the noise she had heard was heels against the hardwood. Miss Waincross was walking very swiftly towards her.

'I don't know. I turned them upside down; the seal broke. I did not peek, I promise!' Pearl stuttered in short, uneven bursts. Her eyes filled with tears and she slumped forward, still trying to hide the papers.

Miss Waincross crouched down, her skirt tight across

her knees, and took them from Pearl. She tapped the bottom of the stack on the floor a few times and they arranged themselves magically into a proper squared-off grouping. Her ears burning, still barely able to take a full breath, Pearl handed her the broken envelope, defeated.

'You must be more careful.' Miss Waincross stood and held her hand out to Pearl, helping her up.

Pearl was surprised at how cool Miss Waincross's palm was against her own hot, sweaty hand. She could not read her supervisor's expression, but was certain Miss Waincross was anything but pleased to stumble across this mess.

'I am so sorry, I, er, cannot say . . .' Pearl fumbled. Her heart still thumped against her ribs.

'Let us not talk of this again, Pearl,' Miss Waincross said, putting a red-tipped finger to her lips. 'These accidents happen. I blame myself, really. I should have been guiding you more. It is my job, after all, to help you grow and develop. I'll take the papers back with me and put them in a new envelope. I have a few scattered about. Why don't you come back in thirty minutes? I should have it sorted by then and you can make your delivery as if nothing ever happened.'

Her face steaming from fear and embarrassment, Pearl couldn't, for once, fathom what to say in response, so she nodded and watched Miss Waincross turn on her heel and walk down the hall. After a few seconds, Pearl trudged in the opposite direction, her mind reeling from what had

25

just happened. Two things stuck out: first, Miss Waincross was not going to turn Pearl over to the authorities for her colossal mistake; and second, there were things happening in the huts at Bletchley Park she had not even dreamt were possible.

Pearl's mind raced as she paired the few words she'd glimpsed on the secret papers with the dribs and drabs she'd overheard as a messenger. Recently, she'd noticed an increase in the number of messages being transported from Bletchley to other war offices, and from hut to hut at the Park. There was definitely a more palpable sense of urgency, with new faces arriving every day to fill the newly constructed huts. Now, from what Pearl had seen on the hallway floor, she was pretty certain they had figured out at least one of the codes the Germans were using in their communications. As her footsteps thudded in time with her heart, Pearl also knew she had worked out something very dangerous.

Exposing the secrets inside that envelope would be like pointing out where all of Britain's warships were in the sea, or what the next move was in the offensive against Germany. Information gathered at Bletchley helped Britain plan their next steps in this awful war. This was why, after all, they had the Secrets Act. If this information got into the wrong hands, even by accident, it could kill thousands of British soldiers in the blink of an eye. And the minute the Germans learnt their code was broken, they'd switch it, leaving Britain clueless about their next move.

Still shaking, Pearl stepped outside the building, gulping in the crisp autumn air as if she'd been holding her breath. She leant against the back wall of the mansion, scanning the row of parked motorcycles for Richard's. He would make her feel better. He always did.

She touched the sprig of lavender in the front pocket of her cardigan for reassurance. It was dry now, little pods of purple likely trapped in the porridge-coloured wool, but she always kept it there until he gave her a new one. Or until it disintegrated.

That was how they'd met, about a year ago, Richard handing her a sprig of lavender as he waltzed into the mansion. She'd never seen him before that day and yet he'd confidently told her she should wear more purple. It brought out her eyes, he'd said. Then he'd introduced himself and told her a funny story about some sheep he'd encountered on the road. Almost every day since then, Richard had given her a new sprig of lavender and they'd continued talking. Pearl wasn't sure what to call their relationship – she'd been thinking they might be more than simply friends, but neither of them had acknowledged it was more, until their dinner 'date' last night. Or rather, she'd thought it was more than just a friendly meal – he'd asked her out and paid for her supper – but it had ended in confusion and a speedy farewell. Her ears burnt just to think about it, so she tried not to. If only she could go back in time and erase all that awkwardness, all her missteps. But of course, if she could go back in time, her priority now would be to make sure to not open the envelope. That was worse than awkwardness with any boy, date or not.

Seeing Richard and his friend, Antony, entering the back gate, Pearl waved and ran her tongue over her teeth, searching for stray bits of toast or jam. She was within reach of the lavender bushes, as usual, and hoped he wouldn't forget. He'd been acting oddly for a week now. Pearl was trying not to associate his distracted behaviour with what had happened last night, but it was hard not to. They'd left the evening on such a strange note.

She was on edge, waiting for Richard to acknowledge her, leftover nervousness from her encounter with Miss Waincross still raging through her veins. Antony laughed at something Richard said, his eyes squinted and head tilted back, as Richard pretended to twirl the ends of his pencil-thin moustache. She waited a beat or two longer, willing him to look up. Instead, he walked on the longer path between the gate and the mansion – not his normal one, which took him by the lavender. And Pearl. As the crunch of his heavy boots on the gravel pathway faded, Pearl felt her shoulders fall. She hated that a silly boy could flatten her like this, reducing her to a pile of insecurities and doubts.

'Don't you have somewhere to be?' a sharp voice from behind her asked. It was Mr St John, who managed one of the huts. Thankfully, he didn't linger for her response, instead rushing off down the path after making a disapproving 'tsk' sound. Pearl's shoulders dropped and what little confidence she had left rushed out of her like air from a popped balloon. Someday, she would love to work with Mr St John, to learn from him and do something other than ferry messages around. Being seen loitering outside the mansion did not exactly put her in the best light for a transfer. Realizing her scant luck today was dwindling even further, Pearl gave up on Richard and headed back inside to re-collect her first delivery.

Pearl made her way towards Hut 4, package in hand, relieved Miss Waincross had handed it to her as if nothing had happened. She was next to the small bike rack outside the bank of long, rectangular huts when she heard someone running up behind her.

'Golly, you are quick,' he said breathlessly. Pearl glanced up to find his tall, lean figure approaching, wavy hair seeming to swirl around his head in the breeze. He smoothed his anaemic, waxy new moustache which had been grown, Pearl supposed, to make him look older. At eighteen, he was one of the younger dispatch riders, but also one of the best. His friend and fellow Don R (as dispatch riders were known), Antony, said he rode the twisty, narrow roads around Bletchley faster than any other bloke on a motorcycle.

'I am sorry, Pearl,' Richard said. 'I didn't mean to shrug you off. Not today, not yesterday. I turned around and you were gone, run away before I could give you these.' He held up a small bunch of coloured leaves. 'Sorry it's not lavender, but that's pretty much done for the year.'

'I know,' Pearl admitted. 'I stood next to it today with nothing much else to focus on than its sad spikes. Last winter, you brought me sweets.'

'I did!' Richard slapped his empty palm to his forehead. 'I'd forgotten. Well, I'll have to stop by the shops on the way back home today. You like lemon sherbets?'

'Sweets for someone sweet,' Pearl murmured. He'd said that once. She'd never forgotten it.

Richard adjusted the bulging leather messenger bag he always wore across his body. 'Sorry about earlier, truly. I've been looking for you, though. I promise.'

Pearl felt her anger melt away almost instantly. When she had Richard's attention, nothing was as important. His words took her above the overhanging cloud of war, the constant threat of loss and pain. Richard's voice, which was deep and soothing, reassured Pearl, bringing comfort like the rumble and clack of a train as you journeyed towards some exciting destination.

'I can't be long. I have deliveries to make.' Pearl paused before she added, 'But it is good to see you.' She wrinkled her nose, wishing her voice hadn't sounded as cloying as a bar of Cadbury's.

'Everything all right with you, then?' Richard asked, his voice thin, like he was expecting bad news.

'Fine,' Pearl answered cautiously. 'And you?'

Richard took in a deep breath, clearly choosing his words carefully. 'My mum heard from a cousin in London. She walked by a pile of rocks the other day on the way to visit a friend and saw a hand. There was someone buried there in all the rubble and no one knew for days. People walked by a body for days and carried on with things.'

'To be fair, Richard, they didn't know it was there,' Pearl started, gently. His breaths were coming quicker, his hands gesturing wildly as he continued.

'The raids in London, naval fleets bombed day after day – it's truly abysmal. We don't see it out here in the bubble of Buckinghamshire, but this war, it's changing people.'

Pearl crossed her arms over her chest and exhaled loudly. He was exasperating when he got this way, over-thinking things like he was a philosopher at university, a place neither of them had been as yet because of the war. 'Richard, I don't think it's true that we don't see it,' Pearl said. 'I do. Well, not *see*, but I hear about it on the radio. It's the whole reason we're working for the Foreign Office, after all.'

Richard waved his hand, dismissing her. 'No, that's not the same. We're bombarded by reminders to keep calm and zip our lips. But we don't see the human cost, nor do the men in power. How much do *they* feel the pains of war when they go home to their posh houses in London? They tell us to save and scrimp, but what does that really mean to people like my mum, who works twelve-hour shifts at the munitions factory without complaining – or that poor sod under a pile of bricks . . .'

Pearl softened her voice a bit. 'Richard, we're fighting this war with everything we do, every single day. Spouting off about the people in power isn't going to help anything at all. It'll make it worse. I can't tell you that enough. Besides, every delivery you make, each day, counts. You know that.'

'Perhaps . . .' Richard's hand travelled to his moustache again, smoothing it over and over. He looked up at her suddenly, his eyes dark and piercing, and threw the fistful of coloured leaves on to the grass. 'Do you ever get the feeling the world is out of balance? Like someone kicked us off our axis?'

'Nothing's right these days,' Pearl said flippantly, annoyed that he'd tossed her bouquet away like a handful of rubbish. It may have been just leaves, but they were *her* leaves; he'd chosen them for her. Didn't he realize how much that meant? She shoved her hands in her cardigan pockets and balled them into fists, trying to contain her frustration.

'No, it's not the regular sense of everything being

off-kilter, like we'll never get back to the place we thought was "normal". It's more than just hating this war and all the pain it's causing. There are things happening – awful things that aren't reported in the newspapers – and don't you think if I see a way to stop them from happening, well . . . ?' he started, then looked over his shoulder before continuing in a hushed voice. 'I feel I should watch my back. A lot. More than simply changing up my routes, keeping an eye out for people following me – those things are routine.' He leant even closer and Pearl noticed flecks of yellow in the deep brown of his eyes. 'Pearl, we've always been good friends, right?'

Pearl tilted her head slightly, unsure she wanted him to continue. His thoughts were all over the place – at one minute dangerous and the next understandable. He was getting like this more and more, and she hated it. One of the things she used to love about him was how sunny he was, so carefree in spite of the war. But that had changed lately. 'I suppose.'

'You know you can trust me, right?'

'I do,' she admitted, trying not to overthink what he meant by this.

Richard's eyes left hers for a moment, like he was expecting someone to wander around the corner. 'I know I shouldn't be telling you this, but I feel like I'm going mad. It is hard to keep everything secret, you know – to stay quiet and keep it inside.'

'I suppose,' Pearl said quietly, though she did know, having just violated the Secrets Act that morning. 'What is it?'

'I've noticed something odd about a few envelopes I've delivered recently. They looked, well, like someone had opened and resealed them. It's not completely obvious, a slight tear or a wrinkle that looks out of place. Pearl, do you think I'm being overly paranoid?'

An image of this morning's tattered envelope flashed through her mind, causing heat to rise in her cheeks. They had been told to report anything out of the ordinary to their supervisors and here it was, the opportunity to gain in Miss Waincross's graces. But she couldn't let her eagerness to atone for her own indiscretion cloud her judgement. She stepped closer to Richard and lightly placed her hand on his arm. She smelt tobacco on his warm breath and closed her eyes briefly, trying to lock his scent in her memory. He was so near to her, her whole body tingled, even her toes, and she had to blink several times to wake up out of her lovesick dream. 'Richard, we are all on edge, you Don Rs especially, on the road at all hours of the night. You need a good sleep, a hearty meal. Perhaps what you think you saw is nothing, a simple case of frugality. Save and reuse?'

'I suppose,' he said. 'But normally, the Bletchley envelopes look crisp and new. Not reused. These hadn't been properly sealed and were a little wavy, like the paper had been steamed.'

'Oh?' Pearl said, her heart pounding, but not completely because of his words. They were still very near to each other. In the films, they would've kissed already. Sure, they'd already kissed once, sort of. It hadn't been a real one. He'd stooped down to brush her cheek but she'd turned her head and their lips touched briefly, which sent a shudder down her spine. It was unintended, based on his look of surprise afterwards. But they'd grown closer since then. Now, she could imagine in exquisite detail what it would be like, how quickly it could happen.

Her breath hitched and she took a step back.

What was she thinking? She had to focus. 'How worried are you? What's your gut telling you?'

He paused for a few moments, then nodded. 'It *is* different. Something has changed. These envelopes aren't right, Pearl. What would you do? I don't know whether to report it to my supervisor or keep quiet. He might blame me.' He looked at her earnestly and of course she melted. 'I trust you. You won't lie or do me wrong. What should I do?'

'Well, you cannot keep this a secret. You have to tell someone. *We* have to tell someone.'

'I know,' Richard said sombrely. 'But who? I don't trust my supervisor. He's only in the position because of his title – Lord something or other. I suppose I could tell someone else, but . . .'

Pearl again thought of Miss Waincross. If these

envelopes really were being compromised, it needed to be reported straight away – if not by Richard, then by her. And if telling Miss Waincross something like this would convince her supervisor she was trustworthy, that was just a bonus. 'What if *I* report it? After all, the envelopes are coming from the Park. I know who to speak to in order to keep this discreet. Besides, you have too much on your hands these days. Let me take care of this for you.' Pearl parcelled out her words slowly, hoping she sounded sincere and considerate rather than the paranoid bundle of nerves she felt.

'You? Pearl, it is my job, my envelopes.' Richard looked down at Pearl's hand, still on his arm. She immediately pulled it back, like she'd touched a hot stove. All he'd said about trusting her – had he even meant it? 'Are you sure you should be doing this?'

'I don't mean to overstep, of course,' she mumbled as she lowered her burning face. His eyes were distant, preoccupied. 'Think about it, will you? But Richard, we both know if there was something wrong with your deliveries, it cannot be kept secret. I can help. Let me do this for you.'

Richard walked a few steps towards the back gate and Pearl fought the urge to trail behind him like a duckling following its mother. He turned around suddenly, his face etched with relief. 'All right, Pearl. If you really, truly can trust this person.'

'I am certain of it,' she smiled. 'I probably should go,

Richard. Work and all.'

'Sure, sure,' he nodded. 'By the way, can you stop by the pub after your shift this evening?'

Pearl shrugged, her heart stupidly galloping in her chest. In spite of all the anxiety from that morning, her heart melted at this personal invitation. She longed to sit beside him all night, taking in his stories and the scent of his hair pomade, even though she always felt slightly unwelcome at Richard's regular pub. 'I'm not certain. Mum might want me home.'

'Ant and I will be there.' Her stomach sank slightly – not another date, then. He backed away, hands clasped as if praying. 'I'd love to see you, too. I promise I'll tell you a good story, give you a distraction from all of this. I know you need it.'

And like that, he was gone, bounding across the lawn as quickly as a spooked deer. She sighed, then shook her head as her pulse returned to normal. She knew she had to tell Miss Waincross about Richard's envelopes. But first, she had a delivery to make.

4

ELLEN

When Ellen was asked to present a permit to the guard, her stomach dropped until she remembered she'd placed it in her coat pocket last night for safekeeping. Once granted entrance, she crept along the dewy, wet path, surprised to see so much activity already at Bletchley Park. In daylight, the mansion was even uglier – red brick, with many different rooflines and ornate bay windows appearing at random places. Clearly, the place had been designed by an indecisive architect with an eccentric client. The mansion looked out on a small pond that appeared popular with ducks. To the left of the pond were several long, rectangular buildings, as out of place as a pile of children's building blocks abandoned in a manicured garden. A car horn honked in the distance, jolting Ellen away from her thoughts.

Inside, the mansion was already buzzing – typewriters

clacking and girls rushing in and out with clipboards and file folders. Ellen returned to the vestibule in which she had waited with Pearl and unwrapped her bacon sandwich cautiously. She felt invisible, but also conspicuous – would someone reprimand her for eating in here? Eventually, a woman in a tweed jacket and skirt came through the doorway and waved her into a room with elegant bay windows overlooking the front lawn – thankfully by this time Ellen had eaten her sandwich and disposed of the grease-soaked paper. The woman had a pair of reading glasses on a beaded chain around her neck, which swung like a pendulum when she leant forward.

'Welcome,' she said cheerfully. 'My name is Mrs Patterson. I think you met my daughter, Pearl, yesterday evening. I hope she was as welcoming as she should've been.'

Ellen nodded, knowing it would help no one if she told the truth.

'Excellent,' Mrs Patterson said, looking relieved. 'Shall we walk you over to Hut Four, then?'

Mrs Patterson was compact but projected an air of confidence, like her daughter. She kept her eyes on Ellen as she collected a few folders from her desk and clutched them to her chest. 'Right. Are you ready?'

'As ready as I've ever been,' Ellen replied, wondering if she was being too eager. Mrs Patterson simply smiled and strode to the door.

They walked out on to the gravel path. Two soggy mallards crossed in front of them; Ellen supposed they were heading towards the pond. Mrs Patterson turned to Ellen and said swiftly, 'You have been told this place is run under absolute secrecy and have signed the agreement. You are not, in any instance, to reveal to anyone what you are doing. You know what to say if you are asked what you are doing here?'

'I am to tell them I work for the Foreign Office,' Ellen remembered, thankfully. They passed two long, rectangular buildings just beyond the mansion. Each had a number by their nondescript doors.

'And the address?'

'Box one hundred, Bletchley.'

'Good. Your first assignment is to join a new group under the guidance of Mr Gilbert St John. Mr St John is a highly esteemed professor of philosophy, with degrees in linguistics, Romance languages, and a concentration in advanced logic. I suspect you will be right at home with his girls.' Mrs Patterson stopped at the door. 'You'll be in room seven. I have to deliver these down the hall in room eleven. Are you happy to introduce yourself?'

Ellen wanted to say, *No, I want an escort because I have no idea what I'm doing and why I'm here*, but she nodded and tried to look fearless. 'Of course.'

'Brilliant,' Mrs Patterson said, opening the door. 'Mr St

5

PEARL

She jogged the last few steps to Hut 4. Since they started building huts, it seemed there was always a new one being constructed just steps from the last. They looked identical, for the most part, except a sign labelling each with a number. Floorplans were similar as well – one long hallway leading to offices or larger work rooms, mostly with closed doors Pearl never got to open.

Hut 4 stank more than the other huts and Pearl pulled the collar of her thick Scottish-wool cardigan over her face in anticipation. She preferred to deliver to the huts with the more modern amenities. Hut 4 was not one of these, with an ancient paraffin stove that let out more smoke than heat. The ventilation was awful due to the sandbags and brick walls built to protect the buildings in the event of a raid. Even if windows were opened, no breeze or natural light would make its way into the rooms.

Stepping inside, she could still smell the smoke through her makeshift mask. The door at the end of the hall was open. Mr St John usually left the door ajar, no matter what people said about security or keeping the heat in. He was a strange and quiet man, but the girls who worked there (only girls, which Pearl thought was refreshing) respected him.

Pearl placed the envelope in the wire basket on his desk, which was buried in other papers, folders and empty teacups. Mr St John was hunched over a table with two girls looking on, pencil scratching as he worked on something. His hair sat on his head like a bird's nest. There was a pencil wedged behind his ear, one she was certain he had forgotten about. He wore a necktie every day, but it was often the same one, stained by egg yolk or pea-green soup. His baggy, striped trousers were worn, and his white shirts were yellowed. No one cared about that, though, even the well-dressed girls who worked for him. His was a case of intelligence outweighing his strange quirks and, oftentimes, mild odour.

The new girl, Ellen, caught Pearl's eye. She was sitting at a desk, papers strewn in front of her. She stood out from the other girls, her skin glowing white like she hadn't been worn and dirtied yet. Everything about her was simple and understated, yet her hair shone as if styled at a salon and her clothes looked bright and well made. She was stunning in the same way a clear blue sky was –

ordinary but sometimes it took your breath away. Pearl was certain she had already made friends with the glamorous debs in the room. Unlike Pearl, Ellen seemed just their type – well dressed, presentable and polite, with a swipe of blush-coloured lipstick.

Ellen looked up as Pearl tiptoed over, trying not to attract attention.

'Pearl! What are you doing here?' Ellen whispered, a hint of caution in her voice.

'Shh. I'm here on official business, but if Mr St John catches me talking to you I'll get booted,' she said, keeping her voice low. The last thing Pearl wanted was yet another reason to lose her job.

'Oh, I am sorry,' Ellen said, her dainty hands fluttering nervously about her thin, pale neck. 'I am a little overwhelmed, confused really. I'm trying to figure out the code in these messages . . .'

Pearl fought the urge to roll her eyes and settled for an audible, exasperated sigh. 'You aren't supposed to tell me what you're doing, remember?'

'Right!' Ellen said. She quickly slapped her hands, fingers spread wide, across the note cards. She was a touch odd, her mannerisms not quite right. 'Sorry. I assumed since you were in here, you would know what we were working on.'

'Oh, I know what you are working on, only you're not working on the right thing.' Pearl watched Ellen, waiting for this to sink in. Mr St John never gave any instructions to the new girls. He expected his room to be full of self-starters. After all, he had his own projects and made it clear he wasn't at the Park to waste time with training.

Ellen looked down, her cheeks turning as red as Pearl's wool skirt. 'What do you mean, it's not right? In my interview, I was given a puzzle. A crossword. Not that I thought we'd have crosswords here, but I figured my work would be somewhat complicated. Oh dear, am I making it *too* complicated?'

She seemed deflated. Pearl sympathized – she had seen many new girls humiliated because they could not figure out what to do on the first day. Only this was the first girl Pearl had wanted to help, though she was unsure why she felt that way. She'd worked out what they did in this room because of something Miss Waincross told her one day. 'Take this envelope to Gil's hut. Number four. And if you could stop by the stationery cupboard under the stairs and bring them some more red wax pencils, that would be most helpful. That room goes through boxes of coloured pencils with that crazy cataloguing system Gil developed.' Between that statement and some basic observation and casual eavesdropping, Pearl was pretty confident she knew what Ellen should be doing.

Pearl glanced over her shoulder at Mr St John and the group of girls around him. He was pointing at something on the desk with his pencil, making loud, sharp tapping noises on the desk. Thankfully, no one was paying them much attention because of it. 'Look, Mr St John expects figuring out your job to be your first puzzle. See how those girls by the window are writing things down on the blank cards with different coloured pencils?'

'Yes . . .' Ellen said hesitantly. When her face flushed red, the colour crept all the way down her long neck. Even her ears were pink. It was impressive and mortifying.

'The girls are categorizing parts of the message for later use. You don't decode them – that's in another hut perhaps. I shouldn't say, really. The whole process is meant to be . . .' Pearl bit the inside of her cheek. She *could* say, but wouldn't.

'. . . secret,' Ellen finished, her face flat. She looked from Pearl to her papers as if trying to decide whether Pearl was joking around.

'You'd be better off to ask one of the girls for their cheat sheet and get cracking.' Pearl nodded firmly. It felt good to help someone with something so concrete, especially after all the complications with Richard. Maybe if she intervened before Richard got to his supervisor, she could solve that problem as quickly, too.

Ellen looked around. 'I would rather not. They have not been friendly.'

Pearl was somewhat surprised to learn Ellen had not become chummy with the other girls, but also relieved. Pearl, too, had struggled with the rather snobbish debs.

This meant Ellen was more like her than she'd originally thought, and perhaps why she'd been motivated to help her in the first place.

'The thing I've heard about Mr St John,' Pearl said, pointing to the papers buried under Ellen's forearms, 'is he gives his girls the clues they need. He doesn't allow just anyone in here – you're of a certain calibre – and he expects you can sort out any issues.'

Ellen's eyebrows were scrunched, jaw muscles clenched. She was probably thinking about whether to show her notes to Pearl. Smart. It showed she'd been listening, another thing Pearl liked about her.

'It's all right. I don't need to peek. I know not to do that,' Pearl said with a nervous laugh. 'You need to find out what your focus is. Cards are categorized by topic, person, location, etc. So, you go through the messages looking for mentions of a specific commander—'

'Yes!' Ellen said. 'I saw a name in there. One. On a card. Wait, should I have told you that?'

Pearl forced a smile and stifled another eye-roll. 'There! Your first mystery solved. Now it is up to you to figure out the classification key – the colours and words they use. That, I cannot help you with.'

Ellen blinked at Pearl for a few seconds and nodded. She opened her mouth as if to talk and then closed it again, like she was trying out the correct sentence in her mind first. Finally, she spoke. 'Thank you. As much as I hate to admit it, I was completely on the wrong track.'

Pearl stifled a laugh. 'You were. But that's all right. Everyone is at some point.'

'I thought I would be doing something, a bit more, well, thrilling.' She sighed. 'You know I love puzzles.'

'I do?' Pearl said, confused. She barely knew the girl.

Ellen fidgeted and nodded furiously. 'Last night, I helped you with your crossword. I said I loved puzzles.'

'Ah!' Pearl was sorry she had not remembered that. With all the worry over Richard, everything else had flown out of her brain. Not that she could tell Ellen that. Ellen's eyes were locked on Pearl's expectantly. She was hardly blinking and Pearl couldn't help but fidget. 'Wait a minute.'

Pearl slipped between two girls at the next table and stole a notecard and pencil. The girls barely acknowledged her, something Pearl was banking on. Then, she stood in the aisle with her back to Ellen, deciding it was best to start with a simple anagram. She jumbled the letters of her message to make new words, an exercise that took no time at all. Most people did not realize Pearl had this special talent when it came to puzzles, but sorting letters and numbers came as easily to her as untangling a knotted ball of wool. When she faced Ellen again, she was pleased neither Ellen nor any of the other girls had noticed her. Ellen, for one, was focused on her work, chewing the end of her pencil like it was a Rich Tea biscuit. This wouldn't

6

ELLEN

She was, essentially, an archivist, hunting for certain people and locations and marking them on cards along with the date they were mentioned. Ellen was confused as to why she'd been made to work a rather difficult crossword as a job interview for this position, but reminded herself this was all for the war effort and she was but one piece of a rather large, complicated machine. Filing information for reference was important, and eventually she lost herself in the hunt for her designated topics. When she finally looked up from her work to blot her cold, dripping nose with one of her mother's lace handkerchiefs, Ellen noticed a little square of paper on the corner of her desk:

FOG HEALTH HITTING. ASHES ETHOS REMOTE.
FURY IRONED,
- P

Ellen rubbed her eyes with the heel of her hand and looked around for some clue as to who had left it. 'P' could be Pearl; at least she hoped it was. Chewing on the end of a pencil, Ellen felt her mind slot the clues into place. It was all orderly and logical, how the letters travelled around to their correct spaces in her mind. She turned the paper over – blank – and then took a sip of lukewarm tea. Remembering a dictionary she'd seen on the shelf, she scrambled for the book to confirm. Then, smiling, she pencilled the message in alongside the block letters:

POG HEALTH HITTING = Tonight half eight.
ASHES ETHOS REMOTE = Meet at horseshoes

That one was tough. Ellen had to assume horseshoes was a place, perhaps a restaurant or teahouse, although it sounded more like a pub. Ellen was not the sort of girl to frequent pubs and wondered if Pearl was.

FURY IRONED

That had to be a valediction, the closing of the letter, and it was easy to move those letters around to form, '*Your friend*', a statement that made Ellen smile.

Tonight half eight. Meet at Horseshoes. Your friend, Pearl

Ellen beamed. True, her *actual* work was in a pile under this anagram and remained confusing and a bit of a let-down, but with this puzzle from her new friend, Ellen had hope. Now, she needed to not mess it up. That was always the hardest part.

'I figured it out!' Ellen blurted upon seeing Pearl across the street from a pub called the Horseshoes, then immediately felt stupid. Of course she had figured it out. If she had not, she would not be here. Why did everything that came out of her mouth sound so wrong? '*Do not react without thinking it over first, Ellen,*' her mother used to say. '*Your impulse is, more often than not, wrong.*'

'That is . . . I meant to say, um, hello and thank you for inviting me,' she said. *Second try was better*, she thought.

'Right, sure,' Pearl said, clearly distracted and not at all put off by Ellen's uncouth exclamation. 'I'm glad you could come. It would not suit for me to meet two boys at a pub alone. I needed someone else to make it, well, proper.'

While it was not an enthusiastic reception, Ellen supposed it would have to do. She smiled sheepishly. It felt fantastic to be out, and with a new friend! Her shoulders felt lighter, the dull throbbing in her temples from being cooped up in the hut almost gone. Then she thought of Mother. 'But Pearl, are you sure we can go to a pub alone, to meet . . . boys?'

'Ah, sure. I know them. It'll be fine,' Pearl added, although she looked far from certain.

Ellen hesitated, nervous about meeting new people as usual, especially boys. But she did really want to do *something* different and get out of the same old routine she had at home of reading alone in her room. Books only did so much to make a person feel alive. 'If you say it will be all right . . .' she said, taking a deep breath of the outside air. She loved feeling the clean, cool breeze rush down her throat after being penned up in a smoke cloud all day.

Pearl simply shrugged and walked to the edge of the pavement, her head turning back and forth as she prepared to cross the road. 'You worry too much. They're mostly harmless.'

'Hold up for a minute,' Ellen called, wanting to slow everything down – the puzzle, meeting new people, going to a pub – it was all so sudden and unexpected. Ellen preferred time to process and prepare for new situations, after all. 'How did you know I would solve the puzzle correctly and then meet you here?'

Pearl stopped, her grin as wide as a generous wedge of pork pie. 'You were *smashing* at my crossword late at night, after a long day of travel. I knew you'd have no problem solving a simple anagram. Now, whether you would show up was a gamble, but you and I seem similar in some ways. I mean, more up for adventure than shopping for,' Pearl looked down, 'new stockings and shiny shoes.'

Glancing down at her scuffed brown Oxfords and thick, itchy tights, Ellen could not argue. Most of the girls in her hut were Hollywood beautiful, with perfectly waved hair and endless lipstick. She'd realized they were nicknamed 'the debs', or debutantes, both because of their looks and their social standing. While pleasant enough girls, Ellen's innate awkwardness had already made her very much *not* a member of their club.

'I think we are very alike,' Ellen agreed and then added, looking at the pub, 'but also very different. I'm not as sure of myself as you are.'

Pearl shrugged, lacing her arm through Ellen's as they crossed the road together. 'I bet you are. The opportunity just hasn't presented itself yet.'

The Horseshoes was a small pub on the high street in town, identifiable only by a black sign with three linked gold-painted horseshoes adorning it. The windows were tiny, nestled deep into the white wall, and covered with a cross-hatch of tape to stop them shattering in a bomb blast. Two old men in flat caps smoked cigarettes under a tree alongside the road, taking in the last bit of sunshine as they gestured wildly towards a rusty old van parked almost entirely on the pavement. Next to it were two black motorcycles.

Pearl stopped short. 'They didn't wait. They're already in there,' she mumbled. She pinched her cheeks and smoothed down her hair, odd gestures for a girl who had her cardigan buttoned incorrectly.

'Are you sure we should be doing this?' Ellen asked. 'Who exactly are we meeting?' Her stomach felt a little strange, gurgling like she had eaten too much cabbage.

'Two fellows. Antony and Richard.' Pearl kicked at the pavement with her brown shoe. 'Look, Ellen, it's no bother to go in and look for them. They said they'd be here and I'm sure we'll find them inside. It is not entirely proper, but once we're at their table, no one will mind.'

Ellen swallowed down her fears. Mother always said a life was best lived outside one's comfort zone, although Ellen strongly suspected this statement did not apply to two unaccompanied girls going to a pub. 'You know them well?' she finally managed.

'Richard, yes. He, uh, we've been pals for ages. More than pals, but not more in that sense. Well, maybe. It's, uh, a bit complicated. You'll like him,' Pearl said, her words coming in a jumbled rush.

Ellen thought of prodding a bit, then noticed Pearl's pink cheeks and neck. 'I'll take your word for it,' Ellen said confidently. 'Let's go in.'

Pearl nodded and smoothed her hair again. 'A warning, though. They might be a little . . . Well, see, they're Don Rs. Sometimes they are not the most sophisticated.'

Ellen nodded, even though she did not entirely understand what Pearl had said. 'Don Rs?'

'Dispatch riders. They call themselves Don Rs for some reason.' With a shrug, Pearl looked back at Ellen, her expression serious. 'Don't feel you have to go in with me if it makes you uncomfortable. I should've been straightforward with you from the beginning.'

7

PEARL

Pearl stopped just inside the pub door, scanning the crowded room for Richard's leather jacket, the colour of toasted bread. She was anxious about running into him after telling Miss Waincross his story about the tampered envelopes. While the conversation had gone as well as possible, with Miss Waincross praising Pearl for coming forward and insisting she'd protect her and Richard, Pearl's head had been throbbing ever since. She'd expected to feel elated, having redeemed herself in Miss Waincross's eyes and solving Richard's problem as well, but instead, everything felt off.

A fog of tobacco smoke hung over the low-ceilinged room and the air smelt like warm alcohol and wet wool. Tables were filled and the crowd was loud and boisterous. There appeared to be only one other group of women; four debs sitting opposite four boys in ties and cardigans with patched elbows, likely from Bletchley, too. The rest were local men with an older, well-worn look about them.

Pearl steered Ellen to a table in the corner, the one Richard and Ant usually claimed. It was empty, but she supposed they'd be there any minute. She simply needed to avoid the questioning eyes of other men in the pub until then.

Ellen looked as nervous as Pearl felt, but kept a smile plastered on her face more suited to an uncomfortable family photo. Yet again, Pearl cursed being so short and stood on her toes to get a better look. 'It's busy. They must be up getting their drinks,' she said, trying to convince herself as much as Ellen at this point.

'You're sure?' Ellen said nervously. She looked over her shoulder and Pearl regretted everything, from the anagram to this messed-up plan. Nothing she planned ever turned out right. She should've anticipated that, based on her horrible track record of mucking things up.

'They'll be here,' Pearl said, trying to look like she belonged. There were a lot of eyes on their table, two young girls alone. Her breath caught as she spied something orange out of the corner of her eye. With a relief she realized it was Ant's shock of red hair, and wherever Ant travelled, Richard was not far behind. 'There's Ant now!'

'Hiya, Pearl. I didn't know you'd be joining us,' Antony said as he approached, dopey smile on his face, plate and pint of ale in his hands. 'Give me a moment while I set these down and get one extra chair. We're expecting another. He's up getting a pint. Do you want anything?'

Pearl's hands went cold at the mention of him and she shook her head. Then, she watched Ant's eyes travel up and down Ellen's face. His blatant gawking made Pearl want to scream. 'Her name is Ellen. Don't get any ideas.'

Ant nodded but still did not remove his eyes from Ellen. The boy was already too far gone. Pearl groaned. Out loud.

'I'm not joking,' Pearl said sternly. 'Your ogling is almost as putrid as that sandwich.'

Ant tucked his head just as his cheeks went as red as his hair, then scurried off to find an extra chair. While he was gone, Pearl turned to Ellen and mouthed 'Sorry', her eyebrows raised, eyes wide. She felt like an older sister, apologizing for her naughty brother's behaviour. When Ant returned, he plopped down and took an exaggerated bite of the crumbling, dry sandwich, washing it down almost immediately with a mouthful of ale. His face was so gaunt, she could see the muscles in his cheek grinding away as he chewed. He pulled a face. 'They said it was ham, but if it is, there's not much of it. By the way, I'm Antony,' he said to Ellen. 'Pleased to meet you.'

'Pleasure to meet you too,' Ellen said softly, her eyes still narrowed, forehead furrowed, taking him in. Ant's face went blank upon hearing her accent and then softened again. He didn't seem to mind a Welsh girl, Pearl noted.

Pearl shifted in her seat, catching a glimpse of Richard walking toward them, his wide toothy smile directed her way. Face burning, Pearl forced herself to focus on Ant devouring his sad brown bread and mystery meat sandwich.

'Pearl! You made it. Excellent,' Richard said, sliding a frothy pint to Ant. 'Who is your new friend and why have you been keeping her from us?' he asked, a note of amusement in his voice. She knew he was showing off for Ellen. Richard loved nothing more than someone who hadn't heard his favourite stories.

'This is Ellen. We work together,' Pearl said, amazed at how high-pitched her voice sounded in response to his chiding. 'Is someone else joining us? Ant said we'd need another chair,' she added, turning to Ant and desperately trying to change the subject.

Ellen paid no mind to Pearl's attempts to reroute the conversation. 'Nice to meet you, Richard,' Ellen said with cheerful politeness, ignoring Pearl. Pearl willed her to stay quiet with a glance, but she continued. 'Pearl's told me so much about both of you.'

'Well,' Richard exclaimed enthusiastically, 'I am flattered. What did you tell her, I wonder?'

Instead of hiding her head in her hands like she wished to, Pearl stared straight at Richard and made her face blank. The worst punishment for Richard was no reaction at all.

His face fell as he reached across the table to grasp her wrist briefly. 'Oh, Pearl. I was only having a bit of fun. You know I didn't mean it, right?' Before she could speak, he turned to Ellen. 'She'd never hold a grudge. She's loyal to the end, our friend. You're a lucky one.'

Ellen nodded, with a sheepish look to Pearl. When Ellen didn't respond any further, Richard slapped his palms together as if just hit by an idea. 'Both of you will stay to meet my friend Dennis, right? He will be here momentarily, hence the fifth chair you were so curious about.' Richard looked at his watch and then to the front of the pub. 'The London train is probably running late.'

'Why is he coming here? And from London?' Antony said, his words garbled around a mouthful of sandwich.

'He was just transferred out here on compassionate grounds. An ailing aunt or something. Regardless, he'll be a great bowler on our cricket team, Ant – and he's wanted to meet my friends for ages,' he added with a chuckle.

'We're finally meeting the famous Dennis then, huh?' Pearl said. 'That's good – I was beginning to wonder if you'd made him up.' Richard had mentioned Dennis before, a bloke he'd met in London after his shift ended, he'd said. He'd taken to gushing about Dennis's many attributes of late. Pearl had been getting a bit sick of Richard going on and on about his generosity and football skills, but she was also terribly eager to meet him. Now she'd see what all the fuss was about.

'Hardly. He's been busy, is all, finishing up his work in London before moving out here.' Richard crossed his arms over his chest and leant back in his chair. As he tipped back slightly, Pearl noticed a loose thread on the collar of his shirt and fought the urge to stand up and pull it out, maybe letting her fingers touch his stubbly neck as well. 'While we wait, shall I tell a story? Hang on, did I tell you how I saved Dennis's *life*?'

Ellen raised her eyebrows sceptically and Pearl rolled her eyes.

'Here we go again,' Pearl mumbled. Still, as she feigned exasperation, she couldn't help but smile. This was the Richard she loved. The confident, boastful storyteller who would do anything for a laugh or applause.

'Oh, not *that* story,' Ant groaned. 'Excuse me if I don't listen. I have heard this one. Many, many times.'

'I haven't told it that many times. You're just bitter because you were home with your ma. So don't spoil the ending, how 'bout?' Richard grumbled, giving Ant a look that seemed angrier than was justified by one cheeky comment. Pearl couldn't help but wonder why they were suddenly quarrelling. They were normally the best of friends and work companions, and as far as Pearl could tell, had been their normal jokey selves up until now. Something had shifted, though, when Richard mentioned Dennis.

'OK, out with it then,' Pearl demanded, realizing as she did that she was poking the bear a bit. 'Tell us, did you stop a bullet with your fist? No wait, I bet you knocked a German bomber from the sky with a slingshot.'

'Ah, Pearl. You know me too well. I *am* quite burly, but no, I can't stop weapons or moving vehicles. I'm only human.' Richard smiled at her, his eyes wide and sparkling. He was happier than when she'd seen him this morning and while she was glad, she wondered what it was that was making him so giddy. 'As I was saying, about Dennis, I've been delivering to him at Whitehall in London for some time now and one day we started talking. We'd been chatting for some time because, see, he plays football in a league. If you can believe it, chaps from *Whitehall* have a team.'

Ant elbowed Richard at the mention of Whitehall. Richard elbowed him back. Pearl noted the look of caution in Ant's eye. Even though Richard and Ant were both Don Rs, they were not to discuss their deliveries even with each other. If Richard saw Ant's look, he ignored it.

'One late afternoon, he invited me out to the pub to talk about football. He even had the class,' and with this he looked at Antony, 'to buy me a first-class train ticket and leave it for me at Whitehall to collect during one of my stops.'

Antony rolled his eyes. 'I've told you before, that's plain odd. Does he think you're poor? That it's charity? I don't like—'

'It's *class*,' Richard emphasized, looking directly at the

girls. 'He knew I'd have turned in my motorcycle for the night and would need transport. It's being thoughtful. Now, where was I? Ah yes, this was the first time I met him at a pub he said was a regular for Whitehall chaps, although I wondered as it was dark and a bit dingy and out of town. Still, I was excited to meet some of his friends. The people he plays football with sound like crack-ups. Although the blokes who showed up were mostly from the factory nearby, the type you wouldn't want to run into after dark, if you know what I mean.'

'Uh, Richard, are these details important to the story?' Ant asked, his brow scrunched in a concerned knot. Pearl felt her shoulders rising, too. Richard was teetering on the edge of telling too much. If he went much further, she would have to stop him. Though she suspected Ant might as well.

Richard pushed up the sleeves of his khaki shirt, exposing tanned forearms and the shiny gold watch that had been his father's. 'After a few hours in the pub, the ground shook and plaster crumbled from the ceiling. Dennis, well, he screamed something I can't repeat in the presence of a lady.'

'There are *two* ladies here, you know,' Pearl grumbled.

'I knew then we were in an air raid,' Richard continued gleefully, ignoring Pearl.

'What made you think that, Sherlock?' Pearl mumbled, rolling her eyes. She was trying to appear sarcastic, but she couldn't help hanging on his every word. Mostly because she was worried he'd say too much.

'We hadn't heard the sirens, if there were any. A loud *blammo!* Buildings shaking, people screaming. Without even thinking, I shoved Dennis under a table and seconds later, a shelf fell right where he had been standing. It would've fallen on his head – glasses, plates, everything. *Right* on his head.'

'Well,' Ant said, pushing his empty plate towards the centre of the table. 'You're clearly a hero, then. Saving lives in an air raid. Got a medal from the King yet?'

Richard whacked his friend playfully on the arm. 'Oh stop, Ant. You're jealous because you've yet to save anyone.'

Ant rubbed his bicep theatrically. 'Hardly,' he said. 'I am a lowly dispatch rider, saving lives one delivery at a time.'

'That is not something to shrug off,' Ellen said quietly.

'Eh, he's not that great of a rider,' Richard grumbled, flashing Ant a look of annoyance. Pearl picked up an edge to his voice she was not used to hearing. Richard had some beef with Ant beyond his friend's tepid reaction to his story.

Ant's ears turned red as a poppy. 'At least I don't tear around the countryside or flap my lips when I'm not supposed to – caution is everything. Guys like us die every day on the road. Did you hear about Jensen? Broke his collarbone and three ribs because he took a corner too fast.' Although Ant was speaking boldly, his posture told a different story – shoulders caved, chin lowered, back concave. 'And that fellow who never showed up for his shift last week. I heard he was taken from his house by the police. Word was he was a bit too open about where he was delivering things. Told some fellow at the petrol station what route he was taking.' Pearl watched Richard's Adam's apple bob as he swallowed, casting a quick look in her direction. She tried to remain calm, but felt her pulse racing even as she took in a long, deep breath. She had fixed his problem, after all. He mustn't create another.

'I'm safe,' Richard said through gritted teeth, clearly taking offence.

Pearl noted that he did not go any further in his protestations.

'You know I've been riding since I was in short pants, and after that, in the clubs. That's how they found me,' he said for Ellen's benefit, 'straight from the racing track, based on my reputation. They knew everything about me – my standing in the races, my knowledge of mechanics – and I had only to study up on Morse code before I was cleared to ride. I have a map in my head,' he knocked on his skull, 'which is pretty helpful.'

'Plus,' Ant added, 'now that Richard's so busy saving the lives of the lords and ladies at Whitehall—'

'Look! There he is!' Richard interrupted, pointing

eagerly to the front of the pub.

Pearl swivelled in her seat and saw a tall blond man – it had to be Dennis – striding into the crowd. His face lit up when he spied Richard, who was waving eagerly. Pearl knew instantly why Richard had been drawn to Dennis. He was as handsome as a gallery painting, with a smile that gleamed in the smoke-filled room. She stupidly wanted to do something – cough or spill a drink – to draw Richard's attention to herself. Ant shook his head and looked away, his lip curled in disgust. It could not have been from his sandwich. There was something he didn't like about this fellow.

'Well hello,' Dennis said in a voice as smooth as toffee. After shaking Ant's and Richard's hands with gusto, Dennis raised Pearl's and Ellen's to his lips. While Pearl wanted to yank her hand back, she was aware of how carefully Richard was watching her. For him and for him only, she tolerated Dennis's show of formality. He removed a soft-looking navy overcoat to reveal a smart, tailored suit and perfectly folded red pocket square. As he hung his dark grey hat on the back of the chair, he added, 'What a pleasure it is to finally meet you all. I cannot thank Richard enough . . . or can I? Shall I get the next round?'

'Let me help you,' Richard said, jumping to his feet.

Pearl clenched her fists in her lap as she watched them together, laughing as they waited for their drinks. Ellen asked her something, but she wasn't paying attention and was relieved when Ant responded in her place. She couldn't tear her eyes from the bar. The camaraderie between Richard and Dennis was so chummy and enviable. Dennis clapped Richard on the back as Richard doubled over in laughter. She wanted Richard to joke with her like that – a few weeks ago, he had done. Why did he have that with Dennis now and not her? Had he swapped one friend for another? Still, he had told her about the envelopes, a secret so great Pearl hoped she was the only one he could trust with it. Why, then, didn't he look at her the way he was looking at Dennis?

Dennis's eyes were crinkled in amusement as Richard spun his way through another story. Richard, for his part, loved any audience participation, and his voice crescendoed at the story's climax. He looked so satisfied. So fulfilled. Just by a silly story of how they all had been anticipating Dennis's arrival. Pearl felt her jaw tighten as she watched Richard, *her* Richard, act the jester for this fancy, perfectly polished man. If she could've got up and left right then, she would've. Instead, she was paralysed, afraid if she moved she'd either dissolve into tears or throw her chair in anger. Either way, she was such a fool to ever think he was more than a friend to her. She bit her lip and for the first time ever, hoped for the wail of an air-raid siren to end her torture.

8

ELLEN

Dennis was, by Ellen's estimation, nearly four inches taller than the two other men at their table. He'd most definitely had a privileged upbringing. You could see that by how he carried himself – confident, chin up and shoulders back. He'd clearly been subjected to etiquette lessons and the best education, and he exhibited the sort of detached politeness she had seen in peers who had boarded at school. His skin was tanned but not weathered. Dennis was no stranger to the outdoors, but more the type who holidayed on the coast and rode horses on the weekend than pulled potatoes and carrots in the victory garden. Dennis was exactly the type Mother would've urged Ellen to talk to at a party – dashing, polite and in the class to which her mother had always aspired.

When he took Ellen's hand to kiss it, she wasn't at all surprised by how soft it felt. He knew how to flatter a girl, that was for sure – the gesture was old-fashioned but charming all the same. When he started talking, his polished and soft accent perfectly matched the profile she had constructed.

When he and Richard returned with the drinks, Dennis sat next to her at the end of the table, pulling in the chair so his forearms, covered in the deepest blue wool sleeves, touched hers. Warmth flooded her face and she folded her hands in her lap. It appeared accidental until he smiled at her, his gaze intense and purposeful. It seemed like he could see inside her – that he knew she was timid, afraid and unsure around the opposite sex. Then, she felt uncomfortable. She did not like to be left wondering what people wanted from her, especially men.

She hated people staring at her, but the more she took him in, the more his engaging behaviour made her wonder if her assessment was off. Someone of his upbringing would not normally be casually having drinks at a local pub with a bunch of middle-class workers. He should've been more at home in a private club, yet he seemed content to stoop to their level, so to speak. Ellen squirmed, wondering where her analysis had gone wrong. Perhaps he hadn't grown up rich. Perhaps he'd come into a windfall of money, an inheritance that gave him the beautiful clothing and granted him an upper-class education. She bit her lip, going over the facts again, almost frantically. If her process of analysis was broken, Ellen didn't know how she would approach meeting new people. Before she developed it, her mother used to drag her kicking and screaming into new situations. Ellen swallowed against her now-dry throat and pasted on a smile. She simply needed to collect more facts. Her system was not broken. There was no proof of that.

'It is a pleasure to meet you all,' Dennis said, taking his pint from the three fresh glasses Richard had brought back. 'You especially, Antony. I have heard so many tales of your adventures on the road.'

Antony's eyes bugged out of his head. 'You have?'

'Don't worry. Richard is always discreet.' Dennis tipped his glass in Richard's direction as he spoke, his accent as polished and smooth as a marble sculpture.

'Of course,' Antony said. He hunched his shoulders and looked at his lap, his lower lip pushed forward in a definite pout. Ellen put her arms back on the table, hands accidentally brushing Dennis's sleeve again. And again, an electric current ran through her body. No one appeared to notice how close Dennis was sitting except Antony, who shook his head disapprovingly. Antony had an axe to grind with Dennis and judging by the tension earlier in the evening, it was because of something Richard had done.

'So, tell me about yourselves. Richard has spoken so highly of his friends – but we live in strange times, don't we? A few years ago I would have asked about education and profession and interests, but all of those seem wrought with potential landmines.' Dennis made prolonged eye contact with each of them as he spoke, holding glances for a second longer than made Ellen comfortable. His eyes, though, were icy blue. Arresting. She looked away, catching Richard's glance. He beamed at her with an eager pride. There was something childish about how he nearly vibrated with excitement. Dennis ran the show and Richard would do anything for him.

'Some of that is safe, though,' Ellen countered. 'University, for one. I attended university in Cardiff, first year, before I came here.'

'School of hard knocks here,' Richard said, pointing at his chest with both thumbs, 'but you weren't asking me, were you, Dennis?'

'No, no. It feels as though we have always known each other, does it not?' There it was again. Richard's gleeful smile at Dennis. Ellen could not determine if Dennis noticed Richard's adoration – although she was unsure how he could not – as he continued his questioning. 'I have heard stories of Richard's riding, though. Are they all true, Antony? Is he really that fast on a motorcycle?' Dennis leant in further, his long arms nearly stretching to the other end of the table. As he moved, Ellen gazed down at his sleeve. The jacket was made of such fine material – no frayed cuffs or missing buttons like most people's had, especially now clothing was rationed. Make do and mend. Dennis certainly had no need to do that.

'You shall have to come ride with me some time,'

Richard said eagerly. 'You can see for yourself.'

'You know he isn't allowed to do that,' Antony grumbled. 'It is firmly against protocol. Our routes are top secret.'

'I didn't mean during work hours. Protocol doesn't control what I do with my dad's bike,' Richard shot back.

'*Common sense* should control what you do with the motorcycle,' Antony said, looking down at the wood table.

'Where did you go to university, Dennis?' Pearl asked, clearly keen to change the subject. Ellen wondered at first if it was because Pearl was too young to have gone to university, but then sat back from the table so she could get a better look at her friend's face. Pearl's eyes were narrowed, her hands clasped firmly in her lap. Pearl was not diverting the topic of conversation from her education; she was digging for something else.

'Cambridge,' he said.

'No surprise,' Pearl said with a firm clip. Ellen folded her arms and considered Pearl. She was up to something.

'Really?' Dennis countered, a twinkle in his eye. 'Is it that obvious?'

'Yes.' Pearl's face was blank, the edge to her voice verging on outright rudeness. Ellen narrowed her eyes. What was she on about? There was no way she could've known he was a Cambridge fellow any more than, say, Oxford. She was more combative with Dennis than Ant had been, and for no reason Ellen could discern.

'It is a big university,' Dennis said with a shrug, 'and

73

not that special.'

'It was special enough to get you a posting with the Ministry of Aviation,' Pearl retorted.

Dennis raised an eyebrow. 'Is that what Richard told you? Old friend, you cannot go telling people what I do.'

Ellen could tell he was teasing – he'd probably been told to say he worked for the Ministry of Aviation like they had been told to say they worked for the Foreign Office – but Richard blanched, his eyes wide. It struck Ellen that Dennis had power over him, enough to frighten him over a small jab.

'But, y-you know what we all do!' Richard stammered. 'You told me yourself you're high enough up that they tell you those things.'

'Ha! You always take things too seriously, Richard!' Dennis laughed. He stood up and ruffled Richard's hair, a playful yet oddly intimate gesture. 'We both have tremendously important jobs and what I know is of no matter to any of you. Just as what you know is no matter to me. My job is no more important than yours, remember? Yours is so very, very critical.'

Richard puffed out his chest, beaming back at Dennis like no one else was in the room. He glowed under Dennis's gaze, which was warm and proud. Ellen's heart lurched as she suddenly realized why Pearl was so hostile. Was she actually seeing this, right here, out in the open? Richard did not simply like Dennis. He adored him.

Oh Pearl, Ellen thought, glancing over at her friend. She must see it, too. How could she not?

Ellen gazed down at her hands folded on the table, then looked up at Dennis. What she could not glean was how he felt about Richard. She was surprised Richard would be so daring as to look at another man that way, in public, but she imagined it was horrible to have to experience adoration for anyone or anything in hiding. While Ellen didn't give two figs about who a person loved, she knew the government didn't feel the same way. Ellen watched the two men for a while, suddenly saddened that if Richard did have affection for Dennis and it was reciprocated, they'd never be able to express it out loud.

The subject changed to football and the tension around the table relaxed. A light-hearted conversation followed, with laughs and more pints, and ended with Dennis walking a rather merry Richard to his motorcycle, Ant striding off alone to his, both men driving off in separate directions into the dark night.

Ellen thought the night would end there. But as it turned out, she was very wrong.

9

ELLEN

After Dennis and Richard walked off towards his motorcycle, Ellen said goodbye to Pearl, who seemed rather mopey, and nervously headed for her billet. This was the first time she had walked back from the Park and while she had filed away a few landmarks this morning to help her stay on the right track, it was harder than expected in the darkness. The night was clear and cool, a crisp breeze cutting through Ellen's good wool coat. She put up the collar and ducked her head, walking quickly so as not to catch a chill.

She needed to become accustomed to walking this route at all hours, as everyone at Bletchley worked varying shifts so work could continue around the clock. Although they had started Ellen off on a 'good' shift – eight o'clock until four o'clock – she knew next week would be less desirable, and likely require her to walk to and from the Waverlys' house in the dark. Even with her white reflective armband and a dimmed torch she'd borrowed from Mrs Waverly, the narrow road was full of strange shadows and the sounds of branches snapping and tiny footsteps scurrying. Ellen thought she was managing her fears adequately until she heard something that couldn't be explained by nature: the nearing sound of running footsteps.

Ellen flattened herself against the hedge, as she did when vehicles approached on the road. She pointed her torch in the direction of the noise, which had slowed to a trot.

A man in a long coat and a scarf came into view. Squinting again, Ellen's breath caught. Could it be Richard's friend Dennis? Why would he follow her?

'Ellen? Ellen, is that you?'

It *was* Dennis. *How curious*, Ellen thought. They'd only just met, and briefly at that. Still, her pounding heart settled as her torch found his face, smiling widely even as he panted from the effort of catching her.

'Ellen, finally!' Dennis stopped, bracing his hands on his knees as he caught his breath.

'Dennis, what are you doing here?' she asked. Had something happened that needed immediate attention? Was it Richard? Or Pearl?

'Oh,' he said with a chuckle. 'I thought I saw you up ahead and was trying to catch up. We're heading the same way, it seems. You know, it's safer to walk these dark roads in pairs.'

'I don't,' Ellen replied. 'I've always walked roads alone and I'm just fine.' She knew her tone was abrupt but she couldn't help it. Although the idea of a solitary walk had made her nervous, Ellen had been counting on the alone time to gather her thoughts and decompress from such a social evening. Besides, Ellen didn't like surprises or unexpected meetings, no matter how friendly Dennis sounded. The hair on the back of her neck prickled, perhaps from the brisk wind but more likely from the unease of the whole situation.

Dennis laughed, although Ellen had not intended to make a joke. 'Fair point,' he said, lowering his head, as if sensing Ellen's seriousness. 'I do apologize. I didn't mean to give you a fright.'

Ellen started to walk, Dennis falling into step beside her. 'Why are you heading this way?' she asked. 'Town's in the opposite direction.'

'My Aunt Myra lives down this road. She had a fall over the summer and doesn't get around as well as she used to. I had to request a transfer because I was out here so often. Tomorrow is my first day working in the huts at Bletchley. I should probably get a bicycle, shouldn't I? This is a long walk.' His torch was pointed at the ground, illuminating his shoes, which shined in the light like they had recently been polished. They were not the shoes of someone who'd walked miles on this road every day; they looked new and unmarred by dirt or water. He probably would be better suited to a bicycle if he insisted on such fine footwear.

Ellen blinked at him as he rambled on, his voice animated, as if they were not walking in the cold and dark in the centre of the road. The details he offered and his tone were familiar, like they were old friends catching up, and Ellen had to remind herself she barely knew him. He even let slip the number of the hut in which he was employed, which made her slightly nervous, though on some level, she appreciated the familiarity. Her thoughts were disjointed and unsettled and Ellen didn't care for it.

'I am sorry, I should pick up the pace. I'm already late and don't want the Waverlys to worry.' Ellen tried lengthening her stride. Her hands were shaking slightly, so she kept them firmly in her pockets.

'Of course,' Dennis said, jogging slightly to keep up. 'Aunt Myra will be wondering where I am. I said I wouldn't be long and here it is well past her bedtime. Thankfully, her house is just beyond the Waverly place. Do you know Mill Road?'

That sounded familiar. Ellen felt her shoulders relax. 'Down by the mill, I assume?'

Dennis laughed. 'It makes sense, does it not? But yes, you pass the old mill to get to her house. It's rather pretty down there in the trees.'

They moved on from talk of his aunt and family as they walked, Ellen using techniques drilled into her by her mother to move the conversation along. ('Ask about his favourite books [*The Hobbit*] or foods [cheese].') She found she had not talked so easily with a boy since her brother left home for the Army.

As the Waverly farmhouse came into view against the bright night sky, Dennis slowed his pace a bit, as if wanting to stretch out their conversation.

'It is nice talking with someone who appreciates the same things I do,' he admitted when Ellen asked why he was hanging back. 'Is it selfish if I want to keep chatting all the way to Mill Cottage?'

Ellen felt her ears go warm and swallowed down the weird, fluttery feeling in her stomach. Talking with Dennis had been easy. He didn't make her feel at all self-conscious or nervous about her responses. Still, she deflected his attention, which her mother advised in such situations with men. 'Oh please, Dennis, you must have plenty of friends – Richard for one – who are more conversational than I am.' She hesitated before adding, cautiously, 'You and Richard are quite chummy. You seem to know a lot about each other.'

Dennis looked upwards for a beat and Ellen followed his glance, taking in the fast-moving wisps of cloud against the darkening sky. 'It's *different* with Richard. I don't know if I can explain it. He tells me things. I've asked him not to. But you cannot physically stop someone from talking. Trust me, I've tried.'

'He's telling you about his work?' Ellen pried, her heart racing. Richard *was* being indiscreet.

'I don't know what more I should say. I feel awful about it, as Richard is a good friend, but I cannot violate my own pledge to the King. I told him he had to stop. I told him it wouldn't change our friendship. But he seems to have trouble keeping quiet, especially around me.'

Ellen felt her breath catch. If this was all true, and Dennis told anyone at Bletchley, Richard could be out of a job by morning, and rightfully so. She'd heard rumours of traitors put in prison for life, or even hanged.

Dennis continued. 'Oh, Ellen, I feel horrible telling you this, but tonight, as I walked him to his bike, he told me something, an intention he has towards me. Do you understand what I mean?'

Ellen nodded slowly, glad he could not see her face in the dark. She barely knew either fellow, but felt that whatever Dennis was about to reveal was not a good thing for either of them. Ellen knew exactly how it felt when a friendship fell flat. One person always ended up sad and she knew too well how deeply painful that could feel. 'Oh, Richard,' she sighed, almost to herself. 'I did wonder about the nature of your, erm, friendship.'

'In my mind, it is just a friendship – a highly valued one, but that is it. We are simply pals. I told him as much this evening.' He paused. 'Ellen, I think Richard's ease with information around me, well, I worry he's been trying to win me over with secrets.' Just over the rise, Ellen saw the Waverly farmhouse more clearly now. She would turn on to the gravel drive soon, but was not sure she wanted to leave Dennis in the middle of such a charged conversation.

In the dim light from the half-clouded stars, Ellen could see that his lips were pressed together tightly, as if he was trying to keep himself from saying anything more. But instead of speaking, he grasped both her hands in his. He leant in so his eyes looked directly into hers. 'Thank you for understanding. I feel so much better now that I've told someone. Do you think – will Richard still be my friend, or have I ruined it entirely? Oh, I feel horrible,' he said in a soft voice so full of feeling it sent a jolt down Ellen's spine. 'I hate hurting people, especially my friends, but I couldn't . . .'

'You can't be something you are not, but this is hard on Richard. It is never easy to express your feelings, requited or not. Be mindful of that and perhaps you can preserve the friendship,' she said, instantly aware her hands were sweating and oh my, was he ever close. She could smell the brackish combination of beer and cigarette smoke from the pub along with a soapy odour, like he'd just stepped from a steamy bath. Instinctively, she stepped back, pulling her hands from his.

Dennis let out a long breath. Ellen felt a rush, like a breeze through her body. If Dennis did not think of

Richard that way, he could think of someone else romantically.

'Thank you, Ellen. You're right. I'll tread lightly,' he said softly. 'Your approval means a lot.'

Ellen stood for a few moments, puzzled, before blurting, 'Well, then, goodbye.' She turned on her heel and sped, head down, towards the Waverlys' house, refusing to look over her shoulder no matter how much she wanted to. Why had he cared what she thought? They'd only just met!

But what was even more disconcerting was the way her stomach felt like she'd drunk a pint of seawater – murky, unsteady, and unsure of what was to come.

Work flew by the next day, Ellen's last shift before her first day off, and before she knew it, girls were filing out for their lunch break. She tried to act as if she had not completely forgotten about lunch, distracted by the endless fragments of information that came across her desk. She could not help but feel that someday all the pieces would add up to something very critical.

She jogged slightly to catch up with the girls heading to the canteen. Most ate at Bletchley for lunch, as those billeted in the countryside did not have time to return to their residences. Some girls arranged to collect sandwiches to eat back at their desks, but Ellen had relished the break from the smoky, stuffy room yesterday.

She followed the stream of girls into the bustling canteen, smells of roasted meat and salt assaulting her nose. At university, Ellen had usually opted for soup of some sort and whatever dry loaf they were slicing that day, always choosing a table alone so she could study whilst eating. Here, it was different. She had no excuse to shut out the rest of the world with a book, a practice her mother had warned her was dreadfully antisocial, no matter how much Ellen insisted she needed the solitude. As she waited in the snaking queue, she spied Pearl with a few wrapped parcels. Pearl waved frantically, gesturing for her to join her by the door.

'I have an extra sandwich and apple,' Pearl said, holding out a waxed-paper-wrapped bundle. 'I put in a request for one and because I know *everyone* at the Park, even the canteen ladies, they insisted I take two. My duties definitely have their benefits. But I cannot eat both – would you join me?'

Pearl was in much better form than she had been last night, a relief considering how much Ellen had to divulge after her walk with Dennis. 'Thank you. That sounds far more delightful than standing in that queue.'

'Shall we eat by the pond?' Pearl looked out the window. 'For once, it isn't raining.'

Ellen followed her out the door, relieved she would not have to navigate the social intricacies of choosing lunch companions in the crowded canteen. They walked to a bench by the pond, the sun having warmed the day substantially since Ellen's chilly walk that morning. Pearl told her that the first few workers at Bletchley Park had called themselves 'guests of Captain Ridley's Shooting Party' so as not to draw attention from the locals. Most of the original employees lived on site, though some, like Pearl and her mum, lived in town. Back then, they ate in the mansion's dining room instead of in the blocky, larger canteen building, which had been built later. Pearl talked of gorgeous catered meals featuring beautiful food like local pheasant and puffy Yorkshire puddings as light as clouds. The war, and an influx of workers, put an end to those luxuries. And the Yorkshire puddings, when they happened now, were hard to chew and as heavy as sandbags.

'You seem more content this afternoon,' Ellen said cautiously.

Pearl raised her sandwich to her mouth and paused. 'I *am* rather lousy at hiding my displeasure. Mother has said I'd make a terrible spy.' She took a hefty bite, crunching into the egg-and-celery mess with more gusto than Ellen thought the sandwich deserved. Shoving the bite into her cheek like a squirrel, she continued: 'I was so peeved last night. Richard – he's hopeless.'

'How so?'

'Oh, I . . .' Pearl's gaze dropped to her lap and she

shrugged. 'He was being so childish about his friend, Dennis. You'd think he didn't have any other friends, the way he carried on.'

'Funny thing,' Ellen said, although she knew what she had to say was far from funny, 'is I walked home with Dennis last night.'

Pearl gazed up at her friend through her overgrown fringe. 'That's odd.'

'It was,' Ellen agreed. 'His aunt lives beyond my billet, it seems.'

'Huh.'

Ellen picked at her sandwich nervously. How did one tell someone that the person they adored did not feel the same way? Ellen knew she ought to be delicate, but that was not in her nature. Best to come right out with it, she reasoned. It was what she would've wanted, if she were Pearl. 'Richard confessed to Dennis he has feelings for him – amorous ones – after we left. Dennis was worried, both that he'd lose his friendship and that Richard has been sharing sensitive information with him in an attempt to, I don't know, woo him, I suppose?'

Pearl's head dropped again, even lower this time, as she placed the rest of her sandwich on its wrapper. Ellen held her breath, worried her no-nonsense approach would backfire. Maybe Mother was right – she always said you won people over with honey-coated statements rather than the blunt edge of truth.

'I know,' Pearl said quietly. 'I mean, I did not know all of that, but I suspected. That's why I was angry. It was so blatant, out there for everyone to see.' She sighed. 'He had just taken me out for supper. I thought it meant something.'

'I am sorry. Truly. I thought it was better to know . . .'

'Oh, it is,' Pearl said. 'Still hurts, though.'

'Of course,' Ellen said, though she had no idea. She had never had a boyfriend, or a date for that matter.

Shaking the curtain of hair from her eyes, Pearl sat up. 'What was it you said about secrets? Richard has been telling Dennis things he, uh, shouldn't? Like what?'

'He didn't say, but we saw enough of it ourselves last night. It seemed like Richard has told him quite a lot.'

Pearl bristled and picked at the crusts of her half-eaten sandwich. 'Yes, but, do you trust Dennis? Sure, I just met him, but I got a bad feeling about him. Didn't you? Of course, maybe I'm making it up. Mum says I need to get my nose out of mystery novels and into reality. *"Not every-one is a murderer and not everyone has an ulterior motive."* But when my reality is Mum shushing me for saying the words "Bletchley Park" within a few paces of people we pass on the pavement, how can I not be suspicious? Truthfully, though, something felt off about Dennis and I don't think it's because I'm paranoid or read a lot.'

Ellen took a bite of her lunch, which was on bread so dry she had to work to swallow it. Her instinct said that

Pearl's feelings were those of jealousy, not an accurate assessment of Dennis's character. After all, he'd told her about Richard's amorous confession, and his concern about his oversharing. It did not seem to her that Dennis was hiding anything or had an ulterior motive.

'Look, Pearl, more on the novels later, because I love to talk books, but what seemed off to you? Because he was very straightforward and honest with me.'

'He asked a lot of questions.'

'Yes, he did,' Ellen said. Pearl was edging around what she really wanted to say, looking through her hair and offering very guided, slow responses. 'Clearly his questions made you uneasy, but he was not prodding. There was nothing that stretched the limits of our confidentiality.'

'No,' Pearl said, inhaling loudly through her teeth. 'But he was being very selective. I felt he knew things already and was dancing around implied answers.'

As she searched for an appropriately probing question, Ellen realized she was a horrible interrogator. Her mother had coached her endlessly about how to interact with other people. 'Do not feel the need to *fill* every silence, Ellen,' she would say, buttoning up Ellen's cardigan before she went to class in the morning. 'Let others talk to you. Listen to their stories. Sometimes you'll learn more that way.' Ellen took her mother's advice and pressed her lips together, willing Pearl to continue.

'I just . . . I don't trust him. What if he's telling other

people what Richard told him in confidence? I mean, he's divulged Richard's feelings to you. That's not noble, is it? To blab about something private a friend has shared.' Pearl looked across the pond, chewing fiercely on her last crust of bread. She kept shooting quick glances over at Ellen. *She does not trust me yet*, Ellen thought, and was surprised at the feeling of sadness that accompanied that realization. Finally, Pearl spoke: 'I have to talk to Richard,' she said, flatly. 'Warn him about saying too much to Dennis. This could be serious.'

Ellen stood up, wadding the waxed paper around her sandwich. She would eat it later, with a large cup of tea to help coax it down. 'I concur. After all, we've agreed to tell the authorities if we see anything suspicious, and this seems to qualify. Richard could be in danger if someone else overhears him talking to Dennis.'

'Or if Dennis continues flapping his lips all over town,' Pearl said, her eyes wide and fearful.

'I really should get back to work,' Ellen said.

Pearl stood up, her chin jutted forward, palms open to the sky, surprise in her eyes. 'Well, what . . . how do I . . . say something?'

Ellen realized her dismissal of the conversation had perhaps been too abrupt. She turned around and shrugged. 'Don't talk about his feelings for Dennis, just his, um, indiscretions, and how he should be more careful. Does he like puzzles? Perhaps you could put it in an anagram like

10

ELLEN

For weeks, Ellen thought of nothing but her job. She'd figured out the coding system, the colours used and key words to note on cards so they could archive various messages. She liked finally feeling confident in her work, even when she was assigned two weeks of night shift and could barely hold her head up some mornings. She'd arrive home at the Waverlys' and yawn her way through breakfast, often helping to spoon porridge into the baby's mouth while Mrs Waverly made an attempt at small talk. Though she knew her host wanted her to stay and chat over a cup of tea, Ellen always retired to her room for a few precious hours of sleep under her heavy pile of quilts. When she and Pearl happened to have the same schedule, they'd meet for lunch or tea or just a brief hello by the pond. Ellen didn't ask Pearl about Richard again – it was a sore topic for Pearl, and Ellen didn't want to mess things up even more than she already had.

She'd had a few lucky evenings where she'd seen Dennis while walking to work. He was often on his way to his aunt's on a rickety bicycle he'd acquired, and he'd hop off and they'd stop and chat about nothing in particular. Ellen noted that the nights she saw Dennis were less painful than the ones she struggled through alone. She was not exactly sure what that meant, so she pushed it aside and tried not to hope for more chance meetings.

The first Monday back to a day shift was a miserable day; she was even wearing gloves and her cream-coloured scarf inside, it was so cold. The wind tore through the hastily constructed hut like it was a house of cards. But Ellen was able to lose herself in the messages she was categorizing by imagining she was a spy who had stumbled across secret information while searching a tiny cottage in the dense Black Forest of Germany. She had to work quickly before the Nazis found her and assassinated her on the spot. Even in her fantasy, Ellen knew she would probably cave under the pressure, but it made the time pass.

'*Psst*. Ellen.'

Ellen started, nearly knocking an entire stack of cards on to the floor. Pearl was standing over her right shoulder. Her breath smelt of peppermints.

Ellen instinctively threw an arm over her papers, a move she knew would annoy Pearl.

'What do you want?' she whispered cautiously. 'You're

not supposed to be here. Mr St John hates idle gossip during work hours,' she added, hoping Pearl would not be insulted.

Pearl stepped back and crossed her arms. Her glossy eyes shifted around the room. Ellen had never seen Pearl look anything but confident before. 'I need to talk to you. *Now*,' Pearl said, her bottom lip trembling.

'Shh!' Ellen said, her finger over her lips like an angry librarian. What was Pearl playing at? Mr St John wasn't preoccupied enough for them to chat in plain view like this. Didn't she realize that whatever had upset her, this wasn't the time or place? 'Please, Pearl, you're going to get me in trouble.'

'Ellen. Pearl,' Mr St John said, rising fluidly from his chair, 'I need you over at my desk. Make haste.'

'Me?' Pearl asked, pointing at her chest with a shaking finger.

'I said your name,' he replied, his expression blank as usual. Mr St John was not used to being questioned. When he called your name, you answered. Quickly.

'Hurry up,' Ellen whispered, pushing a bewildered Pearl down the aisle.

'But I . . . I have to tell you something . . .' Pearl stammered, looking at Ellen helplessly. Ellen put a finger to her lips again and pulled her friend to Mr St John's desk.

He sat back down in his chair and opened a file folder on his desk. 'You have both been reassigned, effective tomorrow morning.'

Ellen opened her mouth, but shut it again when Mr St John held up his hand. Was this a promotion? If so, was it appropriate to be pleased? Ellen looked from Mr St John to Pearl and decided to save her excitement.

'Please report to me at eight thirty sharp tomorrow in the large corner room down the hall. I will be your supervisor. Any questions?'

'You're saying I'm not a messenger any longer?' Pearl asked, clearly dumbfounded. Her eyes were wide and her mouth gaped. Ellen's mother would've told her to close it before midges ventured in.

'Correct.'

'Does Miss Waincross know?' Pearl asked.

'Miss Waincross is well aware of this change,' Mr St John said. 'She and others have asked you to be placed under my tutelage, as you could benefit from more direct monitoring and observation.'

'I see,' Pearl said. She took a step backwards, as if someone had pushed her. Ellen frowned. Was she mistaken, or had Mr St John said, in not so many words, that Pearl was being closely monitored?

When she had first arrived, Ellen had heard a story about a girl in her room, also tasked with categorizing index cards. Some of the girl's cards went missing and even though the girl swore she had nothing to do with it, she was gone the next morning. Some naively thought she

94

had been sent home, but most agreed she had been arrested. If she was found to have passed information to the enemy, she would have been executed for treason. There was a rumour someone had turned her in – and another rumour that other girls might've been spying too. One was even so bold as to look warily at Mr St John. Everyone was a suspect, it seemed: even Pearl.

Mr St John gave them a long, hard glare. Ellen couldn't imagine him truly doubting Pearl without solid proof. He seemed to be driven by facts, just like she was. He would collect his own evidence and dismiss rumours, and Pearl wouldn't let him down. She wasn't that type of girl.

'Remember, you are to report tomorrow at half past eight. We have several detailed instructions and rules to review before you get started.' He looked at his watch and then back at the girls. 'Ellen, it is close enough to lunchtime. You're excused for the day.'

'For the day?' she blurted, then added, 'Sir?'

'I suspect it would be more beneficial to have a clear mind at the start of your shift tomorrow. Besides, I have important meetings and can't be here this afternoon. The other girls will carry on. They're used to taking over when needed.'

Ellen nodded and thanked him, wondering what was so important he'd leave an entire room of workers on their own, without assistance. But she tried not to concern herself with it – she was getting promoted, after all. The idea that she was about to get more challenging, important work to help with the war effort was beyond thrilling and she couldn't help smiling as she rushed back to tidy her desk. Then she remembered the odd bit about supervising Pearl, which had struck her as a strange thing to say in front of someone else. Also, it had to have been embarrassing for Pearl.

'Ellen!' Pearl rasped above her shoulder. 'Ellen, can you please hurry up? There is something I have to tell you.'

'I should clean my space for the next girl. It's the least I can do now that I'm leaving this room. You heard Mr St John, I'll need a clear—'

'It. Cannot. Wait,' Pearl interrupted through clenched teeth.

Ellen felt her shoulders rise and she gripped her pencil tighter. 'It'll take five minutes at most. What's the hurry, Pearl?' Her heart sank as she noticed how her friend's eyes brimmed over with tears, her neck splotchy and red. 'Oh dear. What's wrong?'

Pearl walked to the front of the desk and leant down, her face level with Ellen's. Then, she whispered three horrifying words in Ellen's ear: 'Richard is dead.'

11

PEARL

Pearl's mouth was dry. Forming the words had been more difficult than she had anticipated.

Ellen cocked her head to the side like she was having trouble hearing. Her hands still gripped her pencil tightly, so hard Pearl thought it might break, but she leant across the table and answered, 'What do you mean?'

'I mean what I said.' Pearl had enough trouble saying it the first time. She did not want to have to repeat those words ever again. It made the whole terrible thing more real.

'All right,' Ellen said. She put down her pencil and gathered the rest of her cards and pencils to one side. She took ages to neatly pile the cards, square the edges and put the pencils in a box at the top of her desk. Then she swallowed and said, 'We'd best go somewhere we can talk. Mr St John said I could leave.'

Pearl let out the air she had been holding in, relief washing over her. 'We need to talk in private. I don't know where to go.'

'We can go to my billet. It is only a short walk from here and no one will bother us there.' Ellen shrugged into her wool coat and fastened the top button. 'The roads to the countryside are quiet. We can talk along the way.'

Pearl nodded and followed Ellen out of the hut. They walked quickly past the pond and round the front of the mansion, following the driveway to the gate. Once outside the Park, they took the narrow, curvy road that led away from the town. Even though the street was mostly deserted, Pearl didn't feel comfortable enough to speak until they'd got past the rows of houses. Now, only the cows and sheep could overhear their conversation.

Pearl felt her chin start to tremble as she prepared to tell Ellen everything. She remembered her mum's face when she'd told her. Her mum had cried. Her mother, the strong, stoic voice of reason and the unflappable assistant to one of the most powerful people at Bletchley, quickly wiping away tears as she told Pearl in their front hall.

'It's not just that Richard has died . . . it gets worse,' Pearl started, her voice hoarse.

Ellen barely flinched, her stride steady, but there was a softness to her tone. 'I hate to take a venture at what is worse than death, Pearl. Now, why don't you start at the beginning?'

Pearl looked up at the sheet of clouds above – it was as if someone had pulled grey curtains over the sky. The weather had turned, the last few wisps of autumn sunshine carried away on the cold wind that ripped through the trees, reminding them of the frigid winter ahead. She wondered if Richard was cold – he had to be – and where he was. Had someone at least covered him? Pearl pulled her cardigan closer, a chill running down her spine.

'It was so tragic, Ellen. So, so tragic.' She paused, taking a shuddering breath and willing herself not to cry ugly, raw tears. 'Ant and Richard were riding early in the morning as usual and had just left the Park. You know those narrow roads towards London, like curlicues, but with hedges and walls on the sides. Like these.' Pearl twirled around, her arms wide, pointing to the high hedgerows lining the narrow, windy road. She felt unhinged, out of control. None of what she was saying seemed real. Her body vibrated like she was on the back of an actual motorcycle. 'Richard rides too fast.'

'I remember them talking about that,' Ellen said calmly. 'It was an accident, then?'

'They seem to think it was an accident, but there is an official investigation underway.'

'As there should be,' Ellen replied. Pearl glanced across at her. Ellen's lips were pulled down in a deep frown and her eyebrows arched. Worried. She didn't reach out for

Pearl – and that was all right – but she was visibly hurting for her friend. That was enough for Pearl, who hugged her cardigan closer.

'There's more, though,' she began again.

'The worse than death bit?'

Pearl nodded. 'Richard's messenger bag is missing. The bag with all the envelopes from Bletchley Park. He was headed to Whitehall, so those missing envelopes have to be . . .'

'Extremely important,' Ellen finished.

They turned the corner and a tall, narrow farmhouse came into view. 'Here we are,' said Ellen. 'Stay quiet until we get upstairs. I trust the Waverlys, but I would hate to start rumours.' Then she took Pearl's arm and escorted her up the front walk.

The house was quiet, as Ellen had promised. Mrs Waverly was in the garden with the baby and Mr Waverly had gone into town. Pearl and Ellen were able to slip upstairs to Ellen's attic bedroom without any questions. Ellen had not lied about how quiet her room was, but she'd neglected to mention how cold it was. Up in the attic with no fireplace, Ellen relied on Mrs Waverly's worn quilts to keep warm. Her small single bed looked like an illustration from Pearl's childhood picture book *The Princess and the Pea*, stacked with at least six brightly coloured quilts. Ellen sat on the bed and pulled a quilt over her shoulders, her coat still on. She patted next to her and after Pearl sat close to her, she looped the end of the quilt over both their shoulders.

'There. The quilt helps, doesn't it?' Ellen asked gently. 'Now, shall we begin again? Richard died in a motorcycle accident yesterday morning. There is an investigation going on because his bag with envelopes bound for Whitehall has gone missing. You are distraught, as you should be. He was, well, more than a friend.'

Pearl nodded, wiping at her eyes. Even if Richard had not loved her in the way she had him, he *was* more than a friend to her. They had been close and talked every day. She would miss him tremendously. 'Ellen, I won't see him in the mornings any longer. Ever.'

'I know.' Ellen hugged her a bit closer. 'I *am* terribly sorry, Pearl.'

She took a deep breath. 'There is something else. Remember how you told me I needed to talk to Richard? To voice my concerns and protect him? Well, I kept trying to, but it wasn't an easy thing to bring up. For the last few weeks I've either missed him, or I couldn't gather up the nerve to say anything. Besides, he wasn't himself, not since . . .' Her cheeks coloured and she shook her head. 'Finally, I put a letter in his bag the evening before he died. I had hoped he'd find it and read it in the morning, when he was sorting out his deliveries. Perhaps he saw it. Perhaps he didn't. Only, I have no way of knowing and now he's gone. For ever.'

'Relationships and men are nothing but confusing. Far worse than the hardest puzzle, in my opinion,' Ellen said. 'What exactly did you disclose in the letter?'

Pearl hesitated. Even though she wanted to tell the whole truth, it was complicated. She would not tell Ellen anything about the envelope she'd opened accidentally, what Miss Waincross saw or about Richard's concerns over his tattered envelopes, all of which added to the worry churning in her mind. 'It was mainly about our relationship. But I warned him about Dennis, like we discussed, telling him to be careful what he told others. I probably wasn't subtle enough. I wrote things down I should not have.' Pearl felt heat rise to her cheeks. 'What was I thinking? I'm going to be in so much trouble.' She buried her face in her hands.

Ellen put her cold hand awkwardly on Pearl's knee, so stiff and unnatural, it felt almost like a porcelain doll's hand lying there. Ellen spoke softly: 'I hate to say it, but if someone stole Richard's bag, someone who intends to share that information with the Nazis, they likely will not pay much attention to your letter. They'll not be able to focus on anything other than the fact that we've been able to decode some of their communications. They won't care about Richard's loose tongue.'

'I know. I *know*. But I need it back, Ellen.' Pearl waited for Ellen to pry into the specific things she had written, but she did not. 'Even if it's just found by the police, I said things I shouldn't. I won't be allowed back at the Park. Or worse.'

Knowing Ellen, Pearl expected more questions, asking for details. Instead, Ellen asked, 'What would you like to do, then?'

'I want to get it back.' Pearl wiped her eyes with the back of her soggy sleeve. 'I don't know how, but I have to find it.'

Ellen inhaled deeply. 'All right, then. We'll look for it.'

'Are you sure?' Pearl asked, swallowing loudly. 'You'll really help me?'

Ellen nodded. 'There's no harm in looking. Perhaps it's as simple as scouring the accident scene and four eyes are better than two, after all.'

'That is true,' Pearl asserted, managing a smile. They made a plan to go to the accident site early the next morning, before there was much chance of passing traffic, and Pearl felt something like relief. With Ellen's help, she might just be able to squeak out of trouble yet again, although she knew nothing was ever that easy. Not for Pearl, at least.

12

ELLEN

The next morning, before it was even close to being light, Ellen opened her attic door to find a jug of water and a clean hand towel waiting outside as normal. She wrapped her hands around the warm porcelain, trying to make her teeth stop chattering. It was a freezing six o'clock in early November. Winter was going to be miserable without a source of heat in her room.

After splashing her face and thawing her numb fingertips in the bowl of warm, soapy water, Ellen layered two jumpers over her wool skirt. She was nearly cold enough to wear the horrible thick tights her mother had sent, but she didn't want to stand out. All the other girls wore stockings.

In the dining room Mr and Mrs Waverly sipped tea in silence. The baby slept in a cot near the fireplace, which filled the room with an inviting warmth. Ellen was lucky the Waverlys had a wood fireplace, even if the heat did not reach her attic room. She had heard tales of other girls having to hunt down paraffin for the tiny, inefficient heaters at their billets and they were often unsuccessful and, therefore, even colder. At least Ellen knew the dining room would always be cosy at breakfast time.

When Ellen entered, Mrs Waverly poured her a cup of tea and pushed a bowl of porridge her way. A pile of almost burnt toast sat on the sideboard, crumbs scattered across the runner like sand on a beach towel. Ellen selected two darkish slices and slathered them with home-made jam. She was grateful to Mrs Waverly for having preserved tons of fruits and vegetables in the summer with the products of her plentiful home garden plot.

'You're up early this morning. It's not even half six,' Mrs Waverly said when Ellen finally sat down. 'I thought you had the afternoon shift this week.'

'I'm meeting a friend. We are going, uh, for a walk.' She paused. 'Also, I've been reassigned, so now I'm on mornings again.'

'A walk?' Mr Waverly said, spooning raspberry jam on his burnt toast. 'It's barely above freezing outside. Have you gone barking mad?'

'Andrew, hush,' Mrs Waverly exclaimed. 'Be nice. I am sure it will warm up . . .'

'They're forecasting freezing rain,' he said, pointing at the newspaper with a small silver baby spoon. 'But I suspect it will be nearly tropical once that ends.'

Ellen looked out the small window. It was dark and grey but had been for the past two days. As long as she and Pearl could investigate the scene of the crash before it started raining, it would not be a problem.

'Don't mind him, Ellen,' Mrs Waverly said, smiling broadly. 'If you need to take a walk to clear your head, that is what you need to do.' She lowered her voice and leant in. 'I have heard you girls are under immense pressure working for the Foreign Office, is that right?'

Ellen simply took another bite of toast and smiled. Mrs Waverly knew Ellen could not answer that question. Still, every once in a while, she would prod, slightly, with an envious, eager look in her eye. Ellen knew that if Mrs Waverly didn't have the baby, she'd probably have been recruited to the Park. She was smart, always reading dog-eared Agatha Christie and Dorothy Sayers novels by the fireplace. But unlike Ellen, Mrs Waverly had married early and had a baby. Another reason why Ellen hated the heat that crept across her face whenever she thought too long about Dennis – she did not want to end up like Mrs Waverly, unhappy and stuck at home.

Ellen looked at the clock. It was almost seven. She stuffed the last of her toast in her mouth and washed it down with weak tea.

'Sorry – got to run. Need me to pick up anything in town?'

'No,' Mrs Waverly said, her voice soft as she looked down at the tablecloth. The baby cried out and Mr Waverly shot her an angry look.

'June, take care of that child,' he snapped.

Ellen slinked out of the room before a row started, crouching in the hall to tighten her shoelaces. She hated being a fly on the wall of their family home. She felt awful when they did anything normal couples would – fought or held hands under the table. Her goal was to be as invisible as possible so they would not kick her out – the freezing attic room wasn't that horrible and she was able to walk to work in thirty minutes, unlike most girls who had been billeted further into the countryside.

Luckily, the row didn't really start at all – as Ellen straightened up, the baby quieted and Mr Waverly started to talk as his wife hushed the child. 'Fran Farland came by last night after you went up, all shook up from some accident on the main road to town.'

Ellen stopped beyond the door frame, clinging to Mr Waverly's words.

'Oh, poor fellow. He wasn't hurt in the accident, was he?' Mrs Waverly asked, her voice quiet and cautious.

'Not Fran, but a motorcyclist. A grisly accident. The boy had skidded out before Fran came round the corner in his dad's van. It was all over before he had a chance to help, poor lad.'

'Did the van hit the motorcycle?' Ellen blurted from

the hall, instantly regretting it when she saw the shock in Mr Waverly's eyes. She should've stayed quiet, but how could she? He was talking about Richard. She pushed the door wider sheepishly. 'Sorry. I didn't mean to eavesdrop . . .'

'So, you heard about it, did you Ellen?' he replied, spacing out the words thoughtfully.

'Not really,' Ellen answered, edging back into the dining room slightly. 'I heard there was an accident, but I had no idea there was a van involved, just that the road was treacherous and the motorcycle rider died.'

'Well,' Mr Waverly said firmly, 'Fran did not hit the motorcycle. He swerved and hit a wall at the roadside, smashed his headlamps but nothing else. Fran's father has his own demons from his short stint in the war. He was badly injured in training camp when another lad flipped their vehicle over. It killed the friend outright and between injuries from that accident and his heart troubles, Farland's aged tremendously since returning, poor fellow. Which is why Fran was behind the wheel. He's an overly cautious driver, especially when his father's in the passenger seat. Slower than a grandma with a cane, he is. I suppose he'll be even slower after seeing blood all over the road and a boy's head smashed in like a pumpkin destined for the pig trough.'

Ellen closed her eyes at his last statement, wishing he had spared her the grisly details. Then she looked at Mrs Waverly, who had gone as pale as a sheet.

'Bless his soul,' Mrs Waverly gasped. 'I've always told you people drive far too fast on those roads. It is so dangerous out there, between the bombs and the—'

Mr Waverly nodded in agreement, cutting her off. 'Those show-off military blokes need to slow down, show some respect for the roads. Too many of them flipping over, dying in the fog out there. Fran said it was a tricky part of the road, one that *locals* know to be wary of. He said there was no *reason* for the accident. None at all.'

Mrs Waverly bowed her head.

Ellen licked her lips to avoid taking in another shuddering breath. Richard *was* a local, though. He would've known to be cautious on that curve, wouldn't he?

Mr Waverly had already turned back to his newspaper.

'Be careful out there, dear,' Mrs Waverly said as Ellen retreated, her stomach and mind churning.

'You needn't worry about me,' Ellen said as she shut the door, shooting the woman a quick smile.

Something had made Richard crash, but not the delivery van. That, coupled with the missing bag and the letter Pearl was desperate to get back, made everything about Richard's death very curious. While Ellen knew she was getting ahead of herself, she also knew this was shaping up to be a proper mystery, and she loved a good mystery.

13

ELLEN

The moment Ellen saw Pearl running down the road she felt even colder. Why was Pearl not wearing more than that ratty old cardigan? Ellen had wrapped her long scarf over her head, burying her nose and mouth in its scratchy folds and breathing in the natural, wheaty smell of wool. As Mr Waverly had predicted, rain started as soon as Ellen left the house. Chunky rain. Ellen stuffed her gloved hands in her pockets and bounced on the balls of her feet.

'Sorry, sorry, sorry!' Pearl called out as she jogged down the road. 'Mum was up early and insisted I sit with her and eat a whole bowl of porridge. A *whole* bowl!'

'It is frigid out here. Best get moving before the clouds really open up,' Ellen said, marching forward. Once the blood started moving again in her limbs, she did not exactly thaw out, but she could finally think of something other than how icy she was. A bitter breeze lashed against her exposed cheeks. She looked at the road, shiny with a layer of frost. Could it have been this cold two mornings ago? If so, they had an obvious cause for the accident.

'Have you heard anything more about what happened to Richard?' She needed to be delicate with what Mr Waverly had revealed. First, it would be upsetting. Second, she suspected Pearl's mother would have heard more reliable information.

'Nothing much. Richard came into a curve well ahead of Antony – which is not surprising of course, because of how fast Richard always rode – and crashed.' Pearl looked at Ellen blankly.

'That's all?'

'I suppose?' Pearl said, then put her hands on her hips and stopped walking. 'What are you after, Ellen?'

Ellen sighed. Her sleuthing needed some work. 'They were alone on the road?'

'I don't . . . why? You're digging for something, aren't you?'

Ellen could not help but smile. It *was* nice to have a friend who knew her well enough to recognize these things. Upon smiling, though, she realized Pearl would probably take this the wrong way – she was not, after all, mocking her – and she immediately explained. 'Look, this morning Mr Waverly told me what he had heard about the accident. They weren't alone on the road. There was a local grocer's delivery van that either happened on the accident afterwards or may have caused it.'

'The van . . . was it Mr Farland's?' Pearl asked.

Ellen nodded. 'I think so. Along with his son, who was driving, according to Mr Waverly.'

Pearl looked at Ellen sceptically. She did not speak for a while and when she did, she was cautious. 'Well . . . it makes sense that there was someone else involved. Richard was fast, but he was a really good rider, and he knew these roads really well. Ellen, did you know Don Rs have to know every route in and out of any pickup or delivery location, both backwards and forwards? He said the other night they could never take the same route twice for fear of being followed. They know the roads round here better than a London cabbie knows Piccadilly Circus. No, there must've been something different about the situation, something unexpected, for him to get into such a bad accident.'

Ellen wiped a thin layer of cold moisture off her forehead. It was sleeting in earnest now, drops that pierced like needles before melting in an icy sheet over her exposed flesh. Fog had blanketed the sky. 'Couldn't he have heard the van approaching?'

'His bike sounds almost like a small train when you're on it. Sort of a chugging noise on top of a low rumble – so he might not have heard. But he didn't only depend on his hearing, Ellen. He told me once he practically felt the

112

road under his legs, like the bike was part of his body. It never made sense to me, but if that was the case, wouldn't he at least have *felt* the van's presence before it hit him?' Pearl looked at the sky and blinked rapidly. Ellen could tell this was all very, very hard for her. Ellen knew she needed to be careful, steer away from emotional memories and make Richard's death more like those old 'when a train leaves a station' word puzzles.

'Pearl, I'm not sure it did hit him. The van was damaged. Mr Waverly said its headlamps were smashed, but I saw the Farlands' van out making deliveries yesterday – so it can't have been too bad. It ended up crashing into a stone wall. Think about it – why would the van continue on and hit a stone wall after hitting Richard? It would have stopped immediately. Especially because Mr Waverly said Fran is an overly cautious driver,' Ellen said.

'The way the road curves, it's a blind corner on both sides – you'll see in a minute, we're nearly there. The point is, Fran Farland wouldn't have seen Richard, not at first. Oh, Ellen, are you sure Fran didn't hit him?' Pearl said, her voice high and thin and almost frantic. 'Maybe something happened to the brakes.'

'Hear me out,' Ellen pleaded. She had lost Pearl and needed to get her back to that analytical space. 'I don't think the van caused the accident. It's not possible, not with such minimal damage to the vehicle. Most likely, the van hit the wall to avoid crashing into the motorcycle, which was already down in the road.' Ellen ran to the hedgerow and pulled back some leaves, exposing the sturdy but ramshackle rock wall that ran underneath. The road was lined with this hedgerow and rock wall, nearly to the neighbouring town. 'Think about how gruesome his injuries would have been had he been tossed over the front of the van – it would not have been clean enough to do today's deliveries, let alone yeste—'

'Ellen, please,' Pearl interrupted, squeezing her eyes shut. When she spoke, it was more air than tone, breathy and light and easily drowned out by the sound of the wind. Ellen had to strain to hear her, for once. 'There *was* blood everywhere. Maybe not on the van, but on Richard. He hit his head. Richard's mother couldn't view his . . . his body, because it was so bad. Can you imagine?'

Ellen remembered what Mr Waverly had said about the smashed pumpkin and took a deep breath in, the cold air biting at her throat. Instantly, she saw her brother's face, bloody and pale, and her throat closed. She had not expected such a visceral reaction and when she looked at Pearl's pained face, she felt terribly sorry for her grieving friend.

'I am *so* sorry,' Ellen said. 'I truly am.'

'Thank you,' Pearl said with a meek smile.

The wind had picked up, which meant that not only was the sleet hitting them square across the face, but the earthy, pungent smell of cow dung from the surrounding

114

farms overcame the cleansing power of the wet snow. Although they could not clearly see the fields beyond the tall, dense hedgerow, there was no doubt the cows were there, every so often emitting a gentle moo as a reminder.

'Here,' Pearl said, 'the crash site is further along the road but it'll be faster if we cut through this field. Following the road takes ages, it's so loopy.' She rubbed her hands together and blew on them.

'I'd give anything for a little sun right now,' Ellen said as Pearl unlatched a gate. They entered a lush green field dotted with black-and-white cows. The shorn grasses crunched under their feet and dark mud tried to suck their shoes into the earth – Ellen wondered if the road might've been better after all. Pearl pulled Ellen closer to the fence, on to a wet, rutty path and away from the cows huffing angrily. Once up and over a small hill, the countryside expanded before them, or at least as much as the close cloud cover would allow. The snake of a road came into view.

'Is that it up there?' Ellen asked, pointing to a lane that curved and cut through the green farmland.

Pearl nodded, her teeth chattering.

'Here, you must be hypothermic. Take my scarf.' Ellen didn't wait for Pearl to respond, trying to ignore the freezing rain that struck her neck as she unwound it. Her own worn wool coat was no match for the brutal weather, but poor Pearl only had that silly, soggy cardigan.

Pearl nodded and wrapped the ivory scarf around her

head, Ellen's hands guiding it into place and tucking it under the collar of her cardigan. Ellen grabbed Pearl's hand and they walked down the hill to the gate to the road, which Pearl closed behind them. They approached the curve cautiously. They could not see anyone coming into the corner. The fog was so low it was now covering the road, perhaps as it had the morning Richard died. Ellen wished they had brought torches.

As they entered the turn, Ellen's senses heightened as if she were an animal on a hunt. Her ears pricked at every sound: the faint swish of the wind in the grass and the low moaning of the cows beyond the hedges. Her eyes scanned the shrubbery and the dark, wet road and came to rest on a curiously dark spot of pavement.

'What is that?' Pearl asked, pointing down at it.

'Petrol,' Ellen said with confidence, 'spilt from the accident, most likely.'

'Is it from Richard's motorcycle or the van?' Pearl asked cautiously. 'Or maybe it could be . . . something else?'

Ellen could hear Pearl's raspy, shallow breaths and knew she was wondering if the stain could be blood. She tried patting Pearl on the back slowly, hoping it was soothing. 'The way the water is beading up on it is more indicative of petrol.'

Pearl visibly pulled herself together. 'If this is where the bike lost its petrol, where would Richard have landed?'

'Landed? Are you saying that he was catapulted from his motorcycle?'

'That's what Mum said, yes,' Pearl said, shrugging out from under Ellen's awkward patting. 'Which doesn't tell us much about how it happened. Ant told me once that riders flip over their handlebars all the time. It's like initiation for a rider. It could have been as simple as oversteering into the curve or,' she scuffed the road with her shoe, 'a slick, icy surface. I don't remember there being fog the day before yesterday, but it could have settled in quickly like it is now. You know how the weather is here.'

A wave of disappointment overcame Ellen. Was this simply driver error – Richard riding too close to the edge of the road and catching a rock or sliding on dirt? But surely Richard was too skilled a rider for that. 'Are you sure? You and the others have said he was the best rider out there – wouldn't he have been used to challenging conditions?'

After a pause, Pearl nodded. 'You're right. He rode like he was invincible, but he was a more than competent rider. Once, he took me for a picnic and he drove this road so fast, the wind dried my eyes out. It was scary and exhilarating – I understand why he loves – loved – riding fast. But I never felt unsafe with him. He knew this road well – and how to drive in ice and fog and all sorts of conditions. He had maps in his bag and he studied them before he took any unknown route. He was thorough. No, I can't believe it was just bad riding that caused this.'

Ellen combed the side of the road, finally finding what she was looking for – fine crystals of glass peppered in the dirt.

'This must have been where the van crashed,' she said. She crouched down and looked at the bent and broken branches of the hedge. 'Right here.'

Ellen's gloved hands shook as she moved the broken limbs aside. There was the wall hiding behind the leaves, a few large rocks at its base. The van *had* crashed into the wall, not into Richard. 'All right, the van did not cause the accident and was clearly not the source of the petrol spill, which is several feet away. Something else made him crash. What was it?'

Pearl shrugged. 'Ellen, does it matter exactly how he crashed? I just want to find the bag, I'm not sure I need to know how Richard died.'

'If we can pinpoint where he landed . . .' Ellen trailed off. While she had not been concentrating on finding the bag, she knew that theoretically, if she uncovered how the accident had happened, she could figure out roughly where the bag ended up (computing angles and curves was her strength, after all). This was not, however, something she wanted to tell Pearl.

Thankfully, Ellen spied something out of the corner of her eye.

'Look!' she said, running over to Pearl, who was pacing slowly back and forth along the side of the road. 'Over there. See that?'

'What?' Pearl said, her voice barely above a whisper.

Ellen stood behind Pearl and pointed at a large branch at the side of the road – it looked oddly out of place. 'What if that was in the road? Could it have caught Richard off guard, causing him to stop short and fly off his bike?' Ellen asked, kicking the branch with the toe of her shoe. 'It wasn't windy or stormy. He might've expected ice or fog but not a branch of this size.'

Pearl nodded sombrely. 'If this was in the road, it definitely would've surprised him. It is long enough; he couldn't quickly swerve around it. So, it *was* an accident,' she said.

Ellen said nothing. Pearl's whole body sagged, as if suddenly deflated. But something was itching at Ellen's mind. Sometimes the simplest solution is the best one. Sometimes, though, it is set up to *look* that way.

'The only tree close by is over there.' She pivoted and pointed to a large tree coming out of the curve, several yards from the severed branch. 'This branch is not from that tree. Look at the thickness and colour on the bark. Pearl, see how thick it is compared to that tree there? Where did this branch come from?'

14

PEARL

'What you're saying is Richard's death might not have been accidental?' Pearl touched the branch lightly with the toe of her shoe. She took a shuddering, deep breath and wiped her nose on the back of her damp mittens. Every part of her was cold and soggy, and her hair must have looked like a wet horse's mane. She bounced from foot to foot, hoping to get circulation in her numb feet. 'Someone put the branch there on purpose?'

'I suppose it could've fallen off the back of a truck . . . but also, yes, someone could've put it there. We can't rule it out.'

Pearl hugged her cardigan closer and stepped back from the branch. Her head throbbed and her knees felt weak. She needed a chair. This was amounting to so much more than finding Richard's bag and the letter she'd written him. What if the branch was there because of what she'd told Miss Waincross? Had whoever was responsible for the tampered-with envelopes found out that Richard had reported it, and decided to kill him as a result? What if this was all her fault? What if she, too, was in danger? What if they came after her next?

The timing of her reassignment, right after Richard's death and the bag's disappearance, made her wonder if there *was* a link between her and what had happened. Pearl glanced across at Ellen. She wanted to tell her about that day she'd dropped the envelope . . . but she couldn't.

'Let's set this aside for now and focus on the bag,' Ellen said, appearing to sense her friend's distress as she patted her shoulder rhythmically. 'Could it have been thrown from his body somehow?'

Relieved, Pearl shook her head. She preferred thinking of the concrete: the missing bag, the marks on the road, even the strange branch, rather than wondering about what lay beneath. 'Richard wore the bag across his chest, per regulations. He once told me that was to keep his "trigger hand" free.'

'Did he carry a gun?' Ellen asked with wide eyes.

'I have no idea,' Pearl said with a shrug. It was silly how little it mattered now. He had died regardless.

Pearl looked over her shoulder at the low, menacing clouds and slick, wet road. A chill ran down her spine, even though her armpits were sweaty and hot. 'Ellen, move away from where you are standing. Please? It's a blind curve and has got incredibly foggy.'

'Right,' Ellen said. She had been crouched down in the centre of the road, inspecting the surface so closely her nose was practically pressed to the ground, but quickly moved to the ditch next to Pearl. 'Let's have a look in the hedges, in case the investigators missed something.'

They combed the hedges – on opposite sides of the road – to no avail. Finally, Pearl stopped and hugged her arms to her chest. Her cardigan was no match for the sleet, which had picked up to a downpour. The wool hung heavy on her shoulders, the loose weave doing nothing to shield her from the cold wind. 'This is hopeless and I can barely feel my lips. We should go.'

'Yes, they are quite blue – and we'll be expected at the Park soon. You should've worn a proper coat in weather like this. Why do you insist on wearing that cardigan all the time?' Ellen asked, tentatively.

Pearl bristled, even though it was a question she heard quite often, mostly from her mother. 'It was my father's. He wore it all the time, but mostly when he was sick and could never seem to get warm enough. It used to smell like the smoke from his pipe and liquorice, but that was years ago.' She sniffed it as a child might a security blanket, pretty certain she caught a hint of anise. 'Besides, it is far warmer than you would think. Thick wool and all that.'

'Yes, wool is warm, but hardly waterproof.' Ellen put her arm around Pearl's shoulders. They began walking across the foggy road towards the field gate, Pearl's shoulders sinking when they stepped into the soft mud on the farm path. Ellen gently pointed to a copse of trees further along. 'I wonder if the branch could have come from there?'

Pearl did not answer immediately. The copse was the closest to the road and the trees did appear similar to the branch. But it was a considerable distance to drag a large branch. This was absurd, wasn't it? 'I don't know, Ellen. It all seems pretty far-fetched. It's easier to believe it was an accident.'

'That's what they always want you to think,' Ellen mumbled.

Pearl couldn't help but smile. The same exact thought had run through her mind, but she'd brushed it off as a result of too many mystery novels. Despite the rain, the air was still, the peaceful quiet that came before a snowstorm, when all the town was inside waiting. Pearl felt like that too. She was waiting. Only she was not sure for what.

Nearly half an hour later, they approached the Park. Pearl's stomach sank when she saw Miss Waincross walking down the path towards them, a black umbrella held stiffly above her head. She wondered if she should ask about her reassignment. Was Miss Waincross trying to keep her safe . . . or was Pearl under suspicion?

'Hello, Pearl,' she greeted her politely before turning to

Ellen. 'And you must be Miss Davies. I am Miss Waincross. I've heard about you from Mr St John. Pleasure to meet you.'

'I'm flattered,' Ellen said. 'Nice to meet you too, Miss Waincross.'

'Gil has been quite impressed with your work thus far. I do hope we have a chance to work together in the future,' Miss Waincross said, her voice warm, 'or at least grab a friendly cup of tea.'

'It would be my pleasure,' Ellen said, her eyes downcast.

Then Miss Waincross stepped in front of Ellen and grasped Pearl's shoulders. 'I heard about your friend, Richard.' She smelt of lilacs and talcum powder and wore a vibrant red raincoat that matched her lipstick. 'Pearl, I am so very sorry. I know how it is to lose someone special to you.' She looked over Pearl's shoulder at Ellen, who was politely keeping her distance, and lowered her voice so even Pearl struggled to hear her words. 'You must be concerned about this and your reassignment, but do not be. You need not worry about anything right now.'

'Thank you,' Pearl mumbled, her shoulders slumping from relief. She hadn't wanted to bring up the matter with Miss Waincross again and was grateful she didn't need to. Although her last sentence was a tad curious. *You need not worry about anything right now.* Often when people said you didn't need to worry, it was because they knew you had reason to. And if not 'right now', then when? Before Pearl

15

PEARL

Pearl followed Ellen through the door to her new job without any fanfare, walking in like she wasn't pre-occupied with Richard's death, which looked less and less like an accident the more she mulled it over. Confidence was a state of mind, she told herself, walking past others rushing to their desks. Soggy and shaking from the cold, she looked at some of the girls again. What if they knew more than they let on? What secrets did everyone else have at Bletchley? A shudder ran down her spine. With all the things kept hidden at the Park, it was possible no one was what they seemed.

Pearl followed Ellen into the corner room and hung her sodden cardigan on the row of hooks just inside the door, then sat next to her friend at a table near the front. The layout of the space looked very similar to most of the rooms Pearl had seen – four rectangular tables and chairs, one blocked window, a few wooden cabinets lining the walls. The only difference, really, was the table arrangement; they were grouped in a collaborative 'U' shape in the middle of the space, which somehow felt a tad more inviting. As they waited, Pearl grasped Ellen's cold hand under the table for reassurance. Ellen shot her a startled look, but Pearl didn't let go. She needed to feel someone else beside her, someone she could trust.

'Now what?' she whispered, even though the other girls weren't sitting close enough to eavesdrop.

'I have no idea,' Ellen replied as she looked around the room. She seemed as fascinated as Pearl, which was odd as she had been in a similar room since she had arrived. Then, Pearl noticed more subtle differences – wire baskets on tables, handfuls of pencils scattered about, a map of Europe on the far wall. 'But I'm surprised Mr St John is not waiting for us. He practically sleeps in this hut.'

'I heard that, Miss Davies,' Mr St John said from behind them, sounding both exhausted and annoyed. 'I have a home, like you, and it is impolite to judge a person based on their waking hours. Some of us simply need less rest. It is a scientific fact I can back with evidence if you would like.'

He stood in front of the open door, a stack of papers in one hand, the other stroking his chin and its somewhat darker stubble growth. Pearl wanted to laugh and say, *You have not been home! It is completely obvious!*, but she knew better.

'My apologies, Mr St John,' Ellen mumbled, smoothing her wet hair back from her face. 'That was out of turn.'

'Indeed,' he said with a nod. The room was so quiet they could hear the faint *scritch scritch* as his fingers stroked his new beard. He studied them for a moment and then walked in, closing the door behind him.

'This is a tad unconventional, starting you off together as new members of the crib team on the same day, but I decided you two could help each other out. Ellen, you have shown great promise in the few weeks since you started. I'm proud to have you in the crib room and do not doubt you're up for the challenge.' He then looked directly at Pearl and added, 'I had no choice in your change of position, but that said, I am well aware that both of you are equipped with the learning to excel here if you put your minds to it and follow the rules.

'Let me start from the beginning, and remember, what I am about to tell you is confidential. It does not leave these walls. If I or anyone else finds out that it has, there will be serious consequences.' Again, he looked directly at Pearl, who could not help but squirm under his gaze. 'When we get messages from the various listening stations around the country, they are delivered here, as they are not in plain German. They are in a code, as you may have surmised, and our job here is to decode those messages. It is critical to the war effort and protecting our soldiers on the front line. To that end, we have people in this room looking at the messages in order to create what are called "cribs". Cribs are our best guess at standard messages – greetings, weather reports, basic enquiries – that appear at the beginning of any communication. If we know where the message has come from, we have a bit more to go on. For example, Army? Navy? That might help us understand how to make our best guess at decodes.

'In addition, if we can figure out the cribs, we have half a chance at decoding the more important parts of the messages. Another team has the means to attempt to decode the entire message but need the help of your cribs. Of course, the Germans, squirrelly little bastards, send a lot of inconsequential messages – or even gibberish.'

'They do this to confuse us?' Pearl asked.

Mr St John nodded. 'And to maintain a steady flow of messages. They bombard us with messages, hoping it masks any uptick in important activity.'

'Which would indicate an operation being planned,' Ellen said dreamily. Pearl could not help but smile at her. Ellen was in love with puzzles and mysteries in the same way most girls were obsessed with fetching film actors like Cary Grant. To be fair, if Pearl had not been so nervous about why she was given this new job, she would be equally giddy.

'Exactly,' Mr St John said. 'And the most troublesome part is that the Germans change their codes every day. You have a twenty-four-hour window in which to come up with a crib. When you get something that seems plausible, you hand it in most urgently and then it travels to the next stage. Your part in this process is critical, do you understand?'

'Cribsters,' Pearl murmured. She'd overheard the term in the canteen once, and despite not knowing exactly what a cribster did, she wanted to be one. And now she was.

Mr St John raised an eyebrow at her and kept going. 'The key to finding a successful crib is working quickly through the messages. They will not make sense at first, but as you get more accustomed to messages, you will begin to see patterns. It is essential you pay close attention to the messages and do not waste others' time. Time is of the essence. Always. Last week, a group found a crib at exactly one minute after midnight. Their work was then irrelevant and we were not able to find the location of a German naval ship which later attacked one of our own.' Mr St John placed a thick folder on the table in front of them. 'I should not have to reiterate this, but security is essential. If any information is removed from this room, you will also be removed from this room. For ever.'

Pearl shuddered. There was something in the way he said it that made her feel like he was speaking solely to her.

'We need more people reviewing and creating cribs if we are going to get more effective at breaking them. The more messages that come through, the more attempts we need at creating a successful crib. We also have word from one of our prisoners of war that there is a raid expected. Soon. We need all the help we can get in identifying where it is planned and when. That is news that cannot leave these walls, because if the Germans get word that we have cracked any bit of their code at all, they will change the code and we will *lose* the war, understand?'

Pearl tried to maintain eye contact with Mr St John, catching his glance each time he looked up from the papers on the table. Even as she wanted to impress upon him that he could trust her, her mind was racing. She wondered, just for a moment, if he was watching her for another reason. Not because she couldn't be trusted, but because he knew something: that she was in danger, too. It was a big leap to move from menial messenger to the crib room, but Pearl knew she had the ability to solve these puzzles, just like the other girls. Their university degrees meant nothing in here. It all came down to who could make sense out of senseless letters. So, whether Mr St John was testing her or protecting her, she needed to prove this placement hadn't been a mistake. She'd heard there was a huge room with giant machines to translate the codes. How amazing would it be to work on those someday? Pearl swallowed down her fears and tried to appear obedient and engaged.

'Think of today as your training day. You'll be working on previous messages side by side with the cribs that were successful. Hopefully it will help you understand how the cribs are formed. Tomorrow,' Mr St John said with a satisfied nod, 'I throw you to the wolves. I am not protecting either of you from anything, no matter what your past posts were like. Here, we are serious, intense workers with a goal in mind. If this becomes too much, you are welcome to leave. Today, I'll go easy on you. It will be the *only* time. This war is rushing forward and we do not have time to mollycoddle anyone from here on out.'

And with that, he turned on his heel and left the room, shutting the door behind him. Ellen looked at Pearl, then at their brown box of papers. Within moments, the door opened and the room filled with others, talking quietly among themselves as they sat down quickly and started work. The room was made up of mostly women – only two men sat in the corner together – and no one looked twice at the two new girls at the table in the centre of the room. Soon, the only sounds were the scratching of pencils and the occasional flip of paper.

Ellen reached for the stack of papers and handed Pearl a pencil. Theoretically, there was not as much urgency as on a normal shift because these were old intercepts from a previous day. Still, nerves coursed through Pearl like an electric current and her fingers shook.

'By the way,' Ellen whispered with a sly smile, 'you never told me you know German.'

'No, I did not. And, for that matter, neither did you.'

Pearl paused a moment, wondering if she should continue. She lowered her voice even further. 'Do not tell anyone I know this, but there is a lot Mr St John didn't tell you. I overheard him a while ago talking about the German code. He didn't know I was there, and as soon as I realized it was sensitive information, I stepped away from the door. It was open, Ellen, don't look at me like that!'

Ellen looked at her hands and said softly, 'I suppose if the damage has been done, you can share the information with me. If you think it'll help our efforts.'

Feeling vindicated, Pearl continued. 'The code the Germans are using is formed using a machine. To encode their message, they choose a three-letter setting on the machine. Sometimes, they choose easy settings like AAA or BBB, but that morning, Mr St John was talking about one fool who used the first three letters of his girlfriend's name – once they figured that out, it was super easy. But let me take a step back – the crib is, like Mr St John said, a guess or clue at what the settings of the machine should be to decode the message. What we're here to do is figure out what some of the letters are, so that they can test them somehow to try and figure out the entire message.'

Ellen looked at her with wide eyes.

Pearl shrugged. 'When people think you're unimportant, you're often invisible to them.'

16

ELLEN

Ellen's first day at her new job went by quickly. She was surprised at how busy she and Pearl were, with no gaps in which they could talk about anything but the strange, jumbled messages at hand. They studied the intricacies of each message in the pile, noting the Germans sent weather reports quite regularly. Figuring out the basics of how the code worked also helped – for instance, if a message started with the letter 'V', the underlying, decoded message could not also start with a 'V'. Due to the nature of the machine the Germans were using, a letter could not be coded as itself. There were other little tips and secrets Pearl had learnt through what she said were her sources (Ellen was positive Pearl was simply excellent at eavesdropping) that helped them somewhat. Even though Mr St John had given them a lot of weather reports as their practice examples, there were so many variations that Ellen had no idea how she was going to hold her own while combatting the distraction of Richard's mysterious death.

At half eleven, Mr St John appeared and told them they would only get a short break for lunch. 'Do not linger.' He narrowed his eyes and pointed at each of them. 'I am taking a risk on both of you. Do not let me down.'

Ellen felt her face get hot. She hoped he did not mistake her redness for embarrassment. She wanted to retain a place in the crib room so badly, she felt the desire bubbling up inside her like a force that needed controlling.

'We would never let you, or our country, down,' Pearl said solemnly.

Mr St John looked at them blankly, then added, 'I hope you would not, Pearl.'

They were silent as they rushed through the blustery weather to the crowded canteen. They found a quiet corner and ate their dry fishcakes and soggy, vinegary cabbage wordlessly. Ellen thought about all the times Mr St John looked pointedly at Pearl when talking about traitors and decodes gone wrong. She chewed a bite of faintly fishy potato thoughtfully and wondered if it was a bad idea to trust her friend. How was she to know whether Pearl was as innocent as she claimed? Something had obviously happened to warrant the close observation – something

Pearl wasn't telling her. Although they had been friends for what seemed like ages, it amounted to only a very eventful couple of months. Ellen wondered if she truly *knew* Pearl.

The canteen bustled all around them, the vegetal cabbage smells mixed with a cheerful rumble of idle conversation. Still, they sat in silence, as if someone had placed a bell jar over their lonely, quiet table. Finally, Pearl opened her mouth. Then closed it. Ellen could not take the suspense, even if she did welcome the silence.

'I am excited about our promotion,' she said innocently. 'Are you?'

Pearl cocked her head to the side and swallowed. Her hair had fallen from the pins that held it back, and Ellen realized Pearl had actually *troubled* with her hair this morning. In fact, her clothes were nicer – a pressed blouse with a small gold pin at the neck under her dad's old cardigan. How had Ellen missed the effort that her friend had put in for her first day? How had she neglected the most cursory of observations?

'Of course I am, Ellen,' she replied. 'It's what I've always wanted. Honestly, though, I'm having a hard time concentrating with everything else.' She paused and took in a shuddering breath. 'I want to think of the cribs, really I do, but the biggest puzzle in my brain is Richard's death. Full stop. I cannot stop thinking of that branch, whether it simply fell into the road off the back of a truck or if someone put it there. If so, that someone must've known he, or another person, would hit it. Was the branch intended for Richard? Or was he in the wrong place at the wrong time?'

Ellen blinked at her friend. Pearl stabbed her pile of cabbage with an unnecessary amount of anger and chewed the bite loudly. Pearl would never win over Mr St John if she was frustrated and preoccupied. 'Well, then,' she said, 'it looks like neither of us will be able to focus until we figure out what really happened to Richard out on that road the other day. There is clearly more to this than a road accident. I know you simply wanted Richard's missing bag, but we appear to have opened Pandora's box.'

Pearl stopped mid-chew and stared, her mouth hanging open slightly. 'Are you serious?' she said through a mouthful.

'We have to be able to concentrate on our work for Mr St John as much as the Richard bits. He's watching you carefully, and me as well. We cannot fail on either front.'

Pearl dropped her fork and swallowed. 'I promise.'

'Good,' Ellen said, 'because we have to agree that our official work is the most important. Now that we have that bit squared away, how should we approach our, erm, new project?'

'What do you mean?' Pearl took her last bite of cabbage. She must've been incredibly hungry, Ellen thought. It smelt like dirty socks.

'Well, what will we do first? We investigated the scene

of his death and that brought up some questions about what happened. Who would be able to tell us more about the accident?' Ellen pushed her fishcake aside and laced her fingers together on the salt-covered tabletop.

'Ant,' Pearl said without question. 'Mum said Ant was with Richard that morning, which doesn't make sense. They usually rode separate routes for safety. Still, if she's correct, Ant must know more.'

'Also, he seemed angry with Richard a few weeks ago when we all met Dennis at the pub. Wasn't that curious?' Ellen added. 'So, we will talk to Ant. Then what?'

'Look,' Pearl said, letting her fork fall to her plate with a clank. 'There are three people we need to talk to: Ant, Dennis and Fran Farland. Ant and Fran were at the accident site and Dennis had a close relationship with Richard. He might know something.'

'That makes sense,' Ellen agreed. Her heart did a tiny flip at the mention of Dennis. She did not want to sound too eager, but hoped she would be the one to question him. She liked talking to Dennis. Sometimes she liked talking to him even more than she liked talking to Pearl, which made her feel a little guilty. He was so straightforward, so open – whereas Ellen found Pearl's moodiness difficult to navigate. She drew her attention back to the matter at hand. 'I don't know Fran . . .'

'I do. I've known him for ages. His gran lives down the road from me, so I see him on occasion bringing a cake or trimming her hedges. I'll take him if you take Dennis.' Pearl made a face like she'd just sucked a lemon slice. 'I can't stomach much of him, you know.'

'Fine,' Ellen said, biting the inside of her lip. If only Pearl knew how much she *wanted* to talk to him, she probably wouldn't talk much to Ellen either.

'Then we can both attack Ant,' Pearl said with a sly smile, 'so to speak?'

'Yes, after all, he was there when the accident happened. I imagine he'll give us answers no one else can.' Ellen wished she had a pencil and paper – she would have loved to start a list of questions, but at least they had the first few steps laid out. It would be up to her how she approached Dennis and when and for how long. *Golly*, how her palms got sweaty just thinking about arranging to meet him rather than simply bumping into him by chance. 'I'll need to write down some interview questions first.'

'Me too,' Pearl agreed, pushing her empty plate aside.

'Right. Let's take tonight to write down our questions. We can review them at lunch tomorrow and then find Antony after our shift. Do we, erm, tell him to meet us somewhere, or . . .'

Pearl chuckled. 'No, let's just figure out where he'll be after our shift and surprise him. If he thinks too much about it, he might get nervous and call it off. We don't want to give him an option to refuse.'

Ellen stood up and pushed her chair into the table.

'I like that idea.'

'I'll think of where best to find him. Maybe his house? I'm not sure if he's still frequenting the pub after his shift, but I'll do some sleuthing.' Pearl rubbed her hands together like a villain in the films. Her mood had changed entirely during the lunch break; her grief over Richard had lost a little of its bite, at least for now. And Ellen was relieved. It was hard to find hope these days. Ellen was glad she'd given some to her friend, even though she knew it was only temporary.

17

PEARL

Pearl's mother had a small, unused reporter's style notebook in the top drawer of her desk: perfect for stealing in the few minutes before she came home. After supper, Pearl holed up in her room and wrote down what she hoped were the most important questions to ask Antony to unravel the mystery of Richard's death.

Pearl was so excited to get to work the next day, she didn't even mind that it was yet another Bonfire Night without a celebration. She stepped out of the door and almost jogged down the road in the wind and rain; it was no matter that she didn't have an umbrella and had forgotten her white gloves and armband at home. She felt invincible with the notebook tucked into the waistband of her plaid skirt and, for once, wasn't tipping her ear to the sky to listen for the grumble of German planes. As she waved to one of her favourite guards, Reggie, and exchanged pleasantries while he checked her permit, she realized how much lighter she felt. She had a purpose, a plan, and that alone gave her a new energy.

Almost without realizing it, she wandered behind the mansion where all the Don Rs entered the property, leaving their motorcycles in a quiet location away from the huts filled with thinking, puzzling scholars. She could almost imagine Richard standing by his motorcycle, laughing as he tightened the strap on the leather bag he wore across his chest. Instead, in Richard's normal location, was Antony. He stared blankly at the mansion, his goggles and gloves still on. Pearl's breath caught in her throat and she felt her chest buzzing with excitement. Sure, she'd promised Ellen they'd do the interrogation together after their shift, but how could she pass up an opportunity like this? He was alone. Unable to stop herself, Pearl ran over.

'Antony! Ant!' she called. She had her notebook out by the time she got to him, trying to hold it casually as she scanned her boxy handwriting for the appropriate, hard-hitting first question.

'Pearl?' Ant replied, pushing his goggles on to his forehead. He looked and sounded weary, like he hadn't slept in a week. 'What are you doing here?'

'Aren't I always here?' she retorted.

He nodded. 'I guess you are. But you're normally here to see Richard. Not me. I never had people waiting for me.'

'Sorry,' Pearl said, and she was. She had never given any thought to Antony before now, whether he was lonely or sad. Even if he'd been arguing with Richard before he died, they had been best friends for quite some time. 'I mean, I am truly sorry, Ant. Richard's death must be awful for you.'

'Awful cannot even begin to explain how it is,' he said, his tone a bit snide. He took off his leather gloves and wiped his face on the inside of his elbow. 'Sorry, Pearl – you don't want to hear the details and I need to get on my way. The war stops for nobody, right? Not even for mourning or a funeral.'

Pearl's eyes flooded. 'No funeral? How could they not?'

'Apparently, the investigators have not released, er, Richard to his mum. It could be a while, so it's back to work for me, her and everyone else.' Antony strode purposefully towards the mansion, gravel crunching loudly beneath his boots. Pearl jogged to keep up. She couldn't lose him, no matter if she was holding back tears.

'Antony, wait,' she called, a few steps behind. 'I understand how you feel. Well, not entirely because I wasn't there that morning, but I miss him, too. Fiercely. As you must.'

Ant turned, his eyebrows drawn to a peak on his forehead. 'He left such a huge hole . . .'

'I know.' Pearl felt an ache in her heart. It seemed so cliché, but she had not known how much she'd miss

Richard until he was gone for ever. Taking a deep breath, she tried to stay focused. 'Ant, I know that morning must've been awful. And reliving it must be even worse, but what happened? I need to know, well, how he died. Did he suffer? Did he,' she struggled, as her voice caught, 'have any last words?'

Antony's head slumped as if it had suddenly become too heavy. Pearl caught up to him and put her hand on his arm. He wasn't wearing the coat he and Richard normally wore, the long light-brown trench with the narrow belt and the white-and-blue reflective armbands. This one was different, shorter and worn. The cuffs didn't reach his wrists.

'Ant, where's your coat?'

He yanked his arm away and turned towards her. His eyes were closed, his mouth pinched tight. Without opening his eyes, he answered, 'At Richard's house.'

'What?'

'I used my coat to cover him up that morning. He was cold, shivering. The officers gave it back to Richard's mother, along with his. I have to collect it later, but I just cannot imagine . . .' Antony paused and opened his eyes. 'Pearl, I think he knew he was going to die.'

Pearl tried to swallow. It was not easy. 'What do you mean?'

'He gave me something before we set off. Told me to hold on to it for him. In case, well, just in case.' Antony looked over his shoulder. The path was deserted, but still, he was nervous. Pearl shuddered.

'What did he give you?' Pearl demanded.

'I, uh, it's for me. Shoot, Pearl, I shouldn't have said anything. It's mine to figure out. You should stay clear of it all, OK? Look, I have to run. Work and all.' Again, his eyes shifted as he talked, keeping an eye on the dispatch riders behind them and people entering the mansion. As he started to walk away, Pearl grabbed his arm again. Harder this time.

'No,' she said firmly. 'Look, Ant, I need to know what happened and you are going to tell me.'

He shook his head. 'Pearl, you don't want to get into this. What happened that morning has haunted me every second since. I cannot stop seeing him on the road, bleeding. Do *you* want that nightmare in your memory every single moment?'

Pearl inhaled sharply, feeling heat rise to her face. Didn't he understand that not knowing was worse? Her list of questions flew out of her mind. 'Ant, listen to me, until I find out what really happened to Richard out there on the road, why he ended up dead and not anyone else – not you or Fran and his father – I am going to have the worst possible images in my mind that will keep me awake all hours. I *have* to find out what happened to him or I'll never be able to let it go. Do you understand?'

After several moments of silence, Ant spoke. 'All right.

I'll tell you. You're right. Maybe talking about it will make the pain go away, or at least hurt less.' He glanced at his watch. 'But Pearl, I have to go. They'll be waiting for me and won't be happy if I'm late. Especially now.'

'Can you meet me at the Horseshoes after my shift? At our table in the back? Please? At five?' Pearl's shoulders lifted in anticipation.

'I don't know. I have to help with my brothers. Plus, I should really go see Richard's mum. Get my coat.'

'Say,' Pearl said, cupping her notebook with both hands, 'what if you didn't have to go to Richard's alone? I can go with you. I know his mum from way back. Maybe that'll make things easier?'

'You'd do that?' Antony sounded genuinely surprised. Pearl supposed he was right to be - she'd never volunteered to do much of anything for him. He had always been Richard's annoying sidekick in her mind, to be avoided if possible. But now he was her only link to Richard, the key to the last few minutes of his life. She needed Antony.

'Of course,' she said.

'All right.' He swallowed and looked over his shoulder quickly. 'Quarter after five. Our table. Then we'll go to Richard's.'

'It's a deal,' Pearl agreed.

She watched him walk quickly into the mansion, looking over his shoulder every few steps as if he were being followed. If Richard had told Dennis too much, what was to say he hadn't done the same with Ant? What else could make the poor fellow so paranoid, so nervous about the truth? But even more importantly, what had Richard given Ant before he died and why had Ant kept it a secret until now? Pearl shuddered, hoping Richard hadn't told Antony too much. No one else needed to know their secrets, especially if it put them in danger.

18

PEARL

It had taken some explaining at lunch, but Pearl finally got Ellen to not only agree to meet Antony after their shift, but to understand why she'd cornered him the way she had on the way in. Initially, Ellen had been less than pleased, saying she thought they had agreed to work together, that they needed to trust each other.

'We will never get to the bottom of things if we're not honest with each other,' Ellen had whispered as they sat huddled over their latest work. 'If we make a plan, we have to stick to it.'

Because Ellen had chosen to make her point in the middle of the crib room, Pearl had no choice but to agree with a firm nod of her head. 'Partners. Completely,' she agreed, and they shook on it. While she felt somewhat guilty for keeping pieces of the truth from her friend, Pearl was confident she was doing it for all the right reasons.

Over a lunch of salty vegetable stew, they discussed the questions each had written, running a line through any repeats or those Ellen thought too risky. For the most part, their objectives were aligned and Pearl felt a gentle hum through her body as they walked down the road towards the Horseshoes at the end of the day. It was dark enough that Ellen had lectured her about leaving her reflective items at home and insisted Pearl wear one of her white gloves. The left one. As they approached, however, Pearl slapped her forehead with the gloved hand.

'Ugh, again!' she wailed. 'Every time I forget that women cannot go into pubs unaccompanied. We should've arranged for Ant to meet us outside. I'm so used to Richard waiting to walk me in, I simply take it for granted.'

Ellen laughed. 'Look, he said he'd meet us here at Richard's regular table. We're five minutes late, besides. I suspect he's in there.'

'I need to get a wristwatch,' Pearl grumbled, annoyed once more at the freedoms denied to women. She was certain she'd never get used to it, nor did she ever want to. Still, a watch would help.

The pub was not very busy, which was to their detriment. As they wove between empty tables, Pearl felt the eyes of the old men lining the bar on her back and it took every ounce of willpower not to turn around and say something. Thankfully, Ant stood up and waved and Pearl felt the men look away.

'Ellen, I didn't expect you to come too. Hello.' Ant looked surprised and embarrassed, straightening the collar and cuffs on his ragged work shirt. It made no matter, as his hair stuck up in weird carrot-coloured tufts and his eyes were red-rimmed atop dark circles.

'I hope you don't mind,' Ellen said with a reassuring smile.

Ant looked more nervous than angry, continually glancing at the table behind them as if, like earlier, he was scared of being watched. 'I thought this was about you finding out what happened, Pearl. For your own sake.' His eyes slid to Ellen and away uncomfortably.

'It's about finding answers,' Pearl said firmly. 'Plus, if we're going to get to the bottom of Richard's death, we'll need her help. She's smart.'

'I remember,' Antony said with a nod.

'You remember Ellen or you remember she's smart?' Pearl asked.

'Both,' he said. Finally, he smiled and looked a bit more like the fellow Pearl remembered. Most of the time when she saw Ant, he was smiling and laughing at something Richard had said. He had a nice smile, Pearl realized. 'What did you want to talk about, Pearl?' he asked, his warm gaze turning cloudy, guarded again.

'First of all, we need to know what Richard gave you the morning he died,' Pearl said cautiously. 'You

150

mentioned it earlier, then quickly backtracked. Why?' She would've preferred more small talk first, easing him into it, but she knew they needed to get to the point.

Ant lowered his head to his arms and moaned. 'Oh, what a mess.'

Pearl exchanged a worried look with Ellen and felt her stomach rumble with traces of cabbage and dread. Ant looked like he wanted to walk away.

Pearl watched as Ellen's neck lifted a bit like a periscope on a submarine. She scanned the surrounding tables and the men at the bar before returning her gaze to Ant. After studying him for a while, she let out a long breath and said, softly, 'Antony, you need to trust us. We all know there is an official investigation underway, but you and Pearl will see things that they miss – you both knew him better than anyone. We just want to help.' She paused. 'Let us help.'

Like Ellen, Ant lifted his head and scanned the room. Then, he waved the girls closer. 'Push your chairs nearer. Just in case.'

When they had done so, he continued. 'Pearl, it was awful out there.' He shook his head.

'It was cold that morning, correct?' Ellen asked. Her tone was direct. She and Pearl had scooted their wooden chairs to either side of Ant, the friends hunching together closely at one half of the circular table.

Antony cocked his head. 'It *was* cold. The frost on the

fields hadn't melted yet – it was only just dawn – so it may have been slick on the roadway. Though I never slipped.'

'But Richard was going faster,' Pearl added.

'He was. But he was a better rider. A little frost wouldn't have taken him down.'

'Pearl and I went there yesterday,' Ellen said quickly. 'There was a large branch on the side of the road, and I started to wonder, what if that had been in the *middle* instead?'

'If anything had been in the road, branch or otherwise, he would have avoided it. I swerved to avoid his downed bike and managed to stay upright.' Antony folded his arms across his chest.

'But the branch was rather large. You didn't notice it?' Pearl asked.

'No.' Ant folded his arms on the tabletop. 'But then I was distracted trying to avoid Richard's bike in the road.'

Ellen nodded. 'Can you describe what you did see? Where was Richard in relation to the bike?'

Ant cleared his throat a few times and then nodded slowly. 'He was all the way on the other side of the road. When a motorcycle comes around a curve and hits something, or is overcorrected, what happens does not entirely make sense. Without getting too technical, depending on the rider's skills, the bike *and* the rider can end up flying, tail over tea kettle, at the same time. They are not thrown in the same direction they were heading; more like they take a sharp turn from where they are headed – ninety degrees. It's unfathomable. I've seen it once before – a bloke I was riding with was actually hit by his own bike and broke his collarbone. I don't think it was the same with Richard. He didn't break his collarbone – well, wait, I don't know that for certain. He was on the ground when I arrived. His bike was in the road and Richard was off the road under a tree. Once that sort of accident – a highside crash – starts, it is almost impossible to pull out of it unscathed. Even for the best riders. Like Richard is. Was.'

Ant looked at the ceiling. Pearl swallowed. Richard had been doomed, it seemed, but had he known it was coming?

'Why do you think he knew he was going to die?' Pearl asked. 'You said earlier that Richard had some idea this was going to happen, but how can someone predict a motorcycle crash?'

Ant leant in again, first looking over his shoulder. 'I don't think he knew he was going to die that way, just that something bad might happen. Soon.'

'Explain,' Pearl demanded. 'You said he gave you something. What was it?'

Ant looked uncomfortable, squirming in his chair again, then reached into his front pocket. 'Well, there is this.'

He placed an ordinary train ticket on the table.

'Curious,' Ellen mumbled as she and Pearl leant in over Antony's hands, their foreheads practically touching.

Pearl was confused. What did they care about some old, used ticket?

'He gave you a used Bletchley to London ticket? And that's why you thought he'd predicted his own death?' Pearl's increasingly fast pulse throbbed in her forehead.

'Shh!' Ant hissed. 'Keep your voice down. What did I tell you before? You have to be careful.'

'Fine then,' Pearl said quietly, picking up the ticket, 'but you need to explain.'

Ant glanced to the side. 'How can I explain it? He didn't. But it has to mean something. He gave it to me, after all.'

'Look,' said Pearl. 'There's something written on the back. See?'

'*Cornwall*,' Ellen read aloud.

Pearl traced the writing with her finger. Was it Richard's handwriting? She was almost certain it was.

'Maybe he was going to Cornwall,' pondered Pearl, 'and changing trains in London?' She let out a loud sigh of frustration. 'That's it, then? Ant, come out with it. A trip to Cornwall is definitely odd but it doesn't mean Richard thought he was in danger. We all know better than that.'

Ant stared down at the table. Why did Pearl get the sense he wasn't telling the whole truth?

Ellen gnawed on her thumbnail and furrowed her brow. 'Tell us again what happened when you came around the corner and saw Richard on the ground. Did you see him immediately?'

'Well,' Ant said with a sigh, clearly relieved Ellen had diverted their attention from whatever he was withholding, 'yes, I saw Richard in the ditch almost immediately. His body was by the tree down there and his bike was in the road.'

'Was there anyone else there?' Ellen asked.

Pearl sensed a slight hesitation, but Antony cleared his throat and continued, 'I was focused on Richard. No one else mattered.'

'The only person you saw was Richard,' Pearl confirmed.

'Yes, initially. Before Fran and his da crashed.'

'They crashed *after* you arrived,' Pearl confirmed again. 'And before then, there was just you and Richard.'

Antony scratched his forehead. 'Sorry. This is all so jumbled. The van crashed moments after I got there. Or right as I got there. I didn't see what happened.'

'Interesting,' Pearl muttered, looking directly at Ellen. Antony was dodging the questions quite a bit, but if she had noticed, Ellen was hiding it well – her expression was neutral.

Finally, Ellen cleared her throat. 'At that point, did Richard have his bag over his shoulder still? Or was it no longer there?'

Pearl couldn't help but smile. *There you go, Ellen. Don't forget the bag.*

'I, uh, I can't . . . I don't know. Maybe? He must've, yes, it was still over his shoulder when I went over there. Yes, it was,' Antony said with a firm nod. 'I do remember thinking that I should maybe remove it so the messages didn't get, well, bloody.'

'Did you?' Ellen continued.

'No,' he said. 'I did not. I didn't touch anything. I was reminded afterwards that protocol dictates I was supposed to take his bag and continue on my route. I knew that, on some level, but I also knew I couldn't leave him. You can't leave your friend on the road when he's like that. You can't. Everything else flies out of your mind.'

Pearl's heart felt like someone was wringing it like a wet dishcloth – despite the questions Ant had appeared to evade, that part really rang true. Seeing Richard on the side of the road, fatally injured, would have ruined her, too. She wouldn't have been thinking about protocol either.

'Is that when you put your coat over him?' Pearl asked gently. It felt better somewhat to know that Richard had been comforted by his friend at the end.

'Yes,' Ant said, glancing over his shoulder again.

Pearl felt something behind her, like the subtle breeze when a person walks by too closely. Turning quickly, she scanned the pub. Nothing unusual. No one was near. Just that prickly feeling up the back of her neck.

'Antony,' Ellen prodded, 'why are you so frightened?

Was someone else there? Did Richard say something? You really have to trust us if we're going to help.'

He held her gaze for a few seconds, then sighed. 'OK, fine. There's something else,' he relented. Ant reached into the other coat pocket. He placed a piece of paper on the table. It was crisp and white, and had block letters written in black ink on one side. It looked fresh, new. 'He handed me this in a sealed envelope, just before we left that morning, and told me to read it if something went wrong. He didn't give me the ticket then – it was on the ground after the accident, after they took him away. It must've fallen from his pocket.' Ant shook his head, his eyes downcast. 'I shouldn't have lied, but I panicked. I knew you wouldn't leave without something, so I gave you the ticket. But this, well, he gave it specifically to me. I didn't know whether I should show it to anyone else. Plus, I wanted to figure it out myself, but when it proved more difficult than I expected . . .'

A chill ran down Pearl's spine, a feeling her mum said meant 'someone walking over her grave', a pretty appropriate statement at this point. She took the paper from his shaking hand. Tentatively, she unfolded it.

It was a line of block letters, written in black pen:

TRIEIET DDIBRIES ALVAYO EW EV I IDEL EIBI

'It has to be a code, right? He was trying to tell me something,' Ant said. Pearl felt her eyes narrow as she studied his expression.

She turned to Ellen. 'It does look like a code, doesn't it?'

'I'm assuming you did not tell the investigators about this?' Ellen asked Ant, by way of reply.

'No,' Ant said with a shrug. 'Perhaps I should have, but Richard gave it to me. I assumed he wanted me to have it. Not them, not you. But I'm no good at this sort of thing.'

Ellen pressed her lips together and pushed a stray piece of hair behind her ear. 'Tell me, was Richard fond of puzzles? Or games?'

Pearl shook her head almost instantly. 'He wasn't one for helping with the Sunday crossword, if that's what you're asking. He must've had a very important reason for writing this.'

Ant nodded in agreement. 'He went through a phase where he sent away for decoder rings and invisible ink pens, like all boys do. But that's it.'

'Curious,' Ellen mumbled. 'Can you tell, is that his handwriting?'

'It is,' Pearl said before Ant could answer, her lips set in a firm line.

'You're certain?' Ellen pressed.

'Of course I'm certain,' Pearl shot back. Then she faltered, confessing softly, 'He didn't write me many letters, you know, but I'd still recognize his handwriting.'

'I understand,' Ellen said. 'We can assume it is his unless you feel otherwise.'

Ant looked over his shoulder again. 'Hey, Pearl, are you still going to come with me to Richard's mum's place? It's getting late.'

'Can I keep the train ticket?' Pearl asked tentatively. She felt bad asking without saying anything to Ellen first, but once the idea popped into her head, she couldn't help herself. She glanced over at Ellen. 'You see, I know someone who works at Bletchley station, an old friend from school. I could go right now and ask him before his shift ends. Maybe he'd be able to tell me where Richard was going or help me figure out what the markings mean.'

'Super idea!' Ellen said, clapping her hands together. 'Then, Antony, I will accompany you to Richard's mother's house. That way we can carry on talking.'

Ant looked nervously from Pearl to Ellen and finally sighed, 'All right. But I want Richard's secret code back. He gave it to me, after all.' His voice was tight – Pearl could tell he regretted showing them the message at all.

'Of course,' Ellen said, pushing it back at him. 'Maybe after you take a crack at the code, you can bring it to us? Three minds are better than one, obviously.'

Pearl could not help but smile. Ellen was not going to let that paper go so easily. Pearl knew Ellen would have it back someday, now that she had her eye on it.

'You'll tell me what you find out about the ticket?' Ant asked Pearl as the three stood up.

'Absolutely,' Pearl said, though she knew full well it

depended on what she learnt.

They filed out of the now-crowded pub and walked down the pavement together for a bit until it was time for Pearl to break off and head to the station.

'Come here,' Ellen said, drawing her into an awkward and uncharacteristic embrace. Ellen held her there long enough to whisper, 'Something still doesn't feel right about Antony's story. Be careful.'

Then, just as Pearl was about to remind Ellen that *she* was the one who should be careful, walking alone with Antony, Ellen broke away and fled down the road to catch up with him.

19

ELLEN

The streets were deserted as night fell quickly under the blanket of heavy grey clouds. Snow was drifting down on to the soggy roads and Ellen lowered her head into the upturned collar of her coat as she followed Antony towards Richard's house. Ellen loved the peaceful feeling of the first falling flakes before the roads became slick and impassable. She tried to focus on the quiet evening, for a while, rather than the sense of unrest that nagged at her. The story, the coded message, the train ticket – nothing was adding up. Antony, with the dimmed torch, marched purposefully ahead of her, paying no mind to her efforts to keep up.

'Antony!' she called out. 'Wait!'

She was aware he would've preferred Pearl on this venture, but Ellen hoped her company was better than nothing at all.

'Oh!' he exclaimed, his eyes narrow slits as if he'd recently woken up. 'I'm sorry. I didn't realize you'd fallen back so far.'

Ellen inhaled deeply, relieved he wasn't actually trying to lose her. 'It's all right. It's got quite cold. Let's hurry.'

'You're right, it is cold,' he said, looking into the sky in such a way that made Ellen wonder if he'd seen the snow before that moment. But he slowed down slightly and Ellen fell into step beside him.

Soon they turned down a long gravel drive to a small bungalow which would have been better suited for the countryside than a few streets away from Bletchley train station. 'It was Richard's gran's place,' Ant offered. 'He grew up in London but when his father got sick, they moved up here for the country air. This house was quite different from their terraced home in Kensington. I think Richard was a bit ashamed of it. I stopped by here a lot to collect him, but he never once let me inside.'

'That's sad,' Ellen said. She wondered if that partly explained his attraction to Dennis. Dennis didn't know Richard's history and Ellen remembered the unexpected bonus of starting university with strangers – none of her classmates had any idea of who she had been and what she'd done even the week before. She imagined a person would want to reinvent themselves, as she'd been tempted to had it not seemed so overwhelming.

'It is,' Ant said. 'I never judged him for that. Never once.'

'I believe you,' Ellen said as they stood before the awkwardly cheery yellow door to Richard's house. 'I bet Richard knew it as well.'

Ant nodded.

They stood for a while before Ellen gently added, 'You can knock now, maybe before we're stuck in a fully fledged blizzard.'

'Right,' he said and tapped the door knocker several times.

They waited, side by side, for what seemed like ages. Ellen hugged her arms to her chest in an attempt to warm up, tucking her icy fingers into the cuffs of her jacket. Eventually the door opened, answered by a woman with Richard's high forehead and a puffy red face. She barely looked at Antony and mostly focused on the blue hand-kerchief in her hands.

'I'm sorry I was not able to . . . I'm sorry for your . . . I am very sorry.' Antony couldn't look up from his shoes either and Ellen's chest tightened even though she barely knew these people.

'Antony, help Richard's mother to the lounge and I'll fetch her a cup of tea. Then we will collect what we came for and be out of her hair.'

'Right,' Ant muttered and steered Richard's weeping shell of a mother into a room down the hall.

Ellen didn't have to hunt long before finding the kitchen and a kettle, which she filled and set on the stove.

While the water heated, she tiptoed around the small foot-print of the house, thankful Antony had shut the door to the lounge. There was not much left to the imagination – an open door led to a bedroom with a floral-print duvet, and there was only one other closed door. Hoping the door hinges didn't creak, Ellen turned the knob and slipped inside the darkened room.

She knew immediately it was Richard's room. It had the telltale smell of a boy's room – salty sweat combined with the sour scent of dirty laundry. It was, though, oddly tidy, nothing like her brother's room. There were no clothes on the floor, no piles of books or magazines. If not for the odour, Ellen would've thought the room was unin-habited. It made her think of Pearl's foolish question, asking whether it was possible Richard knew he was going to die. This room did make it seem like either he'd got his personal items in order, or his mother found cleaning a therapeutic way to work through grief. 'Come on, Richard,' she whispered. 'Where do you keep your secrets?'

She opened the drawers on his narrow desk. They had been cleaned out entirely. His bedside table was empty as well. Ellen puzzled over this. She remembered how her aunt couldn't bear to go through her teenage cousin's things for over a year after he died during the first months of the war, saying she wanted to keep them around to remember him by. Richard's wardrobe was a line of orderly shirts and trousers. Could he have kept his room this tidy? And why? Ellen took in the small space, tapping her index finger on her bottom lip. *Think*, she told herself. *Where do you hide your secrets?* Ellen dropped to her knees. *Under things!* Beneath the bed was clean, as was the desk, but as she stood up, she caught sight of something – a small square of folded white paper tucked between the mattress and the bed frame. Without thinking, Ellen grabbed the paper and opened it. At first glance, it looked like nothing, but she knew it was important. Written in light pencil there was a line of block letters, broken into what might've been words, but utterly nonsensical:

MORBE WTN ELIY TWT
CEHTS HIG NAAE ROC

It was a coded message, though different letters than the one Antony had shown them earlier. The paper was similar, possibly the same. The handwriting, though, was smaller, blockier and with a slight slant. Curious that he had two different but similar messages. One so obviously hidden. But why? The kettle squealed. Although she wanted to investigate the note further, analyse the handwriting and paper and ink, Ellen put it in her pocket for later. The last thing she wanted was for someone to find her snooping about in a dead boy's room.

Ellen was pouring tea into cups when Antony rushed into the kitchen.

'We need to go,' he said, so loudly she spilt milk on

to the tray.

'Now? I've just put the tea together.' She looked over her shoulder at him. He had something in a bundle under his arm and looked shifty, like he, too, had stolen something. *Wouldn't that be interesting*, Ellen mused, as she wiped up the spill.

'Now,' he said. 'Besides, she wants to be alone.'

'Does she now?' Ellen paused, watching Antony squirm under her scrutiny. 'Then take the tea in to her and wish her well. I will wait for you outside.'

Although it was difficult, she waited until the front door was shut and they were alone on the road before asking him what was under his arm.

'My coat,' he said nervously.

'Why are you not wearing it? It's snowing.'

'I, uh, I don't know.'

They walked in silence for a while, Ellen puzzling at the lumpy cloth bundle he held gingerly, like it was breakable. 'I know something is wrong, Antony. If you don't trust me enough to tell me, that is perfectly fine. But I would rather you not lie to me.'

'It's bloody, all right? There is blood all over my coat and I cannot face that.' Antony's voice broke as he rushed through the words.

Ellen bit her lip. 'I'm sorry,' she said, as she had no idea how else to respond. She watched her feet as she walked through the light dusting of snow, wondering if there was anything she could do or say that would make this moment better for him. She needed to figure out a more delicate way to ask questions. Antony was not acting normally. Which was only logical: he had watched his best friend die right in front of him. That would've broken anyone.

They walked in silence to Ant's house and he waved at her limply before heading up the path. Raising her collar to the wind and snow, Ellen knew she had to get that coded note back from him. He was right; it had to mean something. She needed to find out what, especially with the second note now clutched in her pocket. With any luck, they might hold the answer to why Richard had ended up dead.

20

PEARL

It was nearly six thirty, and Pearl had to get to the train station before Peter, who'd been a few years ahead of her at school, made his way home for supper with his grandmother. While most men his age were on the front, Peter had lost an eye and could not enlist, instead finding a job at the Bletchley station ticket booth.

The station was bustling with passengers when Pearl walked in. As one of the largest stations in the area, Bletchley saw people passing through from London as well as to the east and west. Voices echoed against the tall arched ceiling. Long queues snaked out from the ticket windows like hosepipes. She stood behind two smartly dressed ladies and did her best to peer past their hats and spy Peter's familiar straw-yellow mop.

'Pearl!' Peter said with enthusiasm when she approached. He smiled broadly, his teeth as brown as the inside of a favourite teacup. One eye twinkled, while the shiny glass one glared straight ahead. 'I thought you'd be at work. But I can get you taken care of. Where you goin'?'

'I'm finished. Earlier shift.' She hesitated, wondering how much to tell him. 'I am here on a bit of business, though. Not exactly travel. Can you make heads or tails of this for me?'

Pearl leant closer to the bars separating them and slid Richard's ticket through. 'Looks like it's a ticket for Cornwall, if that's possible. Can you tell me when that train calls? Or anything at all about it?'

Peter brought the ticket closer to his good eye, squinting at the numbers on the front. He flipped it over and let out an 'aha!' when he saw the handwritten word, *Cornwall.*

'Well, you know this ain't a ticket to Cornwall.'

'Well, no,' Pearl said cautiously, as Peter handed the ticket back through the window. 'Otherwise I wouldn't have found it necessary to wait in that enormous queue to show it to you. Is it old? It looks quite worn. Where would this have taken him?'

'We don't have a direct service to Cornwall. Not with this ticket anyway. This is a ticket to London. Stopping at Leighton Buzzard, Watford and Wembley. One way. And those trains run regular as rain. You, or whoever "him" is, could've been on any one of those lines, really, and got off at any point. It couldn't have been a transfer – the timing is all wrong to catch another connection to St Ives. No, this ticket ends at Euston.'

Pearl felt her stomach sink. She could not go back empty-handed. 'There has to be something. Anything. You see, this was in the pocket of my friend, Richard, who died in a tragic motorcycle accident a few days ago. Can you see when it was issued or perhaps whether it was used?'

'Oh sure,' Peter said, then paused, 'and I am sorry, Pearl. He was a good lad, what I knew of him.'

'Thanks,' she mumbled, swallowing down the lump that always wedged itself in her throat when she talked about Richard.

'This date on the back, the stamp, shows it was used on the twenty-fourth of October this year. I can't tell if Richard used it – tickets are tickets. I could buy one for my gran and hand it to her to give to my cousin, you know? Anyone can use them for a journey.'

'Right,' Pearl said, trying to visualize the calendar pinned to her kitchen wall. This journey was taken two Fridays before Richard died, if she was not mistaken. Was that important? She tried switching tactics. 'Did you see him at the station that day? He was probably wearing his leather jacket with the white-and-blue striped armbands.'

'On the twenty-fourth? That was ages ago . . .' He stopped and scratched his tall forehead. 'Hang on a minute. Let me talk to Harold. He might remember.'

Pearl tried to ignore the grumbles of the impatient

couple behind her in the queue, studying the ticket for any stray mark she might have missed. Peter was right – it was completely normal except for the one word on the back. Logically, Pearl knew she was grasping at straws and, in all likelihood, the ticket was a dead end. She was about to give up and let the angry couple up to the window when Peter returned to his perch.

'I'm afraid I don't have much, Pearl. Harold couldn't say when or if Richard came through on his watch. But Harold had a thought – what if there's a place with Cornwall in the name around one of the stops on the line? The note is handwritten, after all. Seems more like a note I'd write to myself so as not to forget.'

'Yes!' Pearl blurted, her voice catching slightly in her throat. Could he be on to something? 'Where do you think it could be?'

'Oh, I dunno. There are billions of pubs and inns and restaurants in London. Could be any one of those. My local is called the Brighton Arms and the hotel down the road is called the London Inn. Lots of places use location names like that.' Then he leant in, his one eye softening sympathetically. 'But I can't help you any more, Pearl. I have an angry horde behind you and need to get them sorted before they miss their connections.'

'Right,' she said and before she could thank Peter, the impatient couple had elbowed past and pressed against the window. Pearl waded through the crowds entering the station. She paused inside the double door, her eyes travelling from the people milling at the news stand to a couple saying a long and rather gushy goodbye a few paces from the entrance to the platforms. What had Richard been doing with that ticket? Why would he take a train to London and not his motorcycle? Pearl groaned so loudly, the amorous couple stopped kissing and looked at her. Just as she was about to give them a sour look, she heard someone calling her name.

'Pearl!'

Through the crowd, a hand waved high above a bushy, windblown mess of sandy hair. It was Fran, the grocer's son, wearing a slate-grey delivery uniform with his name, *Francis*, sewn in loopy letters on the breast pocket. He was the same age as Pearl, seventeen, and though too young for conscription, he had left school to help his ailing father with the family business. Pearl did not know him terribly well, but the few times they'd talked, she'd always left feeling like he was someone she could really get on with. As happy as she was to see a familiar face, Pearl felt a pang of sadness. Of the men present at the accident, Pearl would've rather been waving to Richard.

'Sorry,' she said, tucking her blouse into her skirt and pulling up her stockings at the same time. 'I am, uh, a bit distracted.'

'Ah sure,' Fran said, his expression softening. 'I thought as much – I called your name three times and you didn't even turn. I wondered if I'd done something wrong . . .'

'Did you? Oh, no. Nothing of the sort; I do apologize,' Pearl said. She didn't even try to explain why she was distracted. Her friend had died. Fran had been there – he'd understand.

'Well,' Fran said, 'I've been the same way, if I'm honest. Can't stop thinking about it, and I didn't know Richard as well as you did. I am sorry, Pearl. There was no one quite like him.'

Pearl nodded and wiped away a tear snaking its way down her cheek. 'Thank you. Now, I, uh, probably should let you get back to work.' She gazed down at the ticket in her hand glumly.

Fran caught sight of the ticket and said, 'If you're heading anywhere north of London, I could give you a lift. I'm headed there now to get replacement parts for the delivery van – parts are hard to come by right now, but a place in Watford told Dad they have all of them, and at a decent price. He wanted me to drive down straight away, so here I am.'

Pearl opened her mouth to tell him the ticket was not hers, but stopped. She looked back at the train station, then at Fran. If he was heading near London, she could kill two birds with one stone – get closer to finding the 'Cornwall' location from the back of the ticket, but also ask him about the morning of the accident.

'Are you passing near any of the stations on the way to

Euston, by chance?' Pearl asked cautiously.

'I suppose I can swing by Wembley if you would like, once I get my parts. It's not too far out of my way, if you don't mind spending an hour and a half or so in the van with me.' Fran scratched his forehead. 'What'cha goin' there for?'

Pearl felt her pulse pick up. How would she explain this? 'I have a hunch about something.'

As they made their way outside the station, Fran paused. 'If it's something to do with what happened to Richard, well . . . I would do anything to help out.'

'Thanks,' Pearl said. She was more than a bit uneasy as they approached the battered van. Looking away from its scarred nose, Pearl focused instead on Fran. 'How did you know it was about Richard?'

'I saw Ant this afternoon – he said you'd been asking questions,' he said as he opened the door for her, 'and I don't blame you. I'd probably ask too, if I hadn't seen a lot of it with my own eyes.'

He climbed into the driver's seat and turned the key. The van started with a rumble of protestation. Pearl looked out the passenger window, watching people scurry on the pavement, the boxes containing their gas masks bouncing from the strings around their necks. She imagined they were rushing home to prepare supper instead of hurrying to avoid being out too late after darkness, handbags and parcels swinging instead of their regulation air-raid protection. In moments like these, it was easy to forget her place in time, to imagine she was looking out a bus window on her way home from school, back when bombs falling from the sky seemed as improbable as pigs flying. She blinked away the tears clouding her vision, surprised at how much her chest ached for that innocent, safe time. She cleared her throat and looked at Fran as he drove. 'It must have been awful there, at the scene of the accident.'

'It was.' Fran gripped the steering wheel and sighed audibly. He drove silently for a while, carefully scanning the traffic in front of them and cautiously turning on to a busier road where, in theory, he could drive faster.

Minutes passed, time blurring like the fields and tiny villages that passed by one right after another. They looked the same, yet different, like an old film reel that kept repeating. After a while, Fran looked at her sideways.

'What is it, Fran?' Pearl asked cautiously.

'They called me in for questioning yesterday,' he started. 'They talked to my father and Antony and, sorry to say, asked for the names of Richard's mates. They might question you, too.'

'All right,' Pearl said, stretching the words as her mind leapfrogged around the various scenarios that came to mind, most of them bad. What if they *had* found her letter? Then what? 'They're just doing their jobs. I wouldn't expect any less.'

'Ah, sure.' Fran looked at her nervously. 'I guess I shouldn't be concerned. You can take care of yourself. Richard used to say that he pitied the man who startled you on a dark lane.'

Pearl smiled. 'He was mostly right about that,' she agreed. 'Who else are you concerned about then?'

Fran swerved to avoid a rut in the road, the van surprisingly agile despite how loud it was. Crates bashed against each other in the back and the seat's springs squealed in protest. With all the clatter made by the van, there was no way he could have surprised Richard, even with the rumble of his motorcycle. Pearl made a note to tell Ellen that later.

'I was in the interrogation room a long time. They asked the same questions over and over – when we started out that morning, what we saw on the road, who was there, and so on. Then their questions became, well, more pointed.'

'Towards what?' Pearl asked, a chill running down her spine. She tucked her fingers under the cuffs of her father's cardigan, balling her fists. She wasn't entirely sure she wanted to hear what he was going to say.

'Towards Antony. They kept asking if I had seen him with Richard's bag or if he had ever opened his own bag and removed anything.'

She remembered how Antony had been acting with the coded message and the ticket – fidgety, nervous, evasive.

Like he was hiding something. It sounded like the authorities also thought something wasn't right with his behaviour. 'And what did you say?' Pearl asked.

Fran glanced across at her. 'That I didn't see anything suspicious. Antony had his own bag across his chest whenever I saw him and I didn't see him remove Richard's. But as I told them, I was concerned with my father. He's had heart issues lately and I was afraid the accident would cause another episode. He's getting on in years and when we crashed, we were both pretty rattled – he nearly died in a road accident when I was a baby. So my attention wasn't fixed on Antony at all.'

Pearl turned in her seat to face him. 'But you hit the wall, not Richard?'

'Absolutely. Oh Pearl, you can't think we hit Richard. How could I be out on the road today if I'd killed a man?'

'I don't know,' she mumbled, feeling embarrassed she'd even suggested it. 'Say, did you happen to see a rather large branch in the road?'

'I don't know. Maybe? I was so focused on my father and the van, a lot of it's a blur. I am sorry, Pearl.'

'I know,' she said, feeling deflated.

She must've let out a tiny sigh because Fran glanced over at her, a pained look in his eyes. 'Look, I didn't know Richard as well as you and Ant did, but I saw him at the pub from time to time and we had a good laugh, we did. I wish as much as you that this had never happened. We didn't see eye to eye on the war or how it should be fought, but I found if we avoided politics, he was a brilliant bloke, always good for a hilarious story. I'll miss him.'

Pearl cringed at the mention of Richard's political opinions. She'd hoped he hadn't blabbed those to anyone but herself – which was worrying. Friends like Fran would've chalked up any off-colour opinions to drink, but strangers would think differently. 'I'll miss him, too. A lot.' Pearl looked out the window at the dark stone walls passing by: sturdy engineered borders that snaked across the countryside like arteries. She felt her stomach lurch as Fran navigated the narrow, bumpy roads, but it wasn't from his driving.

'Also,' Fran said quickly, his words running together, 'they mentioned arresting someone soon. Stealing government papers, of course, is punishable by—'

'Death,' Pearl said, letting out a shaky breath. What if they were going to arrest Ant? Or even her? Perhaps they knew what she'd done? Peeking at sensitive papers, after all, was almost the same as stealing. But Miss Waincross had told her not to worry.

Pearl studied the side of Fran's face, his thin lips, a dusting of pale fuzz on his chin, his bushy eyebrows. He had the rough exterior of someone more comfortable outside than in, but was the type who really felt things. The circumstances around Richard's death obviously bothered him a lot.

'Fran, this is all so troubling. And I can see that you're just as disturbed and confused as I am.' Fran looked at Pearl, his eyebrows tented nervously above his eyes. 'So . . . I need your help, with more than a lift.'

'Whatever you need,' Fran said, turning to her. She had forgotten how *genuine* he was. Her mum had always said Fran was 'all flavours of good' and he truly was. He didn't have to give her a lift or even help her beyond that. With most people, Pearl would wonder what they were after – if they had some other motive. With Fran, it was simply how he was. She looked again at his hands on the steering wheel: tanned, broad, strong. He caught her looking and he smiled, which made her feel warm and protected, like he'd thrown an arm over her shoulders. He was trust-worthy down to his core.

So instead of working her way through the questions she and Ellen had discussed, she told him everything – well, *almost* everything – over the next hour of the drive. Not for any ultimate purpose, but because it seemed right for him to know – and she wanted to hear his responses. She told him about the row between Ant and Richard that night in the pub, a palpable tension she still didn't fully understand. She explained the mysterious branch more, how Ellen thought it might have indicated an accidental fall, but also how it had no place being where it was. Finally, she told him about the coded message in Richard's pocket and showed him the train ticket.

'I have to find out where he went. I know he didn't go to Cornwall – Peter told me as much – but why would he write that on the back of this ticket? I'm trying to make sense of it,' she said as Fran parked the van in front of a row of shops. 'Peter had a hunch that it was a pub or restaurant name of some sort.'

'Hold that thought,' he said. 'I'll be back in two ticks.' He jumped from the cab and ran up to a dark terraced house. He returned a few minutes later with a wooden crate filled with metal parts. He slid back into the driver's seat with a smile and the van chugged back to life.

'I asked the bloke if he knew of a pub nearby called "Cornwall". He said there was one near Wembley train station called the Earl of Cornwall. That sounds right, doesn't it?'

Pearl grinned, her heart lifting. 'Fran, that could be it!'

'It's not far now.' Fran hesitated, his face serious. 'But, well, Pearl, he said it has a, ah, a reputation. It's, well, rough around the edges. I could stop by alone, maybe let you know . . .'

Pearl set her jaw, shaking her head firmly. She suddenly remembered what Richard had said that night in the Horseshoes: that when he'd been in London, Dennis had bought him a first-class train ticket so he could meet him at a dingy out-of-town pub. She peered down at the ticket in her hand. This one was from Bletchley to London, but it, too, was first-class. A tingling sensation ran down her spine. Could it have been from Dennis as well? Could it be the same pub? She had to know. 'No – I want to go. I have to figure this out.'

As they drove for a bit through the slightly busier suburban streets, Fran stayed oddly quiet. Pearl could almost taste the ash in the air as they neared the city. There were more and more buildings against the grey sky. She looked at the assortment of shops and wondered what had made Richard venture so far from home for a pub. And one described as rough at that. Was it just because he wanted to see Dennis? What else had he got mixed up in? Her stomach twisted with worry.

'Look!' Fran exclaimed, slowing even more. He pulled up and parked the van a short distance from the pub's sign, yet Pearl didn't move to open the door right away. She stared at the weathered brick facade, mustering up enough courage to move.

'Shall we?' Pearl said at last, feeling her breath catch as if she had run out of air. Was it possible that a major piece of the puzzle was right there before them?

'Right-o,' Fran said sceptically. 'You sure you want to go in? If you tell me what you want to ask—'

'I need to go,' Pearl interrupted, looking through the windscreen at a line of shops, several vacant. Despite her words, she sat paralysed, her hands clasped in her lap. The shops still in business had windows 'X'ed with tape and sandbags stacked in front, but looked as empty and cold as those with gaping holes where windowpanes had been before. Recent hard times had given this neighbourhood a well-worn quality, but there was something in the carefully painted signs and abandoned window boxes that spoke of better times. Pearl reached for the door handle, wondering what Richard had found in this far-flung pub he could not get in his familiar, safe local.

21

PEARL

The pub was nearly deserted when they entered, perhaps due to the hour of their visit. Most people would have long since headed home to tuck into their evening meal, having already caught up with their workmates over a pint after their shifts at the local factories. Perhaps there'd be another crowd after the next shift clocked off, but that might not be until the morning.

Fran and Pearl walked down a shadowy, wood-panelled hall past a row of empty snugs, which were like little rooms containing a table and benches. The snugs were lit by dim sconces along the wall, which flickered as if they were candles instead of electric light. The stale odour of cigarettes and spilt beer hung over the vacant tables. This would be the perfect place to go if you did not want to be seen or heard – but that wasn't Richard. He had liked crowds – the more people to entertain and joke with, the better. It seemed strange for him to go out of his way to visit a place that seemed a home for loners and drunks.

'Here,' Pearl said, pointing to a lone barman polishing a glass, 'fancy a pint? I'll buy you one for your troubles.'

'Now that's an unexpected surprise,' Fran answered with a wink. 'Of course. I always fancy a pint, but as I'm driving, just a half. Got to protect my valuable cargo, after all.'

Pearl felt a blush warm her neck. Was he implying she was valuable? 'Golly,' she mumbled, pressing a few coins into his rough palm. 'Do you mind doing the talking?'

'Sure. I think I have my story straight. And you'll let me know if I don't.'

Fran grinned at her and then stepped forward to order. When the barman placed the glass on the polished wood bar, Fran gave Pearl a sideways look, then a nod.

'Nothing for the lady?' the barman asked with a smirk.

'No, thank you,' Pearl said, doing her best to appear more ladylike than she felt.

'Say,' Fran began after taking a long swig of his ale and clearing his throat loudly, 'you worked here a while, by chance?'

The barman, a short, balding man with a grey moustache, looked up from the glassware he was arranging on a shelf. 'Me?' he asked, as if there were a crowd of other men standing around.

'A mate of mine recommended this place. Said it was a

fine place for a good pint and conversation,' Fran said casually. 'Came in fairly regular, I think. Wondered if you might know him.' He barely seemed nervous and was doing much better than Pearl would have. To be fair, she had gone over the order of questions and specific information she wanted extracted from the barman before they entered the pub.

Fran took another sip and then leant forward on the bar, his hands clasped. 'He was a military fellow, rode a motorcycle?' Pearl marvelled at how Fran adapted his voice so it sounded more like the local accent – clipped and fast. The barman had stopped what he was doing and, it appeared, was considering what Fran said. 'He was tall with a sad little moustache. Always wore a brown jacket with a blue-and-white armband. Skinny, but loud enough you'd notice him.'

The barman broke his gaze, turning to arrange glassware on a nearby shelf. 'Can't says as I did,' he drawled, his eyes downcast as he bent to retrieve another stack of glasses. Pearl wasn't sure if he was lying outright or avoiding their questioning. Either way, she found it suspicious. 'And I'm not the sort to talk to strangers about customers – military or not – even if I had seen them. You'd best be on your way.'

Then he abruptly left the bar and disappeared around the corner.

Pearl patted Fran lightly on the arm as he sighed into

the remains of his ale. He had tried. Truly. But it hadn't garnered anything at all, not even one little clue that could explain the ticket, the word on the back of it, or whether Richard had even been in this pub.

'I remember him,' came a voice from behind them.

'Who was that?' Pearl whispered to Fran. She turned around, looking for the source of the voice. She had thought they were as good as alone but for the barman; the other two men they'd seen had been so drunk they were now snoring together in a snug. A plume of smoke rose up from behind one of the other snug walls. Exchanging a glance, Pearl and Fran walked over. Pearl's heart was pounding. It was one thing to question a barman in an empty pub. It was another to venture into a creepy, poorly lit snug to chat with the man who'd been eavesdropping on them.

'Excuse me, sir,' Fran started, 'but did you have something you wanted to say to us?'

The man coughed into a handkerchief, a gravelly smoker's cough. He was older, with a few strands of greasy hair plastered across an equally shiny bald skull. The shadows made him look worn and tattered; his shirt appeared dingy and his hands grimy. When he spoke, his voice was low and hoarse, forcing Pearl to lean in to hear him.

'Your friend was here. Sunday before last. Half one in the afternoon.'

A chill ran down Pearl's spine.

'Are you sure it was him?' she whispered loudly into Fran's ear. Both Fran and the man looked directly at her, proving her attempts to be the polite, demure female never worked.

'Are you sure—' Fran started.

'I heard the lass. Don't need to repeat it. I'm sure it was him. Your friend was hardly quiet, like her.' He laughed hoarsely for a bit at his own joke, then continued. 'Him and another bloke were thrown out. Should've been turned over to the authorities for the things they were saying, if you ask me. Drunk, probably, but that's no excuse. We may not all see eye to eye on how the war is being fought, but a lot of us have sons or brothers fighting. You can't go around talking that way.'

Pearl felt her heart sink. No matter how much she'd warned him about this, Richard hadn't been discreet at all about his views on the war. But she should've known. As the man said, he was not exactly the shy, quiet type.

'Who was he with?' Fran pressed, as Pearl had instructed earlier. Sitting on the edge of her seat, anticipation practically buzzing through her, Pearl waited for him to describe a tall, handsome blond man. *Dennis.* She knew he was mixed up in this somehow.

'There was a whole lot of them together that day, all boozing and laughing. Not usual for these parts, but they took up residence in the snug over there. They've been here before, just not so loud.' He began coughing again, rather uncontrollably, and the barman returned.

'Best you two leave now,' he said. 'The place will be busy soon and it ain't a place for young ladies and lads as wet behind the ears as you. Go on, get out.'

Pearl felt her throat catch at the man's words and she stepped back, bumping into Fran. Fran put his hand on her shoulder and steered her out of the pub without another word, his steady, strong grasp guiding her away.

As icy raindrops fell on her shoulders, Pearl took in a long, shuddery breath, the cold air seeming to travel down to her toes like water in a hosepipe. She had never been so relieved to be out of a building, and was surprised by how protective Fran was being. 'Thank you,' she managed to utter.

'Not at all,' he said.

Once they were inside the van, she put her hand on his as he brought the key to the ignition. 'Wait. Did you know all of that already, about Richard's views on the war? That he was a . . . um . . .'

'A pacifist?' Fran finished. 'I suspected as much. But Pearl, being against the war isn't an offence. It may not be a popular opinion, but it isn't as if he's siding with the enemy.'

Rain clattered loudly against the roof of the van. 'I just always hoped he'd only told me about his views. He might not have sided with the enemy, but I knew he felt helpless, frustrated. Even angry sometimes,' Pearl said.

'I know,' Fran agreed, gently.

'Did you ever say anything? Warn him against speaking about it?' Pearl shifted on the ripped bench seat to face him. 'Because I did. When he told me how he felt, I said he needed to be careful.'

'Pearl, I knew a different side of him than you did. You were his friend, but you never saw him when he really let loose. He was proud and confident in his opinions, especially after a few drinks. I suspect he had found his people at this pub, unlike our local. Whenever he got like that, we all hushed him and took away his beer. Here, they probably fired each other up.'

'What did he say, though? Exactly?'

Fran stared through the windscreen. 'To me? He would denounce the war effort as being useless, basically. But he was always peaceful when he spoke to me, always hopeful.' Fran turned to Pearl. 'You know how he loved to tell stories, and outlandish ones at that, so he could have your undivided attention?'

'Sure.' Pearl could see Richard now, his eyes wide and sparkling as he recounted how he'd saved a cat from a broken drainpipe two storeys up. 'We can get going now. If you, well, want to.'

Fran nodded, turning the key. 'I think he was practically a glutton for that sort of attention, the kind that makes you feel listened to and understood . . .'

189

'. . . and loved,' Pearl finished. 'Do you think the men in that pub made him feel loved?'

'I don't know,' Fran shrugged. 'But they definitely made him feel a part of something, even if that something wasn't the best thing for him.'

'He wanted so badly to be loved,' Pearl said. The inside of the van's windows had fogged over and Fran wiped at the windscreen with a handkerchief, making a soft squeaking noise. 'I tried to give him that, you know, if he would've been, well, open to it.' She felt herself blushing furiously, but Fran didn't seem fazed.

'Well, he was mad not to be.'

Pearl's blush deepened.

'You're right though,' Fran said, looking over his right shoulder as he pulled out on to the road. 'He seemed eager to feel liked, to feel part of something. And while I have nothing to back this up other than a hunch, I wouldn't be surprised if that longing led him to make wrong decisions, and maybe even to his death.'

'Do you think?' Pearl asked, wondering what sort of pacifist group would've got someone killed. After all, wasn't that what they were against?

Fran didn't respond, shrugging as he turned on to a waterlogged road. 'Maybe. Maybe not. But Richard had changed lately. I can't be the only person to have noticed it. He seemed quieter . . . a bit down, didn't he?'

'I noticed it too,' Pearl said glumly. Pearl had chalked

it up to the mounting stresses of his job and the world around them – Richard had suggested as much, when they'd spoken that morning after their disastrous 'date' and the incident with the envelope. 'Fran, do you mind if I ask you about the morning Richard died? Is that all right?'

'I suppose,' he said.

'Well, tell me, did you notice anything unusual?'

'The whole morning was unusual, if I'm honest. We were running late because of the weather – deliveries have been delayed this past week and meant we had to work Sunday. I had to scrape the windows free of ice – and then we came upon the accident on the road. My dad got such a fright he reached over and yanked on the wheel and we ended up front-ending the wall.'

'But you saw Antony and Richard on the road?' Pearl asked.

'Yes, and that other fellow. What was his name . . . Richard's tall, skinny friend? The posh, well-dressed one?'

'Dennis?' Pearl supplied. Her heart started thumping quickly. What could Dennis have been doing on that lonely road, at that early hour? It couldn't simply be a coincidence. But aside from that, how could Antony have forgotten Dennis had been there? Pearl tried to swallow, her mouth suddenly dry. Antony had not forgotten. Antony had chosen not to tell them about Dennis. 'Are you sure?'

'I can't be certain it was him' – Fran used the handkerchief to wipe at a line of fog along the windscreen – 'but I'd say so. He was gone in a flash, though.'

'Curious,' Pearl said, more to herself than to him. 'Why did you say you couldn't be certain?'

'My da, you know how his health is up and down? I was so afraid he'd have one of his spells and no doctors near. And Da was breathing all quickly like he did the last time, was as white as a ghost, too. Honestly, Pearl, I couldn't think of anything else. I needed to get him calmed down.'

'And when you did?' Pearl asked.

Fran sighed. 'When I did, the posh bloke was gone and the police had arrived and it was all over.'

'Right,' Pearl said, knowing full well what 'all over' meant. She watched the raindrops slide down the side window, blurring the now-dark countryside, black as ink without the flicker of a single candle or lone street lamp. 'That sounds horrible, Fran.'

'It was,' Fran mumbled. 'Might be a longer drive home, weather and all.'

'I don't mind,' she said, settling back into the lumpy seat. She didn't want to face what was waiting for her back at Bletchley and, for that reason, the peaceful, bumpy ride was a nice respite. Even if she knew she'd have to confront everything soon.

22

PEARL

Distractions were good, Pearl reasoned the next morning, as she scratched under her hairband and puzzled over the crib. *Keine besonderen Ereignisse.* It translated to *no special occurrences* – or, nothing to report. They had been seeing that message more often than not, so it seemed like a good guess for this random string of letters. That was a lot of their job: sizing up the messages for length, positioning, and odds that it could be any string of words commonly used. The easiest way to confirm their guessed phrase was to check that no letters of the translated message and the crib lined up, knowing that a letter could never be coded as itself. For example, you could never have a letter 'e' in your message that was also coded as an 'e' once put through the Enigma machine. If you found a message that did not have a matched letter, you had a potential decode. Pearl lined up the message *Keine besonderen Ereignisse* with the letters they had recorded:

G	E	G	O	H	J	Y	D	P	O	M	I	Q	N	P	J	C	O	S	G	A	H	V	L	E
K	E	I	N	E	B	E	S	O	N	D	E	R	E	N	E	R	E	I	G	N	I	S	S	E

Nope. She tried again, moving the message up and down the row of letters, trying to find a set of letters that did not match up. The work itself was not challenging, just shifting a message and checking to see if there were identical letters in both rows. When she saw a match, she'd shift the translated message to the right or left, leaving the jumbled letters she was trying to decode where they were.

H	Q	E	Y	S	A	W	Q	S	T	N	T	I	L	G	O	K	P	E	S	R	E	V	L	P	Y
	K	E	I	N	E	B	E	S	O	N	D	E	R	E	N	E	R	E	I	G	N	I	S	S	E

Finally, she lined the message up just right. But she had to make sure she was confident that was the message. Was it a 'nothing to report' message or a preamble about the weather? Pearl bit her pencil. *Clear as mud*, she thought.

H	Q	E	Y	S	A	W	Q	S	T	N	T	I	L	G	O	K	P	E	S	R	E	V	L	P	Y
K	E	I	N	E	B	E	S	O	N	D	E	R	E	N	E	R	E	I	G	N	I	S	S	E

All she wanted to do was pull Ellen aside and tell her what she'd found out last night. She'd rushed in to work, verging on late, and had no time for anything except pleasantries. This was not something she wanted to talk about in front of others, revealing that Richard had endangered himself by spouting unpopular political statements, and, worse, Ant might be arrested.

The bit of good news she had to share was that Fran had suggested he arrange a meeting with Ant so they could learn his side of things – for instance, why had he lied to them about who was at the crash site? With all this to think about, Pearl's focus was a bit like a smudged ink blob at best.

'Does that make sense?' she asked, sliding the paper in front of Ellen.

Ellen blinked at her. She wiped her hands on her skirt and nodded firmly at Pearl. 'I'm not able to think straight, are you? I've been dying to talk about what happened,' Ellen lowered her voice and leant closer, 'yesterday at the train station.'

'I've so much to tell you, but not here. Later. I promise,' she whispered.

'More thinking and less talking, girls,' came a voice from behind them. Mr St John. How long had he been standing there and what had he heard? Pearl tried not to panic, but noticed her hand shaking when she took up her pencil again.

'Yes, sir,' Ellen said, her voice trembling. He had scared them both.

'It seems as if you girls do not quite understand the magnitude of your work here.'

'We do, sir. Sorry, sir,' Pearl insisted, but regretted saying anything when she saw his eyes narrow. She should've stayed quiet and returned to her work.

He came around to the front of their table and crouched down, his head almost level with theirs. He put his elbows on the table, shirtsleeves rolled up to expose dark, hairy forearms. The other girls were starting to pack up for lunch. 'It is important you do not take this lightly. I am not sure how many times I must say it, but I will say it again and again. Your work is more important than you ever could imagine. And a loose tongue truly could cost lives. It is possible they know about us, our existence. Then what?' He paused and stared at them both for a long, uncomfortable moment. 'Do you understand what that means?'

Pearl's skin crawled, like a picnic blanket of ants was walking up her legs. 'If they, um, know about Bletchley . . .' she stammered.

'. . . it's a matter of time before they know what we've accomplished,' Ellen finished.

'Precisely. It could be more dangerous than that, truly,' he continued, leaning in closer, much too close even for mentor and students. Pearl could smell the tobacco on his breath. The whites of his eyes held spindly veins of red.

'If they find out we've broken their codes, even partially, they will change those codes. When the codes are changed, we know too well what happens. We have no idea where they are, what they're planning, or how to outsmart them. They will take the lead, again. They might even have the lead now and we do not know. We have to prevent them from learning anything more. If they find out just one little thing about this place, what we're doing, or how we're doing it, well, we'll be lucky to be speaking German this time next year.' He stood up and pulled a pipe from his breast pocket. 'Our actions, *your* actions, have distinct life or death consequences.'

Ellen nodded, but Pearl's eyes flooded with tears as she applied Mr St John's words to everything that had happened the past few weeks. What had she done? Encouraged Richard to cover up a possible security breach? Miss Waincross hadn't told anyone, and she'd said not to worry, so it couldn't be her fault if the enemy knew about Bletchley . . . Could it?

Unfortunately, her impending tears didn't escape Mr St John's notice. His expression hardened – the room behind him was empty now. 'The more time you spend whimpering, the more time you allow the enemy to steal our information. In fact, why don't you both stay in during lunch to make up for all the time you've wasted? Work through, ladies. Show me what you can accomplish.'

Pearl clenched her teeth so she wouldn't burst into a sob. She was so tired, having got home late and stayed up even later fretting about what she'd learnt. Her thoughts were all over the place. Now, at the mention of lunch, she was starving.

'Fear is the ultimate motivator, Pearl. Remember that.' With that, Mr St John closed the door behind him.

By the end of the day, Pearl felt slightly less nervous about Mr St John's words. Her hands had stopped shaking and the sweat spots under her arms had dried, but her temples throbbed, a reminder of how much she had failed. Pearl had felt a certain sense of dread every day since the war started. But this pain was different. It was constant, intense and absolutely her own doing. Why had she been promoted? Why had Mr St John hinted she was being watched? And now he had impressed upon her the importance of silence. She wondered if he suspected something, but reminded herself that Miss Waincross had said not to worry. She let out a long breath and tried to do just that.

After filing away their work, Pearl followed Ellen outside – which was only slightly colder than the hut interior with its old, smoky heater. She was amazed at how refreshing it felt to draw in a breath of clean air after a long day cooped up inside.

'Tell me everything, starting with the train station,' Ellen demanded.

Pearl told her how Fran had driven her to the pub and what had happened inside. 'Richard met others of his own political persuasion there. Pacifists. Unfortunately, they weren't quiet about their opinions.'

'Curious,' Ellen mused, tapping her chin with her finger. 'I can't imagine him being killed because of those views, though. Perhaps we got it all wrong. It could've been an accident somehow . . .'

Pearl shook her head. 'Between the coded messages and the tree branch . . . I don't think it's as straightforward as a slippery roadway.'

Ellen nodded, her finger still tapping away as they walked the darkening path towards the canteen. She was thinking, Pearl realized, turning something over in her mind. Pearl wanted her to come to some of the conclusions on her own, ones about Dennis. She had to realize there was something odd about his involvement with Richard. Why would he invite him to that dodgy pub? And what was he doing at the accident site?

'Fran told me he thought he saw Dennis the morning of the accident,' Pearl tried delicately.

'Oh?' Ellen still appeared distracted, looking far into the distance.

'He couldn't be sure, but I think that's suspect, don't you? What reason could Dennis have for being there?' Pearl hoped she was not pressing too much. She knew Ellen fancied Dennis.

'Furthermore, what reason would Antony have for not telling us this information?' Ellen countered. Pearl stumbled over a root and looked back at her friend, stunned. Was she really overlooking the Dennis bit entirely?

'Both are suspicious,' she tried. 'Dennis probably should've been honest with you, and Antony, too. It makes both of them questionable.'

Ellen was quiet for a while and then mumbled, 'It does.'

Before Ellen shut down any further, Pearl quickly continued, 'Fran was brilliant, though. He suggested we invite Ant to the pub tomorrow evening for another chat.'

'Right. What else did Fran say?' Ellen said, glancing over at Pearl. Pearl hoped she couldn't tell how nervous she'd become talking about Fran. What was wrong with her?

'They're questioning everyone who was at the accident site. And he thought they were going to make an arrest soon.' She eyed Ellen cautiously.

'An arrest? So, they also think it wasn't an accident.'

Pearl stopped walking – still some distance from the canteen – and took a deep breath, trying to calm down. 'Fran thought the investigators were going to arrest Antony.'

Ellen was silent for a moment, then nodded. 'He *was* avoiding our questions, wasn't he? And it sounds like he lied about Dennis being at the accident scene, too . . .' She shook her head. 'Even so, I struggle to believe he's stolen the bag.'

Pearl nodded. 'Me too. We need Ant to trust us, to tell us the whole truth for once, and I'm hoping with Fran on our side, we can do that. Also, it would be handy for you to question Dennis about what he was doing at the accident scene sooner rather than later. Oh, and we have to figure out the meaning of the message Richard gave to Ant. He was trying to tell Ant something. Perhaps he's figured it out.'

'Oh! I forgot to say.' Ellen looked at Pearl sheepishly. 'You see, there's another coded message. I found it at Richard's house when I was there with Antony. I've had a crack at solving it, but can't wrap my head around it. Perhaps later, we can both have a go at it.'

'I'd like to,' Pearl said, a bit annoyed Ellen had not told her of the message before now. But, just as she hadn't had a moment to tell Ellen about the long car ride with Fran, there had simply been no time.

'Good,' Ellen said decisively, 'and I'll need your help determining whether it's in his handwriting or not. What I can't figure out is whether Richard was passing the message on to someone else or if he was the originator. I suppose, just as we can't trust Antony, perhaps we must also have a healthy scepticism of Richard,' Ellen said slowly, clearly understanding how such a statement would be received. 'Come on, let's go in – I'm freezing.'

Pearl bristled as they headed towards the door. She hated to think Richard had not been trustworthy, but what other explanation was there? He had coded messages, after all. Still, he had been so concerned about potential tampering of the messages he was carrying. Someone who was trying to hide something would not have brought that to her attention, or anyone's for that matter.

'What I think we need,' Pearl said as they finally walked into the crowded canteen, 'is a new plan that will result in solid facts. There are too many squishy things rolling around. I don't feel like I know right from wrong these days. Do you agree?'

'Absolutely,' Ellen replied. 'I'm just as muddled as you are. Plans are always the best course of action, regardless of emotion.'

'Agreed,' Pearl said confidently, marching towards the takeaway sandwiches. Since they'd missed lunch, their poor stale sandwiches had been waiting for them since half twelve. As they collected the wrapped parcels, Pearl continued, 'At a very basic level, I think we need more details from Ant about the accident. What else did you learn when you went with him to Richard's last night?'

Ellen took her lunch from Pearl and the two walked outside. Thankfully, last night's snow had melted, but Pearl didn't feel it was all that much warmer. She was, of course, still wearing her father's cardigan. It was not the best shield against the elements, but she refused to acknowledge that. Sometimes, if she held the cuffs to her nose just right, she could swear she smelt his pipe.

They found a relatively dry bench and sat down. Ellen pulled out a square sandwich and slowly began to unwrap it. Pearl had already taken a bite of hers. Ham and some sort of cabbage salad. It was salty and dry, but she chewed a big bite to keep quiet. She knew Ellen well enough by now to understand how her friend needed processing time before actually saying anything, especially if that something was important.

After what she hoped was a respectable silence, she cleared her throat and asked, 'Do you have the note? The one you found?'

'Sure. Take a look,' Ellen said, pulling it from her pocket.

MORBE WTN ELIY TWT
CEHTS HIG NAAE ROC

'Curious. This doesn't look like his handwriting. It leans to the left whereas I've always seen his slant to the right,' Pearl said, putting her sandwich down and bringing the paper closer to her face. 'Do you have a pencil?'

'Sorry, I don't. Let's have a go at it later – I suspect it uses the same formula as the one Antony has.'

'Which we need to get our hands on,' Pearl added. She wondered if Ant would give it to her if Ellen weren't around. 'It might give us clues, like in the crib room. If you're working out a puzzle, you have to have all the pieces.'

Suddenly, Pearl felt sick. She lowered her head between her knees and heaved a deep breath.

'What's wrong?' Ellen said. 'You're pale as a sheet.'

You have to have all the pieces, she'd said – but she was

203

hiding a really big one from Ellen, wasn't she? She suddenly knew she had to tell Ellen everything – about Miss Waincross and the envelopes – now, before it was too late. However sick it made her feel.

Pearl closed her eyes. 'Ellen, I have something to tell you. I never should've kept this a secret for so long. I don't like to lie. I don't. It's just, I was embarrassed.'

'It happens,' Ellen said after a short but noticeable pause. 'I suppose what matters is that you're telling me everything right now. What is it, Pearl?'

Pearl opened her eyes, and though Ellen was not smiling, her expression was neutral, open, non-judgemental. Because of that, Pearl told her everything – from the incident in the hallway to Miss Waincross to Richard's ripped envelopes – and hoped her friend would forgive her for keeping it from her for so long.

23

PEARL

Most mornings, Pearl's mum was out of the house before Pearl woke, leaving just her washed egg cup and plate beside the sink. But today, Pearl was up early – in the kitchen with a full pot of tea and bowl of porridge when her mother came down at half six. It had been a few days since her trip with Fran and their investigation had not progressed at all, mostly because work at the Park had taken priority. This morning, Pearl had set her alarm so she could wake early and have time to think about the jumbled facts while eating breakfast. Her mother, of course, came down early as well and was startled but pleased to see her there. She told Pearl to get out of her dressing gown and accompany her on her walk to Bletchley Park. 'I never see you any more,' her mum said. 'We can catch up. Discuss things that need to be discussed.' *What does she mean by that?* Pearl wondered.

She dressed quickly in her green wool shirtdress and brushed her wild hair into some sort of order that she secured with two combs. Grabbing her father's cardigan from the coat rack by the back door, she ran to meet her mum, who was already stepping out on to the road towards Bletchley.

'Hurry up,' Mum said, her heels clicking loudly as she charged down the centre of the road. 'If we see a car, we can veer to the pavement, but I prefer being out here,' she said, waving a gloved hand towards the road, 'so I can keep an eye on everything.'

Mum walked quickly and Pearl scrambled to keep up. 'Why would you want to keep an eye on everything?'

Pearl scanned both sides of the road, but she could see nothing at all out of the ordinary. It was so early, shops weren't open and few people were out. An old man was taking his poodle for a walk, and he hardly looked dangerous with his cane and wobbly gait.

'Pearl,' her mum said, pulling Pearl's hand and looping it firmly under her arm. She spoke quietly, stooping slightly so she was closer to Pearl's ear. 'What I am going to tell you is top secret. I know, however, that I can trust you – and I need your eyes as well.' She took a deep breath. 'There have been reports that the Park has been compromised.'

'Compromised how?' Pearl asked, fully aware of how her breath was coming shorter now, as if they were

206

running uphill instead of walking slowly down the centre of a flat, wide road. She watched as an older woman in a housedress opened her front door to let a ginger cat outside.

'Top officials at the Park are convinced we might have a spy among our ranks, so it is pretty serious.' Her mum's grip on her hand became firmer. Pearl's heart was pounding. Did they think there was a spy because of her tampered envelope? Maybe Miss Waincross had told them. Maybe *Pearl* was the spy. 'Pearl, I'm asking you to be careful and more aware of your surroundings. If anything happens that is at all questionable, I need you to report it to me.' She paused and glanced over her shoulder. A delivery truck came around the corner and her mum steered them to the pavement. 'We're not to talk of this again, and Pearl, if I hear you've told anyone about this you'll be working as a mother's helper for Mrs O'Flanagan before you've even closed your mouth. Understood?'

Pearl nodded, her mind racing so quickly she couldn't say yes, let alone ask any further questions.

'That's a lot to think about,' her mother said, standing upright and talking in a normal voice again, 'but I know I can trust you. You have a lot on your mind, what with Richard and all. How are you coping? He was a good boy, all things considered.'

What did she mean by that – 'all things considered'? Was she alluding to his political leanings? But how could she know about that? Instead of challenging it, Pearl shrugged. She didn't feel able to speak about him yet – not so casually.

Her mother continued. 'I liked Richard. He was very jovial and polite. I imagine you will miss him, such a good friend.'

'I already miss him,' Pearl said quickly, trying to think of anything else. She would think of the spy. That was distracting. Spies didn't make her cry.

'Of course you do,' her mother tutted and pulled her closer. 'I saw you two together sometimes. I am truly sorry you have to go through this, but many girls these days have this experience, losing a boyfriend or fiancé or husband in the war. It is awful, but maybe you'll find other girls going through the same thing at the Park, especially now you've been promoted. I'm proud of you, you know.'

Pearl shot her a weak, grateful smile, wishing she could be as excited as she should be about her new job. She wanted to tell her that Richard was never her boyfriend, but she didn't. She wanted to tell her that this was so much more than just a broken heart, though that seemed colossal in itself. Pearl longed for her help, really. She needed the reassurance that she was doing the right thing. But it was too dangerous. Her mum couldn't get involved. Pearl didn't want to lose her, too. So, she simply leant into her and tried not to be doubly hurt that she felt rubbish and it wasn't simply because she was lovesick and grief-stricken about Richard. Pearl wanted her mum to fix things, to make the monster under the bed go away, but knew she'd have to be the one to chase away the darkness.

Pearl was mostly silent the rest of the walk to the Park, her mother chatting about things she must've thought would distract her – the weather, their neighbour's kittens, a new book she was reading – until they parted ways in front of the mansion, at which point Pearl nearly crumbled. She let out a scared, gulping sob as she ran to the hut.

24

ELLEN

'Morning,' Ellen mumbled. She rushed into the crib room, practically throwing her coat on the stand near the heater. A few girls were at their tables sipping steaming mugs of tea and talking quietly. Others were wandering in in dribs and drabs, most commenting on the temperature of the room, which was – as usual – icy.

'Best we get started straight away, then,' Ellen said to Pearl, who looked a bit haggard, her wavy hair barely held back from her red, splotchy face by two brown combs.

'Yes,' Pearl said, lining up two pencils in front of her, 'because we're heading straight from our shift to Fran's local. He sent word that he got Ant to agree to our plan.'

'Brilliant,' Ellen said, though she was not entirely sure it was. She was trying not to look at Pearl any differently this morning, but learning Pearl had withheld critical information, and for so long, was troubling. While Pearl had apologized up and down, Ellen worried over whether she could trust her friend. People who had the tendency to lie often did so more than once if they got away with it. Pearl had, for a while, but something eventually made her confess. So perhaps that meant she simply didn't have the constitution to be a serial liar? Ellen had spent a lot of last night tossing in her too-cold bed while obsessing over it. At one point she'd sat up and stared at the jumbled message she'd taken from Richard's bedroom. After what seemed like ages, she'd made no progress and flopped over in her cold bed. She'd slept fitfully, plagued by nightmares about Dennis crashing a delivery truck into a stone wall, and had arrived at work frazzled and exhausted.

Still, she had work to do. Pearl opened the tan folder in front of them to uncover their first message. Sadly, nothing revealed itself no matter how long Ellen stared at it.

FWXTU

'Five letters,' Ellen mumbled.

Pearl nodded. 'Sometimes the answer is right in front of you, isn't it?'

She wrote: $FWXTU = HE \ldots$

Ellen looked over Pearl's shoulder and then continued Pearl's thought, writing:

$FWXTU = HA \ldots$

HALLO!

211

Pearl looked up at Ellen. 'St John said it's often a greeting. Could it be that simple?'

Ellen smiled, feeling a massive wave of relief. Maybe this morning wouldn't be a complete failure. She grabbed the paper. 'Sometimes they are. We can't know until we check.'

Ellen walked, head held high, down the hall to Mr St John's office, where he was hunched over a stack of papers on his desk. 'Excuse me, sir,' she said meekly, 'but we have a crib that might, uh, work?'

Grumbling, he held out his ink-stained hand without looking up. Ellen gave him their paper and walked away, wondering if they'd ·ever know if one of their cribs succeeded.

The rest of the day was not as rewarding. They stopped briefly for lunch, eating quickly on the lawn and returning to their table after fifteen minutes. Then they struggled with one crib for the rest of their shift, to no avail.

Finally, Pearl put her hand on Ellen's arm and whispered, 'I give up. It's time to go.'

Ellen blinked several times, her eyes foggy. 'Is it? I got lost in this latest one. I suppose I'll have to leave it for the next shift.'

Pearl nodded. 'Hurry, will you? We're meeting the boys in twenty minutes and I need to talk to you before.'

'Right,' Ellen agreed. She pushed her hair behind her ears and straightened the collar of her pale pink blouse.

'We should have a plan of how we're going to talk to Ant. Who questions him first, what we ask and so forth.'

'Well, I guess,' Pearl said, dropping to one knee to tie her laces. Ellen continued to arrange the desk for the next girl, then stood to retrieve her coat. 'But Ellen,' Pearl added, 'there's something more important than that.'

'What is it?' Ellen said. She hoped Pearl wasn't going to open up about another batch of secrets she'd been keeping. Ellen wanted to trust Pearl; she simply needed her friend to stop giving her reasons not to. In her gut, she believed Pearl was good and in spite of Ellen's feelings about gut intuitions, she knew this one was right. Pearl meant well. She had simply made some bad choices. 'We have time while we walk, don't we?'

Pearl looked around the room, then ushered her friend outside quickly. With her hand applying gentle pressure to Ellen's elbow, their walk to the gate became almost a slow jog.

'Slow down, Pearl,' Ellen said when she realized she couldn't catch her breath. 'We have twenty minutes. Why the rush? Tell me what's on your mind.'

Pearl looked all around them, like they were being followed, then hissed, 'Not here. It's not safe here.'

'No one is outside,' Ellen protested. 'Can't we walk, at least?'

'I would rather not risk it,' Pearl said, and so Ellen tried to ignore the stitch in her side that was only getting worse the harder she breathed.

Pearl slowed somewhat when they reached the main street in town. But she kept glancing over her shoulder.

'Pearl,' Ellen said between breaths, 'what's going on?'

'Mum walked with me to work this morning. She said she had something to tell me, and I was to tell no one, but . . .' Pearl raised both her hands, as if indicating she had no choice.

'No secrets, right?' Ellen said.

Pearl flushed. 'No more secrets.'

'And?'

'And, it is suspected we have a spy at Bletchley Park.'

'A *spy*?' Ellen croaked. Perhaps Pearl had misunderstood her mother. Because a spy would be one of the worst things to happen to Bletchley. Perhaps even worse than being hit by a bomb, because in that instance, all the top-secret information would be destroyed – whereas a spy could hand the information over to the enemy.

'That's what my mum said. You cannot tell anyone, under any circumstances, because Mum said if she finds out I've told anyone she'll have me expelled from the Park and sent away. You have to promise, Ellen.'

Pearl looked around nervously and finally, Ellen understood her paranoia. She felt herself holding her breath and exhaled sharply. 'Oh Pearl, a spy at the Park would be disastrous.'

'I know,' Pearl agreed solemnly.

'I promise not to say a word, but what are they doing? Did your mother say anything else?' Ellen said. 'Are they trying to find the spy? How did they know? What should we look out for?'

Pearl shrugged. 'Mum said I needed to keep my eyes open and tell her if I see anything unusual. That was it.'

'That brings up a lot – whether Richard's envelopes had been opened by the spy; perhaps he knew of the spy and was killed because of it. Oh Pearl, this is not good.' Ellen was having trouble bringing order to her thoughts. Her mind was flooded with images of people who worked at the Park – any of them could be a spy and she'd never suspected. A shudder ran down her spine. She'd felt safe at Bletchley, in a bubble of security within a world where the sky could explode at any moment. How foolish she'd been.

Pearl nodded, but they were standing outside the pub. 'You cannot say a word,' Pearl reiterated. She put her hand on Ellen's shoulder and got closer. 'Also, I think I should talk to Ant afterwards. Alone. I've known him for ages. If he doesn't open up to all of us, I bet I can get him to tell me whatever it is he's hiding.'

Ellen hesitated. It was on the tip of her tongue to say this was not what they'd planned. They were working together, following a script, laying out a firm path, but then she realized Pearl was probably right. Ant might have been nervous and hesitant around her simply because he didn't know her.

'All right,' she said. She hung back, letting Pearl open the door to the pub first. She looked up and down the pavement before walking in, just in case. It was probably just the breeze, but the back of her neck tingled, as if someone was watching them.

25

ELLEN

Ant's table was tucked in a small nook with two other tables. Pearl slid into the seat across from Ant. Two young men with the barest shadows of moustaches were occupying the other chairs. One of the boys wore a tweed cap and the other probably should have – he had a long, prominent forehead in spite of his baby face. There was a playful twinkle in his eye and, even in the dim pub lighting, Ellen could tell his face was more tanned than Antony's, and his hair was as yellow as hay. He had to be Fran, the grocer's son.

'Ellen needs a place to sit,' Fran said, his eyebrows arching. 'You don't mind, do you James?'

The other lad shook his head and reached down. In one quick movement he stood, tucked a wooden crutch beneath each arm, and saluted them with his free hand. Skilfully, James glided on his crutches to a neighbouring table without spilling his beer, which was impressive as James had one leg.

Ellen slid in next to Fran, a bit embarrassed at their proximity. Fran grinned at her, oblivious. Ellen was surprised by the vegetal, earthy smell that clouded the smoky air around him. She noticed the dark moons of dirt under his wide, blunt fingernails and, under the table, mud-caked boots. He had clearly come straight from working, the lure of an evening pint too great to warrant a change of attire.

Fran turned in his chair to look at Ellen. 'It's brilliant to finally meet you,' he said. He shook her hand with the grace of a gentleman, even though his hands were broad and rough. After he greeted her, he turned to Antony and declared, 'Now that we're all here, who else needs a drink? Your glass is empty, Ant.'

'I suppose,' Antony grumbled non-committally, looking a tad ambushed.

'Nothing for me, thanks,' Ellen said.

'Nor me,' added Pearl.

An older man with a tea towel over his shoulder passed by and Fran raised his hand. 'Mr Parks, can you have three more ales for me at the bar when you get a chance? I'll deliver one to poor James over here,' Fran said more to the table than to the barman.

The old man nodded then leant down and cleared his throat before asking, 'That other bloke, the one who was

218

with you last time. He won't be joining you, will he?'

'No,' Fran said. 'Sadly, he's passed on.'

'Oh!' The barkeep's eyes widened and he lowered his gaze. 'I never expected . . . well, may he rest in peace.'

Fran spoke first, as soon as Mr Parks was far enough from their table not to overhear.

'I'd forgotten about that night,' Fran said, looking at Ant. 'Mr Parks was right; it was the last time we were all here together, wasn't it? Richard had a few too many pints that night, he started talking too freely. Some of the locals got angry.' He exchanged a knowing glance with Ellen and Pearl. Clearly, Richard had been spouting his political views again. 'You had to walk him home, remember Ant?'

'Left his motorbike here, he did, and for as much as he was talking about that Dennis bloke, he was on his own,' Ant said, looking at the ceiling. 'It had started as such a good night, too.'

'It had,' Fran said with a sparkle in his eye. Then his grin faded. 'Can't believe he's gone.' He raised his empty glass. 'To Richard. We had hoped he would live nine lives.'

'To Richard,' they echoed, the girls miming raised glasses.

The pub was so close, so cosy, that Ellen shrugged out of her cardigan, letting her bare forearms rest on the cool tabletop. The rumble of low voices around them was oddly comforting, like a blanket covering everyone's secrets. Fran returned quickly with drinks for himself and Antony, which seemed a sign that it was time to get down to business.

'So, Antony,' Pearl said, diving right in, 'why did you not think to tell us that Richard's friend Dennis was at the accident scene when you arrived?'

If Ant could've crawled into his shirt collar, Ellen supposed he would've. He shrunk in his seat like a turtle hiding in its shell, back caved in and head bowed.

'I didn't think . . . I don't know, Pearl, I wanted to say something, but you know how Dennis fancies— I mean, I . . .' Ant stole a few glances at Ellen.

'Did you not say anything because you think Dennis fancies me?' asked Ellen. 'Because, Antony, that's neither here nor there.' She leant her elbows on the table and cupped her chin in her hands.

Foolishly, she'd wanted Antony to deny Dennis's presence on the road that morning. Fran had been concentrating on his father, Pearl had said, so Ellen had wondered if it was possible he'd been mistaken. She didn't like thinking of Dennis being linked in some way to Richard's death. And despite Ellen lingering hopefully on her walks to and from work, she hadn't actually seen him since the accident. So, Dennis *was* a suspect – she had to admit it. But when she thought of it, wasn't Pearl also a suspect? And Ant, too? At this point, more people *were* suspects than were not.

'I'm sorry,' Ant said, reluctantly. 'I should've been honest.'

220

'And mate, I have to step in, it's not just the bag. It's who they think has nicked it. When I talked to the uniforms the other day, they implied they had their eyes on you,' Fran said.

'So, if you keep withholding information like a numb-skull, you're only going to wind up in jail!' Pearl exploded.

'Pearl, please,' Ellen said gently. 'I think Antony has got the point.' She turned to Antony. 'So, what was Dennis doing at the scene of the accident?'

Ant let out a long sigh and shook his head. 'Dennis was kneeling by Richard when I got there. He said his bicycle got a flat tyre and he was walking it down the road when he heard the crash behind him.'

There we go, Ellen thought, letting out a sigh of relief. A perfectly logical explanation. She remembered the first day she'd seen Dennis riding that bike and what a racket the creaky old seat and wheels made as he'd pedalled the road to his aunt's. She fidgeted as she realized she'd been listening for it on her way to and from work. It made perfect sense that one of the tyres had burst.

Pearl curled her lip and drummed her fingertips on the tabletop. Ellen let her friend tap out her frustration, though she knew it was not likely to make Antony more comfortable in the moment.

'What else did Dennis say?' Ellen pressed, her voice soft.

'He told me what to do,' Ant said quietly, 'and not to

move Richard. He told me to keep talking to him, keep him awake. Then he cycled off on the flat to find help. It was no use, though. Not long after Dennis left, Richard died.'

Fran frowned. 'It all happened so fast. I've gone over that morning time and time again, wondering how we could've changed things.'

'Why, Fran? Do you think you could've done more?' Pearl asked.

Fran swirled the dark amber liquid in his glass as if it were a fine wine. 'Maybe I should have left my dad and helped Ant. Maybe we could've stopped the blood flow somehow or kept Richard talking. I don't know anything about medicine, but I do know Richard was in pretty bad shape. Dad turned out to be just fine.'

Ellen glanced at Ant. He was staring at his beer glass as if trying to disappear into it.

'If my dad was still around and ill, I would've tended to him first, too. And it sounds like Richard was doomed, unfortunately,' Pearl continued, an edge creeping into her voice. 'The only thing you could've done was protect his bag, if you'd known to do so.'

'Did Dennis take his bag?' Ellen asked, her eyes narrowed.

'Not that I saw,' Fran replied quickly, and Ellen felt herself nodding in response. Dennis would know better than to take sensitive materials off a dispatch rider, no matter how dire the situation.

'I remembered later,' Antony said. 'I should've taken Richard's bag and kept on my route. It didn't feel right, though, leaving him or taking anything off him.'

Ellen noticed Antony wasn't making eye contact with any of them; he was looking at his lap instead. Had he, thought Ellen, protected the bag simply so he could grab it at a time when others were distracted? If that had been the case, how would he have taken both his and Richard's bags without anyone noticing? And why? Could he be the spy – or could he be working with them?

But then Antony continued, 'I was trying to do my job . . . but I forgot the rules. I messed it all up.'

Fran sighed. 'You were in quite a state. If I'd known how bad you were, I'd have stepped in. But it all happened so fast. The police were there in a few minutes.'

'When the authorities arrived, what happened?' Pearl asked, still leaning on the table and looking only at Fran.

'The uniforms questioned me and my father,' Fran said. 'They took Richard away and once dad was recovered, we started on cleaning up the veg – the back of the van was in a bit of a state. But I do remember seeing them walk Ant away from Richard. They took you with them, right mate?'

'I told you that already,' Ant said, sounding offended.

'Ant, you have to understand why we're checking your story,' Pearl explained. 'You *lied* to us.'

Fran's eyes widened and he took a long sip of his ale.

'Hold on there,' Antony said, his voice getting slightly

223

louder than was proper even for a noisy pub, 'I only didn't say anything about Dennis because she' – he pointed to Ellen – 'is involved with him. It made me nervous. I didn't trust her. And yes, Fran, I know they're pointing the finger at me as the one who stole Richard's bag. Why else would I be so cautious?'

Ellen blanched at the accusatory way he pointed at her, as if painting a scarlet 'A' on her chest just for having a few friendly conversations with an attractive man. So what if she found him dashing? They weren't 'involved'! Who was Antony to think she'd be so blinded by Dennis she wouldn't be able to think clearly?

'Ant, you can trust us,' Pearl said. She looked over her shoulder and lowered her voice. 'We don't want you to get taken to jail, and frankly, I don't think you deserve to go. I've known you for a long time, Ant. You don't have to lie to me.'

'But I didn't—'

'You did, Ant,' Pearl said. 'You lied to us when you didn't tell us about Dennis.'

'You're not the bloody investigators! I told *them* everything they need to know because *they're* the ones who will arrest the thief, not you. I don't have to tell you anything. Now if you will excuse me, I have to go and help Mum with my brothers.' Ant's lower lip trembled and he stood abruptly, leaving the table so quickly neither Ellen nor Pearl had a chance to respond.

'Well, that backfired,' Pearl said with a snort.

Ellen nodded and swallowed, suddenly parched. She turned to Fran. 'Fran, can you get me half a pint of beer? I know it's hardly ladylike, but I feel like I need it. My father always said a good bitter gave you strength and energy when the going got tough.'

'Is that true, now? Well, in that case, make it two,' Pearl said, then in response to Fran's raised eyebrow, added, 'What? No one can see us back here. Besides, if we're deemed mature enough to work for the Foreign Office, we should be bloody mature enough to drink half a pint of beer to help us solve a murder.'

Fran laughed. 'I'm hardly one to judge, Pearl. Besides, I'd fear anyone who tried to cross you. You'd take 'em out at the knees, I bet. Nah, we're all a bit in awe of you.'

Ellen watched as Pearl turned a shade of crimson, leading her to believe her own earlier blushing had not been disguised by the lighting. Still, she had to agree with Fran's sentiment. They could protect themselves; Pearl especially.

'Go, then,' Pearl teased with a limp toss of her wrist.

Without argument, Fran left the table, a faint smile on his face, and Ellen reached across the table to squeeze her friend's hand. Pearl let out a long breath and gazed back, her eyes dark and troubled. Now that they knew Antony had been lying to them because of the connection between her and Dennis, Ellen felt uncomfortable. She needed to question Dennis, soon, as there were too many un-answered questions left plaguing her. As much as she wanted to believe he was innocent, she knew she could rule no one out entirely. Not Dennis. Not even Pearl.

26

ELLEN

The next morning, Ellen left for Bletchley with plenty of time to walk slowly and increase her chances of 'accidentally' bumping into Dennis.

He had been rather invisible since the accident, leaving Ellen concerned on several fronts. Not only was she worried about his feelings for her (what if he'd tired of her already?), but she wondered why so many of the clues they had regarding Richard led back to him. From his presence at the accident to his invitation to – she presumed – the same shady pub where Richard had got in trouble for his views, Dennis had played a part in whatever had led to Richard's death. Then he had disappeared. She couldn't believe he was to blame – she knew him too well for that; he was a stickler for the rules – but she had some difficult questions to ask. Though Ellen knew she had to be careful, as she did not want to part ways over something she said.

Golly, she fancied him.

The walk was unnecessarily long, anxiety filled. She wondered if she should speed up, slow down, or whether any of her worrying was worth it. In the end, they never crossed paths. Again.

It was a long day at the Park because of her miscalculation. Pearl glowered at the news that Ellen had neither seen nor heard from Dennis. Still, the two worked quietly, with few words exchanged. All Ellen could think about, aside from the piles of letters in front of them, was how she was going to manage to find him. Before, he had always seemed to track her down effortlessly, happening upon her on her way home. Ellen supposed she could call at his aunt's, but did not like the idea of knocking on strangers' doors.

By the time she left Bletchley Park that evening, it was quite dark. She declined a ride in one of the cars taking girls to billets further afield in order to walk beyond the Waverlys' place. She could not face another day of Pearl's sour glances. She would leave a note for Dennis asking him to meet her the following morning. He told her once it was hard to miss, as it was the only cottage at the end of Mill Road, which sounded easy enough to find. Plus, Dennis needed to explain himself.

On a whim, Ellen decided to wander by the train station and into town on the chance she'd encounter Dennis there instead. She watched as shop owners closed their shutters and locked their doors for the night, trapping in any light that might escape into the sky. Bletchley had been lucky so far. No bombs had dropped on the town yet; unlike Cardiff, buildings stood unmarred, streets free of rubble. If it weren't for the sandbags and taped-up windows, Ellen could pretend this was a street untouched by the war. If she let herself go far enough inside her head, she could trick herself into believing she was meeting her brother, David, for a slice of cake as they used to do sometimes after school. That illusion of being carefree, having nothing more important to do than choose between lemon drizzle or honey cake, was a fleeting feeling of normality. She always felt stupid afterwards, like when she used to hide under her childhood quilt in the Anderson shelter in their garden, trying to pretend the weight of the blanket would protect her from the air raid overhead. She was too old and too aware to fall prey to that over and over.

Annoyed with herself, Ellen turned to head back to the Waverlys' for supper. Then she stopped. An older woman was walking next to a tall young man, a stuffed basket of greens and carrots hanging from his wrist. Ellen narrowed her eyes, wondered if she needed spectacles, then decided no. It was Dennis. She was pleasantly surprised her calculations had finally worked.

Instead of running over to him, Ellen lagged behind cautiously, observing from a distance. She could hear the faint sound of their voices and then Dennis laughed, carefully handed the basket over to the old woman, who patted him on the arm and tottered off down a narrow side street away from town. Dennis watched her leave, then looked at his wrist, turned on his heel and headed back down the pavement towards Ellen rather purposefully. He was a few steps away, head still lowered as he walked, before Ellen called out to him.

'Dennis! Hello,' she said with a wave.

Looking up, he flashed a warm smile and stepped forward to grasp her hands in his. 'How *are* you? It is so good to see you again. I've been working all hours. It's a shame I kept missing you on the road.'

Ellen nodded, already feeling relieved that Dennis hadn't actually been avoiding her. 'It is good to see you too.' She paused, then decided to dive right in. 'I have some questions for you, Dennis. I hope it's all right. They're about Richard.'

Dennis narrowed his eyes, but they were soft – as if her straightforwardness amused him. 'Of course. I can't stop thinking about it. It was so tragic.'

Relieved, she pressed on. 'It is awful, isn't it? Do you have anywhere to be right now? Do you mind walking me through what happened?'

Dennis frowned and looked at the ground. He was wearing different but equally shiny leather shoes today. Black wingtips, the laces stiff. How did he keep them so clean? He had a hat on, as usual, but his eyes were arresting even under the shadow of the brim. She was close enough to notice creases between his eyebrows and faint caramel-coloured fuzz on his upper lip. He was not as put-together as when she last saw him. She wondered if that was because of Richard's death. Seeing even a stranger die would take its toll, let alone a friend.

'It will not be the easiest thing I've done today, but for you, Ellen, of course.'

Ellen grinned and felt her cheeks go warm. He was so nice, so generous. But she had to focus. Clearing her throat, she continued, trying to unweave her fingers from his grasp. 'Was that your aunt?'

'Ah, yes. Aunt Myra. Of course. I was helping her with her shopping and she's calling in on a friend for supper. I'm on my own now, so to speak.' He paused and turned her hands over in his so her palms were now facing up. 'Say, I have an idea. Come to dinner with me!'

'Me?' Ellen felt stupid as soon as the word came out of her mouth. No one else was around. Of course he meant her. She stuttered for a bit, unsure how she was expected to answer. Mother would say it was improper. Pearl would remind her this was still part of an active investigation. But Ellen, when she truly thought about it, wanted to keep talking to Dennis. Not just because she had questions for him, but because she liked him. Still, a girl could not be forward in any situation. 'I should really head back. Mrs Waverly . . .'

'Mrs Waverly will understand,' he insisted, releasing her from his grasp and stepping back, waving his hands as if wiping a table clean. 'I cannot have you walking back to your billet alone in this cold weather, not when we could be enjoying the roast supper at the Golden Ball. It's right across the road, I promise I'll walk you home afterwards. Do you have a torch? I have one and we'll be safer as two. Have you had their roast potatoes? Don't tell Aunt Myra, but they're the best I've ever tasted.'

Ellen's chest tightened, both from fear and longing. What she wouldn't give to have Pearl's confidence. She needed to take advantage of the opportunity and use it to get the answers she needed, but couldn't help but worry if dinner out was proper. It would be so public.

As if reading her mind, Dennis clasped his hands together and made one last attempt: 'Look, Ellen, no one ventures out for midweek meals. I'm usually alone when I go to dinner before meeting Aunt Myra. I'd be grateful to have a friend tonight, after all that happened with Richard. He used to meet me sometimes and it's dreadfully lonely now.'

His blue eyes softened and Ellen's heart felt heavy and squished, like someone was stepping on it. Of course, he was lonely and hurting. Richard had been his friend and he'd seen the whole accident on the road. In addition, he didn't seem to mind talking about it – and Ellen couldn't ignore the opportunity to find out more, could she?

'All right,' she agreed and again, her insides did a bit of a flip when Dennis's face lit up. As he led her across the street to the quiet, dark shopfront, she wondered if she was falling for him, like in a romance novel. And if so, would she be able to keep her wits about her and get the answers she needed to prove his innocence? Whatever happened, she would not stay for pudding.

'Have you been here before? You are going to love it. Their evening meal is so lovely. It makes you think you're in a proper restaurant, from before the war. Linen table-cloths, meat that doesn't taste like it came from a tin, sauces lush enough to have been thickened with butter *and* cream.' Dennis pulled open the door and pushed aside the hanging curtain for her. Ellen couldn't help but gasp as the aroma of fatty roasting meat hit her nose. The restaurant itself was small, no bigger than her dining room back in Cardiff, with five intimate tables evenly spaced out. Candles flickered and soft music played from a radio in the corner. Ellen felt underdressed, but Dennis did not seem to mind as he helped hang her coat on a rack beside the door. She felt his eyes travel from her worn Oxfords to her lemon-yellow cardigan.

'You look lovely by candlelight, Ellen,' he practically whispered.

Ellen's face ignited and she ducked her head, following a waitress to their table. What was happening? This was supposed to be no more than a friendly meal, and now he

233

was commenting on her appearance.

When they were seated and alone again, Ellen leant forward. 'Dennis, I do not know what you meant by that statement, but this is not a romantic evening. Just supper. Between friends. Nothing more.'

Now it was Dennis's turn to blanch, his face falling. *Oh bother*, Ellen thought. That was the wrong thing to say. She didn't hate him. On the contrary, she rather liked him. But that wasn't good either.

He nodded and then cradled his head in his hands. 'Oh, I'm saying the wrong thing again. I have so many different emotions coming at me, and sometimes when I'm struck by something – your beauty, for example – the words come out all wrong. You are so poised, so together, you probably don't experience anything like that. I apologize.'

'Oh, but I do,' Ellen said before she could stop herself. 'I say the wrong thing all the time.'

Dennis looked up through his long fingers cautiously. 'You do?'

She couldn't tell if he was playing a game with her – but if he was, it was working. Her palms were sweating, her heart beating so loudly she could hear it in her ears. She had to change the subject, focus on why she was here. 'Richard's death, seeing it for yourself, must weigh heavily on your mind.' Ellen leant her elbows on the table, just inside the perfectly parallel forks and knives. 'Tell me what happened.'

'I'm not sure this is the best place to be discussing it, but' – he looked at the four other tables, at three of which diners were tucking into steaming plates as if nothing else in the world mattered – 'supper appears to be a good enough distraction for our fellow patrons.'

Ellen pressed her lips together and tried not to move, even to swipe at a stray hair that had fallen in her eyes. She had so many questions brimming, but remembered it was sometimes more powerful to listen. She did not want to distract him.

'Ellen, there is a lot of suspicion over Richard's missing bag. I was questioned for quite some time but released. I'm guessing I'm not a person of interest, thankfully. But it is not so for others.' Dennis raised his eyes to the low ceiling, cross-hatched with dark wooden beams. 'Richard would not have wanted this. He was the type who did anything to protect his friends, even if they had different beliefs. He always tried to see the other side of things. But I don't think even he could understand this – someone taking advantage of a tragic accident to steal government secrets. It is such a disaster.'

Forks and knives clinked against plates at the tables next to them. 'It was terrible luck you were even there,' she said, keeping her voice low. 'Did something happen with your bicycle?'

Dennis laced his fingers together and cleared his throat. 'It really was bad luck. I was on my way to catch the train into London for a few meetings – the transfer has been mostly successful, but they do still need me back at the main office from time to time. I'd gone a different route from the one past your billet – one of the blokes I work with lives beyond my aunt's cottage and had mentioned going that way was faster and I was running terribly late. What a mistake that was . . .' Dennis shook his head slowly. 'It was a rather unlucky morning, as also I was riding my Uncle Fred's ancient bicycle. You've seen it – it's horrid. Old, rusty and heavy, but I needed to get to the station fast – and was coming around the corner when the tyre burst and I fell over. Right into the hedges – only a few minutes before Richard came along. I was off the road trying to fix it when the van passed me.'

'You saw the accident?' Ellen gasped.

'Not exactly,' Dennis said. 'I was up the road a bit – I'd walked my bike from the blind curve to investigate the tyre when I heard the accident. I ran back to see how I could help. The van that had passed me earlier when I was fixing my tyre had veered off the road. I saw the van first and then . . . well . . . Richard.' He grimaced, and fell silent.

'Where was Richard when you found him?' Ellen asked gently.

'His motorcycle was still on the road and he was on the ground quite a substantial distance away.'

He had been thrown, Ellen thought. Just as she suspected.

'And was there anything nearby that suggested the cause of his fall? A rock, perhaps, or a branch?' Ellen tried to speak casually and not lead him, but she needed to know whether that large branch had been in the road.

'I don't—' he started, looking up. 'I don't recall. The road was definitely slick. I slipped a few times on the bicycle. It's possible Richard tried to stop and could not because of ice . . .'

Ellen nodded. Like Fran and Ant, he was uncertain but hadn't ruled it out. 'When Antony arrived, what happened?'

'He seemed to have missed any obstacles or icy patches.' He frowned. 'Curious, as Antony always commented how superior Richard was on the road. Still, I didn't see him arrive. I was focused on my friend; it was a lot to take in, Ellen. I didn't want to leave Richard alone, but knew he needed medical attention. The lad in the van was occupied with the older fellow and Antony was a bit distracted. Still, I asked him to look after Richard while I went for help. I had to remind him several times not to move Richard. He wasn't listening. There was definitely something odd about him. It was as if he did not want to help.'

Ellen fiddled with the top button of her cardigan. 'Odd how, exactly? And why would he not want to help?'

Dennis made a 'hm' sound and shook his head. 'I couldn't really tell you. He seemed in shock, like I was, but also a bit distant. I had to repeat his name several

237

times to get his attention, but there could have been many things going on with him. I don't know him; I met Antony the same night I met you. We'd barely exchanged a word. Well, until the accident. Honestly, he didn't give me the warmest reception that night and Richard said not to stir the pot, so to speak. He said Antony was, well, volatile.'

'How so?' Ellen prodded. Antony seemed moody and angry and emotional, but volatile?

'Richard never went into details, but he said Antony was overly competitive and got jealous easily. You heard how upset he was every time Richard told a story at the pub. It was all in good fun, but it seemed Antony didn't want to hear any stories that cast him in a bad light.'

'Antony had known Richard for ages,' Ellen said, thinking aloud. 'He knew Richard was prone to exaggeration. Pearl warned me of that before we met too. I'd be surprised if Ant let that get under his skin.'

Dennis shrugged. 'I'm just repeating what Richard told me. He said Antony had been more and more volatile of late and was challenging everything. Richard wondered if Antony was becoming unravelled, if the stresses of his job or the war were taking hold on his constitution.'

'If he was having some sort of mental breakdown? That surprises me.'

'Well, what I encountered that morning on the road was enough to break anyone, even the most stoic of people. Richard's condition was deteriorating by the minute. I tried my hardest, Ellen, to make sure he was comfortable without moving him or causing more injury. I will never forgive myself for leaving him on the road with Antony. Antony wasn't thinking clearly. He immediately started removing Richard's bag, which jostled his body horribly. I made him stop, but did he continue after I left? Did Antony do more damage when I left to get help? I will always regret that decision.'

Ellen blinked. Antony had started to remove Richard's bag? He hadn't mentioned that.

'By the time I returned, the police were already there – and they didn't let me see Richard. They kept me away from him, down the road, and asked me questions after I told them I'd been there prior. I could've helped, Ellen. I don't know how, but I could have been there for Richard.' Dennis buried his head in his hands for a few moments then looked up, his forehead flushed. 'This is very rude, but I am so very, very cross.'

Ellen wondered how to respond, but thankfully, their meal was delivered – two plates piled with more food than she'd seen in years. It felt decadent and wasteful at the same time and as Dennis beamed at her, she lowered her nose to inhale the fatty, buttery smell of the gravy that ran down the crispy-skinned fowl and on to browned roast potatoes.

'Now,' Dennis said, 'let us enjoy this meal and not talk about anything tragic. In fact, let's pretend there isn't a war going on. It's just you, me and this gorgeous bird. How does that sound?'

Ellen felt her heart clench again, either because of the prospect of a dinner free from stress or the way Dennis's eyes softened as they met hers. She had so many questions, but resolved to let them go, just for a few hours. It was something so welcome, so wonderful, and also something she knew she would regret the next morning.

27

PEARL

It took all the willpower Pearl had ever had to keep her mouth shut when Ellen walked into the crib room the next morning. She had seen Dennis. Pearl could tell. Ellen's cheeks were flushed and she smiled at all the girls she passed before getting to their table. Ellen should not have been smiling. She was late. The floaty way Ellen walked made Pearl want to snap her pencil in two. No investigation went well when the detective fell in love with one of the suspects.

Pearl was burning to say something to Ellen, but she kept her mouth shut, working in a quiet fury for hours. She steamed every time she glanced at Ellen, no matter how confusing the decode was. The only lead she had was that the code was missing one letter throughout. There was no letter 'N'. Did that mean anything? She supposed it could; the biggest breaks in the crib room were often when the Germans did something silly, like set their machines based on their girlfriend's name. *Would Dennis set his machine to 'Ellen'?* she mused, gripping her pencil harder. Pearl fumed over that missing letter for what seemed liked decades with no real victory, until Mr St John burst into the room right before lunchtime, the doorknob slamming with a bang against the wall. He stood at the front of the room, his hair standing on end and his eyes red and wild.

He scanned the room and his gaze finally rested on Ellen and Pearl. 'You two,' he said. 'Come with me.'

'Us, sir?' Pearl managed to croak before trailing after Ellen. Her mouth went dry as they followed him like criminals headed for the firing squad. This could not be a good thing, being pulled aside mid-morning. He led them down the hall, into a room Pearl had never entered, and shut the door with a firm and powerful push.

The room was much like many others Pearl had seen in the hut buildings – close, with a small window, and a single dim light bulb. This one, however, was filled with an eclectic mix of filing cabinets – wood and metal – and barely had any room to work save for a lonely metal desk near the window. A cloud of tobacco smoke rose from the desk, even though Mr St John was not smoking. Pearl could not help but wrinkle her nose as he paced the tiny square of available space behind the desk.

Finally, Mr St John stood still and faced them. 'I need

you to find an entire day's worth of cribs from Sunday the second of November. All the files are kept in here, under my close supervision, but that day's file isn't in its proper place. You must find it. Understood?'

'We'll do our best,' Ellen replied, pocketing the key Mr St John held out for her. Pearl was glad Ellen had taken over, as her reply seemed stuck in her suddenly dry mouth. Sunday the second was the day Richard had died.

'You need to do more than your best. If you can't find them, there will be consequences.' Mr St John looked at them long enough for the silence to be uncomfortable and then left abruptly, locking the door behind him.

'Why did he lock us in?' Ellen asked, whispering even though St John had left.

Pearl shrugged, her heart pounding. Her mouth was too dry to form words. All of it was disconcerting, even the locked door. Mr St John had not said when he would return, but she had a feeling it would be soon.

Ellen continued, 'The second was *that* Sunday, right? Well, then, this has to be connected to Richard. There is no way around it.'

'Perhaps,' Pearl said, her hackles rising again. She lowered her voice. 'Ellen, do you think we're being framed?'

'Oh!' Ellen was obviously surprised. Pearl usually found it endearing when Ellen brightened up thanks to a new idea, but today it was infuriating. They *were* being framed, or at least *she* was, and Ellen was oblivious: all glossy-eyed and lovey-dovey over Dennis. Pearl guessed it had been a romantic rendezvous last night, Ellen too swept away to grill him with the questions they had prepared. 'I don't know. I hadn't given it much thought, but now that you mention it . . .' Ellen whispered. 'You don't think Mr St John is . . .'

'The spy? I don't know. Why else would he frame us?' Pearl started opening the filing cabinets at random, slamming drawers and pulling back chairs loudly. A point had to be made, really.

'What are you doing?' Ellen asked, an innocent, clueless edge to her voice.

'I'm *looking*,' Pearl snapped. 'After all, *I* do what I was *asked* to do,' she said pointedly, slamming another drawer for emphasis.

Ellen blinked at her and unlocked the cabinets. 'Well, then, perhaps you should look where he asked us to look. Instead of simply stomping around and making a mess. You take this drawer with cribs from the month before and I will look at the days following.'

Ellen moved to the cabinet on the outside wall. Typical Ellen, not seeing when someone else was clearly upset. *Stomping*, Pearl thought. *I'll show you stomping.* Pearl pulled out the drawer with a bit more vigour than necessary and was hit instantly by the smell of ink and new paper and mildew. Why had someone stolen those particular files and why ask Pearl and Ellen to find them? If Mr St John was framing them, why have them try to find the files at all? Was it all a show? Did he want to give them a chance to put them back if they had stolen them? That would mean he thought she was a thief in the first place, which made sense. It was likely behind her promotion – not because of skill, but because, as he'd said, he'd been instructed to watch over her. Which meant he knew she'd peeked at the files in the hall. Miss Waincross had lied – or someone else had been watching. Her breath came in short, shallow gasps as she worked faster, fingers flying through the folders. There was no Sunday. Pearl clenched her fingers in a fist and groaned.

'This is really, really bad,' Pearl wailed. 'He knows it's missing. Why is he asking us to find it? Why us? What does he know? What does he suspect? We are never going to find it. Never!'

Ellen sighed loudly, letting her hands flop to her skirt with a slap. Pearl groaned again. Ellen was getting ready to lecture her about something. Did she not understand this wasn't lecture time? It was beyond that.

'All we have to do is calmly explain that we never could have seen those cribs,' Ellen said. 'That's the truth. He'll understand. Perhaps he hasn't done the maths. See,' she began to count on her fingers, 'we started in the crib room two days after Richard's death. Even when Mr St John gave us old cribs for our training, there was no way to know on which day they originated. That information wasn't there . . . was it?'

'I don't think it's a matter of maths.' Pearl's voice was suddenly several octaves higher. And louder. *A matter of maths?!*

'Pearl, you do not need to get testy. Logic will prevail. It always does,' Ellen said, thrusting her nose in the air a bit higher.

Pearl felt anger welling up inside her, like she was a kettle about to overboil. 'Logic might not win, Ellen. The cards are stacking up against us, don't you see? We are being framed here and you can't get your head out of the cloud of love or kisses or whatever it is you're practically floating on.'

Ellen's mouth dropped open. 'I resent that. I . . . I do see the threat. It is palpable. Please, Pearl, do not get ahead of yourself here. We need to stay calm.'

And then Pearl snapped. Like a firework going off, a deep, red rage fizzled in her core and then ignited, rushing out of her so quickly she couldn't extinguish it. 'Calm?! Calm?! Look where that's got us - locked in a room on a wild goose chase for documents we both know will never be found. We're doomed - no, *I* am doomed - because you can't see beyond your polite manners and your puppy-dog eyes for Dennis. No matter what Dennis says, I can't see how his presence on the road makes sense. How does he explain it? The timing is too convenient. He's playing you,

Ellen. Can't you see? He's hiding something and you're too far gone to see it! I bet you didn't even question him last night, did you?'

Ellen bristled, but her face remained oddly calm and blank. Pearl was annoyed not to have garnered more of a reaction.

'I did question Dennis, thank you very much,' Ellen said evenly, 'and he did all he could. He had been on his way to the station when his tyre went flat, just like Fran said. And he telephoned for help almost immediately. He was not there long enough to do harm. He didn't take the bag, nor did he see what happened to it. And he didn't notice the branch, but said it was possible. Really, Pearl, he is as clueless as we are!'

Pearl glowered. 'And you simply believe everything he says?' she said, witheringly. 'You think you're so clever, Ellen. But deep down, you're just like all the other girls. You'd cast me aside in a second for a boy.'

Ellen's mask of calmness crumbled, slightly, and Pearl felt a twinge of mingled satisfaction and the tiniest bit of guilt. Ellen opened her mouth to reply when, all of a sudden, the door swung open.

'Well? Did you find the file?' Mr St John asked. He walked to where they were standing and leant over the cabinet, his straight black tie hanging down like an upside-down exclamation mark.

Ellen swallowed and laced her fingers behind her back.

'No,' she said in an even voice.

'You understand how dire it is to have lost this?' Mr St John walked to one of the open file cabinets and drummed his fingers on its wooden top.

'We understand, sir,' Pearl said quietly. 'I tried. I've always tried to leave my personal feelings behind and focus on what was important. Tried to do everything I could to . . . find the file. Have you, Ellen? Have you?'

Ellen blanched when she called her out and Pearl couldn't help but cheer a bit inside. *Now you know how it feels*, she thought cruelly. *Now you're as deflated and hopeless as I am.*

'I have,' Ellen said between gritted teeth, her eyes filled with tears. Pearl's smugness instantly dissolved into guilt. She shouldn't have said all of that in front of Mr St John. She'd pushed Ellen too far.

Mr St John rubbed his eyes. He seemed exhausted by all of this, but not surprised by their failure. 'This squabbling is not helpful, Pearl. You have let me down. Ellen, you're dismissed for the day.'

'For a break?' Ellen asked. Her eyes were wide and her face had gone pale, almost ashen.

'I said for the day,' he barked. 'Pearl, I need you to remain here with me.'

Pearl felt her stomach plummet, like when she jumped off a high rock into the lake at her cousin's one summer. The ground fell out from under her. She was being blamed for this. But the file wasn't here – none of this was her fault! The envelope was a mistake, she would never do anything like that purposefully! Tears flooded her eyes and she looked to the ground immediately. Ellen could not see her cry. Her anger at Ellen was still bubbling in her chest, even though she would've given anything to take her cutting words back. Now she had no one. Ellen would never forgive what she said and continue to be her friend. Pearl had pushed her too far and here she was, alone again.

It was only after the door had shut that Pearl wiped her eyes and looked up. Mr St John's arms were still crossed as he looked down at her, his lip curled in disgust.

'I have gone out on a limb for you. I took you under my wing to watch over you and help you change your ways. I even gave you an opportunity to return the file. Pearl, normally people like you would be sent away immediately, arrested, no questions asked. I told everyone else they were mistaken. They would see. But it appears I was made the fool.'

'Sir! No, you were not mistaken at all. I am being honest, I promise.' Pearl started pleading but soon realized she should not waste her breath. His eyes were closed, head thrown back as he shook it slowly. He had made up his mind. Perhaps he had made it up long ago – what exactly had Miss Waincross told Mr St John? 'I am sorry,' she continued, softer this time and less desperate.

She tried to remember what Ellen had said about staying calm and sticking to the truth. 'I do not know where the cribs went. We had no idea which day's cribs we were reviewing, after all. If that day's cribs were in the mix of those you had us review, well, there was no real way to tell.'

Mr St John lowered his head slowly. 'I am so tired of the excuses, Pearl. The fact is, you were here, at Bletchley, on Sunday, working as a messenger. You had opportunity, whether you know the contents of the file or not. And, given your previous misdemeanour, I have good reason to believe you are responsible for this.'

Pearl's shoulders sagged. Her instinct was to defend herself, but she knew it was no use. She *had* been at the Park, doing her assigned job, which was taking folders of documents from hut to hut. Any one of those folders could've contained cribs and she'd never have known. Of course, she hadn't stolen those folders, but it seemed pointless to argue this. While Pearl knew someone out there was setting her up, she could not disagree with the facts stacked against her. Whoever was out to get her was very, very good at what they did.

Her heart thumped in her ears and she felt increasingly sweaty. The thought of prison and what was sure to follow petrified her. She already felt as if she were staring down the barrel of a gun, facing the firing squad. That was her fate. Pearl wished Ellen were still beside her, even if her friend did hate her right now. Why had she acted like such a fool?

There was a gentle knock on the door and Mr St John slouched across the room to open it. Pearl's breath hitched when she saw who it was.

'Miss Waincross!' Pearl exclaimed, trying not to betray her relief at seeing her old supervisor. She'd set him straight. She had to be here to offer an explanation, to help Pearl out. She'd said she would, after all.

Miss Waincross turned to her and Pearl's insides dropped. Her red lips drooped into a frown and she closed her eyes slowly while letting out an audible sigh. It was a look of annoyance, like you'd give an incessant fly trapped on a windowsill before you smacked it with a rolled-up newspaper.

'I stood up for you. I believed in you,' she said, her hand clamping down on Pearl's shoulder. 'The time for arguing your case has passed. It's best if you come with me.' She turned to Mr St John and shook her head. 'They all said it would come to this eventually and I should've believed them. I am sorry to have troubled you.'

Mr St John was silent, his head bowed and his hands in his pockets. He did not watch them leave, but walked over to the window and looked out at the sandbags.

Pearl lowered her head, not even bothering to hide her tears. She was done fighting. She was done pretending. She knew it was all over, her future at Bletchley Park finished. Her *future* finished. There was nothing she could do about it. She walked with Miss Waincross out of the room and into the hallway, where two uniformed officers were waiting.

28

ELLEN

Ellen took a long time retrieving her coat, but when Pearl did not join her there was nothing else to do but go outside and wait. Only it was raining, and after only a few minutes, her teeth chattered and her nose dripped. She was shaking a bit, still unable to believe what had just happened. Pearl had been so angry at her – yelling such cruel things. If she'd simply listened, perhaps Ellen could've explained Dennis's story better, and made Pearl believe that she was not blinded by love. How could Pearl not know her better? Ellen had never let her emotions cloud logic before, but had that changed without her realizing?

She took what little shelter she could under the bare branches of a nearby tree. The longer she waited, the more nervous she became. Was Mr St John accusing Pearl of stealing the file, as Pearl had suspected? Had she actually been framed? Ellen couldn't make sense of it. After all,

Pearl's accident with the other files had sounded like a mistake. If she'd truly been a suspect, they wouldn't have let her remain at the Park, under watchful eyes or not. Unless, perhaps, Pearl hadn't been entirely honest. As the minutes crawled by, Ellen's worries festered and grew. Oh, how she wished she could stand alongside her friend – if Pearl could even bear to look at her.

What was more troublesome was that Ellen was unsure what a day's worth of missing cribs could mean. Most times, the cribs they came up with didn't work. At the end of her shift, Ellen was often left with a bunch of useless letters and notes, which she handed to the next girl. Besides, even if they were successful, the cribs only attempted to decode certain letters – never all of them. They were only one piece of the puzzle.

But perhaps the spy didn't need the whole puzzle; they simply needed proof that the code was being broken. If the spy was passing information to the Germans, knowing the code had been broken meant they'd change it up, preventing the Allies from being a step ahead. Knowing the code had been cracked – and cribs were proof of that – meant Britain would be behind again, unable to anticipate the enemy at all.

The rain started pelting harder and Ellen gave up on waiting for Pearl, darting down the path in front of the mansion, trying to avoid a cluster of men and women. Ellen realized she'd have to walk off the path to go around them, but then immediately stepped in a puddle.

'Curses,' she swore, angry about not knowing what was happening to Pearl, and about the muddy water seeping between her toes. No one paid her any mind, absorbed in their conversation. Annoyed with how rude they'd been, practically pushing her off the path and then not noticing when she stepped in the mud, Ellen edged her way back on to the path and used her handkerchief in an attempt to save her soggy leather shoe. It was then she heard it.

'They're here right now, arresting her. Janet saw them all leave out the back of Hut Four. I couldn't believe the numbers of police, but I suppose if a person violates any part of the Secrets Act, you have to assume they're dangerous.'

Ellen froze, her hand midway to her shoe. Before she could stop herself on any pretext of being polite, she stole a look at the people, who appeared to be regular Park workers, and realized they had run out to see the carnage. They were talking about Pearl. She just knew it. Which meant Pearl was the one who had been arrested.

It also meant Pearl was going to be executed.

How is this possible? Ellen thought frantically. Her breath came in ragged, uneven bursts, her face and arms and chest covered in a sheen of cold, clammy sweat. She noticed her hand shaking as she stuffed the handkerchief back in her pocket, oblivious to the cluster of people, her wet shoe, the rain. The only thing that mattered now was Pearl. She was going to die unless Ellen did something to prove her innocence.

Ellen had never felt so much pressure to find the true answer to a mystery, and it was far from exhilarating. It was paralysing. And for the first time in a long time, Ellen knew she couldn't do it.

With increasing evidence against Pearl, and with most everyone, it seemed, believing she was guilty, Ellen worried there was no one left to trust. She knew she didn't stand a chance alone. Before she could second-guess herself, Ellen ran down the path. It was early yet. Because she had not seen Dennis on her way in, it was possible he was doing a later shift. He'd told her his shifts were getting later and longer lately, which was why their morning encounters were so erratic. Knowing she couldn't barge into his hut and ask when he was due at work, she wondered if his aunt might be of help in tracking him down. As much as Ellen didn't want to depend on anyone else, or tell Pearl's secrets, she was in a bind.

It didn't take Ellen long. She was not much of an athlete, but when fuelled by fear and adrenaline, she made it to the turn-off for her billet in eighteen minutes. She knew because she'd noted the time on her wristwatch. It was 12.30 p.m. as she passed the Waverlys' house and continued on down Mill Road, keeping her eyes peeled for a cottage. She picked up the pace further, her lungs burning. She had to find him. There was no one else she could trust.

Around 12.38, Ellen wondered if she'd overlooked a

turn. At 12.44, she spied a squat little cottage, windows black with drawn curtains, ivy climbing up the side as if preparing to reclaim the house for the earth. It looked abandoned, but as she got closer, she saw tyre tracks in the mud, leading to a dilapidated barn behind. There were two walls left of the barn, but the tyre tracks stopped there, as if someone had used it as a carport rather than a home for livestock. There was a mangled umbrella carcass against the wall and a couple of baskets one would use for shopping. While the house appeared vacant, this had to be Mill Cottage.

She had imagined manicured hedges, a white-painted fence, a welcoming red door against crisp white plaster walls. While this was far from that image, Ellen supposed that if Dennis's aunt had been ill for some time, it made sense the place was in disrepair. And a busy chap like Dennis hardly had the time to fix crumbling walls and paint the peeling front door. As she drew closer, Ellen saw that blackout shades covered the windows. It was hard to imagine immaculate Dennis living somewhere so decrepit, but maybe Aunt Myra kept an impeccable house behind the curtains – it was impossible to know.

Looking at her watch again, Ellen rapped lightly on the chipped paint of the front door, waiting only a few seconds before determining that her assessment had been correct. No one was home. Though she was tempted, she resisted the urge to try the doorknob, a bit intimidated by the spooky, abandoned feel to the place. She tore off back towards the Waverlys', lungs aching as she gasped in the knife-like cold air. When she reached her billet, she let herself in, already anticipating Mrs Waverly's questions about why she was home early.

'Hello?' Ellen heard as she attempted to shut the door quietly. 'Who's there?'

'Just Ellen, Mrs Waverly,' Ellen said cheerfully.

'Ellen, dear, I'm in the sitting room.'

Ellen removed her wet shoes and stockings and left them by the front door. She padded down the dark hallway and opened the door to the sitting room, where Mrs Waverly sat by a small fire, baby asleep in her arms, a beautifully wrapped box on the table next to two empty teacups.

'Well, dear, you just missed him.'

'Missed who?' Ellen said, standing behind the sofa to hide her bare legs.

'Shh, dear. Baby just went down. He's been a fussy little sausage lately.' Mrs Waverly wore a mint-green cardigan layered over a faded housedress. Her lips held the faint trace of pink lipstick.

'Sorry,' Ellen whispered, trying to hide the impatience in her voice. 'Did someone call for me?'

'The nice boy you've been seeing. David? Daniel?' Mrs Waverly waggled her eyebrows and smiled.

'Dennis?' Ellen croaked. 'When was he here? Can I still . . . I've been looking for him. I, erm, I need to see him.'

'Oh, a while ago. I wouldn't run after him. But he did leave that package for you.' She nodded at the side table. 'Is it your birthday? Why didn't you tell us? I would have made you a cake.'

Ellen picked up the box, which was surprisingly heavy for its size. The ribbon was dark purple velvet and tied so well, she couldn't imagine Dennis doing it himself. Mrs Waverly leant forward eagerly, but Ellen had no intention of opening the package in front of her. 'Uh, no. It's not my birthday. I'm not entirely sure what this could be. Did he mention anything?'

'No. Just that he was hoping to deliver this in person. He's a lovely fellow, Ellen. You're quite lucky.'

'Right. Well.' Ellen backed away towards the door. 'Thank you. I'd best be going.'

'But won't you stay for tea? It's almost time, well, in a few,' Mrs Waverly pleaded. The poor woman was dreadfully lonely, but Ellen didn't have time to waste making up a feasible excuse; she needed a moment alone. Pretending she didn't hear the woman, Ellen took the stairs two at a time to her room, soggy stockings over her shoulder, cradling the heavy package.

After stuffing her shoes with newspaper, Ellen sat on her bed and tore through the wrapping. She felt a twinge of regret that she could not appreciate this, her first real gift from a man, but had to rip it open quickly and get back to Pearl somehow.

It was a new, leather-bound edition of *Anna Karenina*.

'Curious,' Ellen mumbled to herself and turned the edition over in her hands. It was a gorgeous book, but why would Dennis give her a copy of one of the world's most popular love stories? Then, it was as if her entire body blushed, getting hot and twingy. *Oh.* That *was why he sent it!*

She couldn't think about that. Not Dennis's soft voice and how his hands always seemed warm. Not how he put slight emphasis on the second syllable of her name, incorrectly, so it sounded slightly French.

Golly, this was exactly what she did not need right now. She tossed the novel on her bed and a typed card slid out from between the pages:

```
Ellen,
On one of our walks, you said you were
lacking a good book. This is one of my
favourites and you'll probably see why
almost immediately.
I cannot thank you enough for joining me
for supper and if you are so inclined, I
will be there tonight from five. I would
love to see you.
Sincerely,
Dennis
```

That was that, Ellen thought. Dennis had found a way to get a second date out of her. Not that she didn't want to go, of course. She just wished it weren't under these circumstances. After putting on her one pair of real stockings, Ellen fetched her yellow cardigan. As she pulled it over her shoulders, she felt something stiff in the front pocket. The note she'd stolen from Richard's bedroom. She'd been trying to crack it for days with no luck, always when she was exhausted after a shift. Employing different methods, she looked for a simple code or repeated letter to clue her into the unravelling of the puzzle. Nothing had worked, yet. She needed any possible breakthrough to help clear Pearl's name. Grabbing a pencil and notebook, Ellen sat on the edge of her bed and started rearranging the letters while she waited for her shoes to dry.

First, Ellen wrote out the code again on one line, erasing any spaces. She stared at it for a while, then at the squares of flowered fabric that made up her quilt. She put the letters in a box like the boxes of fabric and then, like working a word search, looked for words backwards and forwards, up and down, right to left, left to right. Then it appeared:

CASTLE BROMWICH AERO N TWENTY EIGHT

No matter how she read it, the message was compromising at best. Castle Bromwich was an airfield in the West Midlands. She knew because of her brother, who upon enlisting brought out maps and books and educated her at length about where he might fly and train. Why would

29

ELLEN

Everything was drenched. Her coat was still sodden, her shoes (especially the left one) squished when she walked, and her legs were like icicles because of her foolish vanity. As her mother said, stockings were almost as useful as nothing, but her mother had never been invited to dinner with Dennis. Twice. As a result, Ellen was chilled to the bone by the time she reached Antony's house, even though she'd walked faster than ever from her billet into town.

When she got to Ant's place, a brick terraced house four doors down from Pearl's with a pile of dirty wellies by the front door, she wiped the rain from her face and combed through her hair with her fingers. Ellen knew she was quite a sight but couldn't worry much over it. She knocked firmly, casually wringing out her scarf as she waited. After Ant had left the pub, Fran had told Ellen and Pearl that Ant had been asked to take a leave from his duties while under investigation. So Ellen knew he would be home.

Sure enough, Antony opened the door slowly, blocking a clear view into the house with his body. The house was warm and smelt of the crispy, browned skin on the outside of a well-roasted chicken. Antony didn't betray any surprise at seeing a drowned Ellen at his front door, but instead looked annoyed, his eyes narrowed as he tapped the edge of the door impatiently with his forefinger.

Before he could say anything, a voice called down the hall. 'Who is it, Ant? Is it Mrs Duneberry? She said she'd stop by for a slice of cake, but Alfie made short order of that sponge an hour ago, the little thief.'

'No one, Mum!' Ant called. Then, he paused and tilted his head. Ellen felt as if he were looking at her for the first time, sizing her up. 'Ellen,' he muttered finally. 'What are you doing here?'

'There's one thing I need and I'll be out of your way.' Ellen hadn't even finished speaking when she noticed Ant shaking his head.

'I can't let you in here. My brothers are home and Mum won't let you alone. She'll have you in for a cuppa before you know it. I don't think you want that.'

'I don't,' Ellen said firmly.

Ant laughed hollowly. 'Yes, I thought you'd agree with me there. Look, I've had a lot of visitors today. Not good ones. I think this might be the last day home with my family before the police bring me in. They're certain I took Richard's bag and they asked some pretty leading questions about Pearl, too. We've been framed, Ellen. They've made us out to be quite the diabolical spies.'

Ellen felt her stomach fall and she braced her hand against the rough, cold brick wall.

'And I suppose you think so too,' Antony said, quietly.

He looked over his shoulder in the direction of what Ellen imagined to be a cosy eat-in kitchen, where no doubt a table full of ginger-haired boys argued over a snack of toast and tea while their mother basted the gorgeous-smelling bird for their supper. When Antony's eyes met hers again, they weren't regretful, but angry. Ellen closed her eyes and took a deep breath. She saw letters against the black of her eyelids, coded messages and the branch, Richard's adoring eyes and Dennis's glinting shoes. There were a lot of things that didn't add up and one of them was Antony. Yet, somehow, even after everything he'd done, all the lies, she didn't truly think he was guilty.

'No. I don't believe you stole Richard's bag, Antony,' she said at last. 'And despite evidence to the contrary, I don't believe Pearl is guilty either. But in order to help you, and her, I need you to stop lying to me once and for all. And I need your help.'

She felt her chest puff up with confidence. Maybe she could do this. After all, between university and the crib room and all those puzzles in the newspaper she had practically been in training for this moment her entire life. However, when she had imagined solving some great puzzle that would garner her fame and fortune, she had never realized how close it would hit her. Because she never imagined it would be about friends. In her daydreams about saving the world, Ellen had not accounted for people who depended on her, people she cared about and wanted to protect. She'd been alone. It had been much cleaner that way, but, she imagined, far less rewarding. 'Antony, *please* help me.'

'I'll be a minute, Mum,' Antony called over his shoulder before closing the door behind him. 'Tell me what to do, Ellen. I'll do anything.'

Ellen put her hand on his arm and her breath caught, trapped and icy in her throat. 'Then, Antony, you need to hand over that coded message Richard gave you. And fast.'

30

ELLEN

As Ellen crossed to the other side of the road, Antony's coded message safely in her pocket, she noticed a car pull up and two police officers get out. She bolted around the corner, frightened. There was always the chance that, somehow, they were coming for her too.

She made her way towards the centre of town and the restaurant. She checked her watch and, upon realizing she had about thirty minutes before Dennis would be at the restaurant, she ducked into a doorway down a nearby side street and pulled the paper out of her pocket. It had crisp, orderly block letters, like the one she'd stolen from Richard's room. Could it use the same simple code? As she considered pulling out the other message for a comparison, a group of men walked by, indistinguishable in their sodden trench coats and limp hats. Ellen stuffed the paper back in her front coat pocket and lowered her gaze, hoping they'd continue walking. The men paused, shook hands, and one broke off. It was then she noticed. The lone man had clean, shiny shoes. Her breath caught.

'Dennis!' she whispered.

'Ellen?' Dennis looked pleased to see her, which made Ellen's neck get warm. She wasn't used to being a girl someone was excited to run into. 'When I left that card at your billet, I never thought you'd actually take me up on my offer. I had hoped, but never fathomed I would be so lucky. Twice in as many evenings!'

Ellen lowered her head in case she was blushing, and said, 'Dennis, I hardly think you're a stranger to the affections of others. You seem quite aware of how to make a girl feel special.'

'I'm glad you think so,' Dennis said, squaring his shoulders and stepping his feet into a wide stance. 'My mother would be proud. She taught me all I know. I have to say, I'm clueless otherwise.'

Ellen raised her head. She wouldn't have faulted him if he was, in fact, a womanizer. It was probably hard to avoid the adoration of many when you were that dashing. He'd even won Richard's affections, after all, without even meaning to. 'You're not that clueless.' Ellen smiled, then pressed her lips together in a straight line. 'Dennis, there is something of the utmost importance I need to discuss with you straight away. Is there somewhere . . . well, we cannot talk about it here. Is there somewhere . . . private?'

Dennis put a gloved hand on Ellen's shoulder. His eyes were soft with concern. 'Are you all right?'

'Yes, I suppose.'

'Then, well, we're a touch early for our booking, but I bet I could convince the owners at the Golden Ball to find us a table. I'm there a lot lately. I cannot ask Aunt Myra to cook for me any longer. It doesn't seem fair in her condition.'

Ellen took his arm and walked across the road towards the restaurant, a closed sign still in the window. 'She seemed quite able when I saw her on the road, after shopping.'

'Did she?' Dennis looked up for a moment. 'Well, I suppose she has her good days and bad days.'

'It must take a lot to keep up the old cottage,' she tried, not wanting to come straight out and admit she'd ventured to Mill Cottage.

'You know how it is,' Dennis said quickly. 'With the demands of my job, I can only help so much.' He paused for a moment, then patted her wrist. 'You wait here for a moment. I'll go in and ask the owners if they have a table for us.'

He left her a few paces from the restaurant and strode to the black front door confidently, smiling once over his shoulder at her. With a firm rap on the door, he disappeared inside. After a few minutes, he waved her in, that vibrant smile still there. He could appear in an ad for

Macleans toothpaste with that grin.

The restaurant seemed different without a lot of people or the delicious aroma of roast dinner. Today, the lighting seemed harsher, illuminating the shabbiness of the curtains and the worn carpeting. And although there were a few couples seated, none were eating, leaving the place awash in the overwhelming smell of bleach and old cooking oil. Still, she was grateful for a private place to talk and followed Dennis to a corner table.

'Is this all right?' Dennis asked. 'They'll bring us menus shortly, but we can start with tea to take the chill off.'

'It's fine,' Ellen said. 'I can't stay long.'

'Oh?' Dennis exclaimed, a note of disappointment in his voice.

'There isn't a lot of time.' Ellen shifted in the wooden chair, which creaked loudly in protest. 'You see, I think I need your help.'

'I'm all ears.' Dennis propped his elbows on the table and leant in.

'I am not even sure what you can do, so don't feel obligated if it's asking too much.' She was stalling. It did not seem right to ask Dennis for a favour like this, yet she truly had no one else to turn to, no one she could trust.

'Go on,' Dennis said. 'I will do what I can. You see, I firmly believe that we are never going to get through all of this without sticking our necks out for someone or something else – a friend, a cause, a movement. I don't think you're the type of person to back something frivolous or act selfishly. You seem more principled than that. I am, too. We're very alike that way and I think that's why I was drawn to you.'

Ellen felt her face go hot again and she placed her cold hand on her neck in what she hoped was a subtle manner. She could not let herself be distracted by flattery, although it was hard not to go weak at the knees. He was appealing to almost everything a girl like Ellen could want. Almost.

'I appreciate that, Dennis. I do.' Ellen wrung her hands out in her lap. One was warm from her neck, the other chilly. She felt like two different people trying to fuse back together. 'What I am about to ask you has to be between us. Do you promise?'

Dennis practically whispered, 'Of course I do.'

'I need your help with Pearl.'

Dennis sucked in air between his teeth and leant back.

'It's not what you think,' she said quickly, her heart thumping that scared way it did when something woke her in the middle of the night. She immediately regretted her decision to tell him. 'She's in trouble but she did not do anything wrong, no matter what people say.'

'I see.' He laced his fingers together and placed them on the tablecloth.

'She's been arrested. Someone is framing her – I don't know who – and I simply need her out of jail so we can figure out how to prove she's innocent.' She took his hands in hers, something that felt so wrong and yet also sent a jolt of electricity down her spine. 'Can you do anything, or think of anything, we can do to get her free? I'm afraid that something rash will happen and she'll be sentenced before morning if I don't act soon.'

Dennis was quiet, his eyes on her hands.

'Please,' she begged. Ellen hated begging.

Dennis leant in. He smelt of pine and mint and something else sweet. 'Ellen, I will do anything. Tell me all you think might be relevant. Then I'll know exactly how I can help.'

So, she swallowed any hesitation, and did.

It was decided that Dennis would leave immediately and head to the station where Pearl was being kept. Dennis was certain he knew where she was being held, and he was also positive he could get her released based on his connections. He didn't mention what they were or what he would have to do to pull assorted strings for Pearl. He simply said he'd do it.

They left the restaurant in the dark and stood on the pavement as Dennis went over his plan. He promised to call in on Ellen after Pearl was released. Then they could discuss next steps. He said he wanted to help her uncover the person framing Pearl.

He held Ellen's hands in his. 'I promise I'll do what I

can,' he said softly.

'I know,' she said, meeting his eyes. Before she could react, she felt his lips on the side of her mouth, like he'd aimed for her cheek and missed. Part of her wanted to step away but the other part leant in, inhaling his piney scent and placing her hand flat against his chest. The kiss lasted for ever, but also not long enough, and when she finally pulled away, he was smiling again.

'Trust me, Ellen. I will take care of you, of this.'

'I don't need you to take care of me,' she said breathlessly. 'Please, help Pearl. That's all I need.'

'Of course,' he chuckled. 'I shouldn't assume you need help. Ever.'

'Right.' She bit her lip and backed up a few steps. She didn't want to turn and leave him, but she had to focus on Pearl. 'You should go.'

'I'll fix this and call to yours shortly.'

'Thank you.'

'Think nothing of it,' he said. He walked a few steps back, still facing her, then gave a little wave and turned on his perfectly polished heel towards the police station.

Ellen was glad he turned when he did because she couldn't help but let out a long sigh. There was so much she'd been holding in – anxiousness, fear, and the strange exhilarating buzz that ran up and down her spine like an irritated swarm of hornets. It was a feeling some part of her wanted to keep going for ever, but most of her wanted to wipe away like soot on a window. She couldn't think clearly. She couldn't breathe correctly. Everything was slightly wobbly and soft, but now Pearl would be taken care of and that was a huge relief.

31

ELLEN

After leaving Dennis, Ellen went back to her billet. At first, she'd wanted to follow him to the station, to be there when Pearl was released, but she wondered if her presence wouldn't be welcome. Dennis would've asked her along, after all. Golly, was there a reason why he didn't want her there? Had she kissed wrong? What if she'd been utterly rubbish at it? With lingering, irrational paranoia, Ellen tried to busy herself until he came to fetch her. He said he'd do that, didn't he? Ellen couldn't remember anything except how warm his lips were and wet and slightly messy, but not in a horrible way.

So, Ellen sat up in her draughty room, touching her lips from time to time (they were still there, still mostly the same), but buzzing with an energy similar to drinking too much tea very late at night. Ellen knew she should harness the buzz, put it to use on the second coded message, but then her mind would wander and she would remember the smell of pine and she'd go look at her face in the mirror to see if there were any changes. There never were.

'Ellen! Come down. I have a nice warm cottage pie for supper. Stop moping upstairs!' Mrs Waverly called.

Moping? Ellen thought, the house getting warmer as she descended from the chilly attic to the dining room. She felt like she was forgetting something important, but her mind floated in and out of that moment with Dennis, the taste of tea on his lips, the deep warmth of his gaze. She'd never felt so utterly outside herself. Perhaps a solid meal was just what she needed to ground her again.

Mr Waverly tended to the fireplace while Mrs Waverly scooped out a very thin cottage pie on to her pretty flowered china. The baby sat in a wooden highchair near Mrs Waverly and every once in a while, she'd lean over and spoon mince or peas into his mouth. The baby wore a cloth bib over his jumper and squealed happily, mash in his dark hair. Ellen took her place at the table, almost across from the baby. Her portion was mostly potatoes and carrots, with a hint of greyish mince.

'Nasty weather out there,' Mr Waverly said, sitting down in his chair, back to the fire.

'Oh, Ellen, before I forget,' Mrs Waverly said, 'a messenger on a bicycle dropped this off for you a few minutes ago. Poor lad being out in the rain and sleet. I offered him a cup of tea but . . .'

'Just hand her the paper, won't you?' Mr Waverly interrupted.

'Right!' She pulled a small envelope from the pocket of her apron and held it out. Without reading the front, Ellen knew it was from Dennis. Why had he called in and not asked for her?

'Who was the man on the bicycle? What did he look like?' she asked tentatively.

'It wasn't your Dennis, if that's what you're asking,' Mrs Waverly said with a sly smile.

Ellen let out a long breath through her nose. Thank goodness. He wasn't avoiding her. Her lap almost burnt when she put the envelope there, but she knew better than to open it under the prying eyes of Mrs Waverly.

'Is it from him?' she asked. 'Dennis?'

'Yes. Yes, it is.' Then, in order to change the subject, she added, 'He lives beyond the old mill with his aunt. Myra, I think her name is. She's quite frail and even though Dennis worked in London, he moved out to care for her. Isn't that nice?'

'What's her name?' Mr Waverly asked, putting down his fork and knife.

'Myra?' There was something about Mr Waverly's voice that made Ellen nervous. 'They live in Mill Cottage just down the road, Dennis said.'

'No, they don't.' Mr Waverly crossed his arms and leant back in his chair. 'No one has lived in the old Mill Cottage for years.'

'But they do,' Ellen blurted. 'I've seen it.'

'Sweetheart,' Mrs Waverly said, her tone that of a mother talking to a toddler, even though she was only two years older than Ellen. 'Mr Waverly is certain of this because his old business partner, Ronald McGovern, owned Mill Cottage. Just as this farmhouse was in Mr Waverly's family, Mill Cottage has always belonged to a McGovern.'

'But perhaps—' Ellen started and Mr Waverly cut her off with a wave of his hand.

'No,' he said sternly. He pushed aside his half-eaten pie and patted his shirt pocket for a cigarette. 'I'm sorry, but this pie is inedible. Make me some toast, dear.'

Mrs Waverly's face fell, but she stood up and plucked the baby from his seat in one strong, and clearly irritated, movement. 'Toast,' she muttered, her lips tight. 'Of course.'

The minute the door shut behind his disgruntled wife, Mr Waverly took a deep puff of his cigarette and used it to point at Ellen. 'I know there isn't anyone living at Mill Cottage. Do you know how? Ronald McGovern was an only child, never married, and died in a tragic accident before the war. The house has been vacant ever since.'

Mr Waverly took two puffs on his cigarette and smashed it in the remainder of his cottage pie with a sizzle.

'Well, it's possible we're talking about two different houses.' Ellen's heart raced like it had on the run back from the cottage. She had seen it with her own eyes. While it looked abandoned, there were fresh tyre tracks. That broken umbrella! Someone had been there, living there. And if not, where did Dennis live? It seemed a rather silly thing to invent, after all.

'There are no other houses on Mill Road. It is a dead end.'

Mr Waverly stared at Ellen, daring her to contradict him one last time. He had to be mistaken. Why would Dennis make up an aunt and a house that was just beyond her billet? Hands over the note in her lap, Ellen suddenly wanted to rush away from the table, to disappear to her room and not hear anything else Mr Waverly had to say. Dennis wouldn't lie to her about such a silly thing. If he had wanted to walk her home, he could've simply asked.

'In fact—' Mr Waverly started, but before he could continue, Ellen put her napkin on her untouched plate and pushed back from the table.

'Thank you for this information. Now, if you would excuse me, I think I need some rest.'

She left before she could see the shocked look on Mr

Waverly's face. He was a man who did not like to be interrupted.

Once in her room, she didn't even bother to go to her bed, just sank to her heels with her back against the closed attic door. She rubbed her forehead against the heels of her hands, trying to relieve the sudden, pulsing pressure that had built up. Why would Dennis lie about that, of all things? Perhaps he'd made the story up that first night in order to walk her home and then the lie grew, but that seemed childish.

But Mr Waverly didn't seem to be one to make things up either – he had lived in this farmhouse his entire life. He knew the area better than anyone else around. There had to be an explanation, a misunderstanding, perhaps. Ellen tried to shrug off the uncertainty as she tore open the thick envelope with her name on it and read the carefully typed card:

```
I was able to get Pearl released on bail
this evening. Unfortunately, she escaped
before I could bring her to you, breaking
any good faith agreement I had in place
for her. She's a wanted criminal. They
found the bag just beyond her garden.
There is mounting evidence against her.
If you find her, she has to go to jail.
Ellen, I know she is your friend, but
```

we need to stick together. You and I can
find the truth. I will call back to the
Waverlys' at half seven, on my way
home, and we can sort through this mess.
Together, we can solve this and any
problem.
Yours truly, Dennis

Pearl had escaped! Which meant she was alone somewhere, in the horrible weather, risking capture yet again
while Ellen was no closer to proving her friend's innocence. A rush of fear hit Ellen and she threw on her damp
jacket and scarf. With a regretful glance at the still-coded
note from Richard's pocket, Ellen tucked it and Dennis's
card into the waistband of her skirt. How did he have the
time to type the note so cleanly when so much was at
stake? She didn't have time to puzzle through any of it
right now. If Pearl had not gone with Dennis, something
had to be terribly wrong. Perhaps she'd seen the spy or
had a clue who it was. Danger was so close; Ellen could
feel it like a ghost at the door. Only she had no idea what
to fear. As much as Ellen wanted to rescue her friend, she
felt woefully inadequate. She needed help, more facts,
another methodical brain. Ellen could only think of one
other person who might be able to help Pearl now: her
former supervisor, the person Pearl had trusted from the
beginning. Miss Waincross. If Ellen told her what she

knew, Miss Waincross might change her mind about Pearl's guilt, and start to see that she was being framed. She dashed out the front door, letting it slam behind her. She had to get back to Bletchley Park.

32

PEARL

Pearl hid in the rubble at the brickworks until the light started to fade, her stomach started to rumble, and her fingernails tinged blue. Eventually, she went home not for any good, logical reason, but because she was hungry and cold. Besides, her father's cardigan was there, left on the radiator to dry last night. She knew it was the most obvious place anyone would look for her, but as she crept through the Tillersons' back garden and over the hedge into her own, she hoped they'd already searched her house and left.

The plan was to sneak in, grab a scone and her cardigan and hat, and leave without notice. It was highly probable Mum wasn't home from work yet – unless they'd let her go early because of the situation – but as she approached, Pearl was relieved to see that the back of the small house was dark. With any luck, she could dip in and out without a trace.

She knew she was in serious trouble now. The stunt she pulled at the station was not exactly the smartest thing she'd done, but the minute she'd heard *his* voice, Pearl knew she had no choice. Dennis, with his posh accent, asking the officer how much it would take to get her released *just for the night*. Saying he'd bring her back first thing in the morning, because *he, too, believed she was guilty.* *No thank you*, Pearl had thought, but instead asked politely to use the loo when the policeman took her from her dark cell.

She'd guessed no male officer was going to accompany her, and her gamble paid off. There was a window above the basin, small but not too small for a girl who had been ridiculed for her size since she was able to understand the short jokes. Pearl wondered how long the officer waited outside the door to the loo before charging in. It must've been a while, because she got all the way over to the brickworks without anyone on her tail, as far as she could tell. Now, though, she feared it would not be long before they tracked her down, which was why she couldn't be at her house for long. It was dangerous being outside, cowering in the hedges, and she hoped Ellen was doing something, anything, to clear her name. She was more than aware that Ellen must've been behind her getting released. So at least she wasn't angry enough at Pearl to let her rot in jail. Even if sending *Dennis* was the worst thing she could've done.

Movement caught Pearl's eye and she crouched down even further, her face almost in the wet earth under the hedges. A few branches poked at her legs – she was sure her tights had ladders up them now – but she tried to remain frozen. There it was again. Someone in the house. Then a light. Maybe a torch? Yes, another beam of light. Two now. Definitely wasn't Mum. Then one opened the back door out on to the step. He wore a hat, a long coat, and Pearl would've bet her entire salary he was a policeman.

He shined his light over the garden for what seemed like for ever. Pearl was shaking so much she was certain the entire hedge was moving. She held her breath, afraid he'd hear her short, fast panting. He swept the garden with his torch once more, then quickly turned and went back to the house, leaving the door open. Pearl heard something crash, glass breaking and a loud thud. Her eyes flooded with tears. They didn't need to destroy her house.

Then, just like that, the noise stopped. The torchlights disappeared. The house was dark again. Pearl waited, counting silently to one hundred before she half-ran-half-crawled to the back door. Peeking inside, she had to clamp her hand over her mouth to muffle a scream.

The place had been destroyed. Pearl picked through a few broken picture frames, rescuing a photo of her parents, and surveyed the damage for a few moments. Tables had been cleared and drawers had been opened, but the worst of it was her mother's large wooden desk by the window. Every drawer had been overturned, every file emptied on to the worn rug. They had been looking for something, but why in her mother's desk? Did they think her mother was involved somehow? Oh gosh, were they after her, too? Pearl quickly grabbed her father's cardigan, buttoning it as she dashed across the wet lawn and into the neighbour's garden. If they thought her mother was part of it all, they would likely head to the Park next. Pearl started running, hoping she would get there before they did.

33

ELLEN

A bicycle would've been a smart investment. Lungs burning, Ellen ran towards Bletchley Park and the one person she thought could help Pearl: Miss Waincross. Ellen had to find Pearl's ex-supervisor fast, before her friend was captured again, with the charge of absconding from bail now added to her laundry list of criminal activities.

She sped down the road, unnerved to see the shadowy figures of two men standing at the sentry gate. They might've been workers arriving for their shift, but they looked stockier. More menacing. Perhaps it was their broad shoulders. Very few mathematicians had an athletic build. Their coats were long, trench style, and flapped open in the wind. Ellen hung back, watching from behind a tree in someone's front garden. Breath coming in short, shaky gasps, she leant against the cool, wet bark and waited for them to move on. Whoever they were, they were inspecting some papers with their torches, definitely spending more time at the gate than someone in a rush to get to their hut. Finally, they walked off towards the mansion, pocketing some of the paperwork. Ellen shuddered. After waiting two beats, she ran up to the sentry. 'Here you are. Ellen Davies. Hut Four,' she said, practically shoving her pass at the guard, all the while thinking, *Hurry up!*

The guard, a bearded man she'd never seen before, looked her up and down and then retreated to his little brick house. If he hadn't taken her pass with him, she would've run off. Instead, she bounced from foot to foot, craning her neck every few moments to see around the brick building to the mansion. The stocky men were inside now.

The guard peered out his window at her, consulting a large book on a table. Waiting like this was not unusual, but had never seemed so inconvenient.

'Those men that were here before me,' Ellen called out, hoping to sound innocent, 'they don't work here. Were they police?' She had never asked questions of a guard before. Only answered them. Pearl had told her to be quiet and she'd be processed quickly. But while Ellen wanted the guard to move things along, she also wanted a preview of what she might encounter in the mansion. If it was, in fact, the police, she felt preparation was key.

The guard didn't answer; he kept flipping through the

book, then wrote something down. He came to the door and handed back her pass. 'You're clear, Miss Davies,' the guard said, leaning against the door frame. 'You can go ahead. Don't know what those fellows are after tonight. You'd best steer clear of them. Stop asking questions.'

Ellen waited, hoping he'd say more. He stared back, then shook his head in the direction of the mansion. He wasn't going to tell her anything else.

The wind had picked up and Ellen looped her scarf around her head in an effort to protect both her hair and her ears, which had gone icy cold. As daylight disappeared, the bad weather took over, filling the shadows with swirls of wet leaves and sudden downpours. She ran to the mansion. Catching her breath in the doorway, she paused to fix her appearance before stepping inside.

The rich, wood-panelled front hall was empty. There wasn't even anyone on the staircase. Ellen shuddered. She was cold, but the stillness in the mansion was not right.

Without hesitating any further, she turned right, into what had likely been a sitting room before the war. It was now Pearl's mother's office. It led into another office, the two rooms separated by regal-looking double doors. She would take a quick detour – tell Pearl's mum what was happening – then attempt to find Miss Waincross's office. Not seeing Mrs Patterson, Ellen grabbed a pencil and piece of paper from the corner of the blotter and wrote a brief, cryptic message. If Pearl came here, she'd know where to find Ellen, but hopefully it wouldn't mean much to anyone else.

As she finished writing, she heard voices emanating from the interior office. Mostly male, low octave, short words. Then she heard a woman. Could it be Pearl's mum? She tucked the message under the blotter and approached the door.

Normally, she would've knocked politely – or found an assistant and asked if it was all right to interrupt. She didn't have time for that. Pulling open one of the heavy wooden doors, Ellen realized she was too late. Pearl's mum, Mrs Patterson, was already in handcuffs.

'What's going on?' she asked.

'Who are you?' a rather large police officer demanded. His sidekick was short and was thwacking a baton into the palm of his hand in a threatening manner.

'She works here, sir. She means no harm,' Mrs Patterson said, her head tipped forward so that Ellen could not see her face, just the short pin curls that fell forward from their combs. Pearl's mum was normally so put-together. It bothered Ellen to see her in disarray. 'Ellen, dear, all is well. You should leave,' she said without lifting her head.

One of the officers dropped Mrs Patterson's arm and stood by the door. 'Unless you want to take a ride down to the station, too, I'd follow her advice.'

'I, uh, I'm sorry Mrs Patterson . . .' Ellen backed out

quickly, tripping over her own shoes and stumbling over the threshold. As soon as she was in Pearl's mum's office, the door slammed behind her and she caught her toe on the rug, falling to the ground with a loud, painful thump.

A woman's voice came from above her. 'Oh! That's some exit. Are you hurt?'

Ellen rested for a breath or two, feeling too dazed to reply. Her tailbone and ankle throbbed. The woman's hand appeared in front of her face, pale red-tipped fingers outstretched helpfully. Reluctantly, she took the woman's cool hand in hers and looked up.

A sense of relief washed over her as she recognized the woman, allowing herself to be helped gingerly to her feet. With her perfectly styled hair, thin red lips, and fashionable navy pencil skirt with matching jacket, there was no one else quite so movie-star perfect at the Park. 'Miss Waincross,' Ellen said tentatively, 'thank you.'

'You're most welcome.' The woman's red lips smoothed into a thin smile. 'Now, Miss Davies, you can stand just fine?'

Ellen tested her ankle which, although tender, wasn't broken by any means. 'Yes. I am so sorry for nearly falling into you like that. But oddly enough, I was looking for you.'

'Hm,' the woman said, her hand still holding Ellen's protectively. 'I had an appointment in there, but it does

34

ELLEN

As she walked down the empty hallway lined with firmly shut doors, Ellen tried desperately to employ calming techniques from her childhood. Deep breaths. Visualize a happy place. Feel your fingers, toes, top of the head. None of them worked. Her mind was still a bird's nest of uncertainties, facts that she couldn't quite prove, things that simply did not add up. Still, she followed Miss Waincross, and not because she thought it was the right thing to do. It was the only thing left.

Miss Waincross walked across the wood floors, her shoulders square, her head held high. *I need to be more like that,* Ellen thought, *self-assured in the face of a storm.* She would never make sense of everything if her mind *was* the storm.

'Here we are,' Miss Waincross said, unlocking a door at the end of the hallway.

She switched on the green desk lamp, throwing a globe

of yellow light over a perfectly empty desk. Her blotter looked pristine, with a pen and pencil lined up at the very top. The surface wasn't even littered with a stray teacup, which made Ellen wonder if Miss Waincross did much work here. Everyone needed a cup of tea to get through their day, didn't they?

Ellen closed the door and stepped into the small, stuffy room. Thankfully, it was warm, and smelt of carbon papers and pencil shavings. Miss Waincross made a sweeping gesture with her hand, indicating Ellen should sit in one of the two high-backed wooden chairs facing the desk.

'So, tell me,' Miss Waincross started, sitting down and crossing her legs at the ankle, 'how can I help you?'

'Pearl is missing. I have to find her. She's in great danger and being framed for a crime she did not commit. Have you seen her? Do you know where she might be?' she blurted.

Miss Waincross stood up and went to sit in her rather creaky desk chair. 'She's suspected of spying, stealing and treason. When you steal cribs and tamper with other top-secret files, well, it's quite bad.'

'I know it appears she's guilty. But she isn't. You have to believe me.' Ellen sat forward on the chair. 'They've arrested her mother; they're hunting for her now. She's in danger!'

'All right,' Miss Waincross said, lacing her long fingers together, 'I have to be honest – I had a hard time believing

Pearl could be a spy. You know I've always looked out for her, taken her under my wing when she needed protecting. I'll say it – I have a soft spot for the poor girl. Tell me what you know. Perhaps I can help in some way, though I doubt there is much I can do at this point.'

'Right,' Ellen answered, collecting herself. 'When Pearl's friend Richard died, Pearl was, well, upset wouldn't describe it, really—'

'I noticed how Richard's death had affected her,' Miss Waincross interrupted, smoothly. 'But it seems Richard himself may not have been entirely blameless. I've heard he was socializing with some unsavoury types. Pearl's involvement with him does not reflect well on her.'

Ellen chose her next words carefully. 'Pearl was worried about him, too. In fact, she left a note in Richard's bag, warning him to be more careful, but then the bag was stolen, perhaps by the very people who might've been responsible for his death. I think whoever it is, they've framed her. We have to find them and arrest them. Instead of Pearl.'

'But who are these mysterious, sinister *people*?' Miss Waincross leant forward and Ellen could smell her flowery perfume. 'I am trained to look at the facts, Miss Davies, the hard evidence. And I see a girl who peeked at top-secret messages and is implicated in missing cribs. We have to remember that sometimes the people you do not want to be guilty, well, they are.'

Ellen felt the paper at her waistband crinkle – her trump card, the proof that *Richard* had been crooked, not Pearl. *He* was the one hiding coded messages in his room and spouting off in dodgy pubs. If she looked at the facts and tried not to imagine the tears welling in Pearl's eyes when she talked of him, Richard *had* to be the one to blame. The evidence was there, in black and white. And like Miss Waincross, Ellen liked the certainty of black and white, even when life was all too often in shades of grey.

But Pearl? Or even Antony? No, they couldn't have been involved in this. Ellen felt it in her heart.

Ellen leant back in the chair and pulled out the coded message. *You have one more chance to make it right*, she told herself. 'Richard gave a message to Antony before they set off, the morning he was killed,' she said, quietly. 'It might hold some of the answers. May I?' Ellen asked, picking up a sharpened pencil from the edge of Miss Waincross's blotter.

'Of course.'

Ellen uncrossed her legs, both feet solidly on the floor. Her knees were shaking along with her hands, and it seemed even her breath was trembling. Carefully, she unfolded the paper Richard had given Ant, side by side with the decoded message she'd found in Richard's room. With any luck it was the same cipher.

TRIEIET DDIBRIES ALVAYO EW EV I IDEL EIBI

There were thirty-two letters. Simple maths said four

columns, eight rows. Easy enough.

```
TRIE
IETO
OBRI
ESAL
VAYO
EWEV
IIOE
LEBI
```

Starting at first in the bottom-right, then to the left and up, then there it was. Clockwise. Ellen tried to swallow, her mouth dry as she gazed down at the result. Her chest tightened. *Poor Richard*, she thought.

I BELIEVED I TRIED I LOVED I WAS BETRAYED

'Oh!' Miss Waincross said, clasping her hands over her heart as if personally injured. 'Tragic.'

The note seemed to be a confession. *I believed. I tried.* He had believed in the wrong cause, tried to undermine the war effort. But *I loved, I was betrayed*? What was that about?

She pushed the second message towards Miss Waincross. 'Same decryption. Different handwriting,' she said. 'This one slants to the right, which Pearl said was more like Richard's. I'm sure we can find a comparison to confirm.'

Ellen watched Miss Waincross as she absorbed the two

messages and all that they entailed. All the pieces now pointed to Richard and although they would absolve Pearl, Ellen felt like she had betrayed her friend, somehow, by tarnishing Richard's memory.

'You know what we need to do,' Miss Waincross said softly, reaching her hand across the desk to gather up the messages. 'We need to tell the police straight away.'

Ellen nodded, already standing up. A gust of wind dashed rain against the tiny office window, a noise like pebbles thrown at the glass. Pearl was out there – cold, frightened, alone. But Ellen had help now. And proof. *I'm coming, Pearl*, she thought.

'There's no time to lose.' Miss Waincross grabbed the handbag at her feet and shrugged into a navy mackintosh. 'We will drive. It'll be fastest.'

Miss Waincross opened the door and dashed through the sideways sheets of rain to the long, squat brick garage that served as a holding place for Don Rs and service vehicles. Ellen followed, wondering if she should alert someone else at the mansion to her whereabouts, but then thought otherwise when she heard the rumble of a car being started nearby. She had to clear Pearl's name before it was too late.

35

PEARL

The rain had turned to sleet. The wind to a relentless blast of cold, painful snowy pellets. An overgrown rhododendron was doing a horrible job shielding Pearl from the elements. Also, her cardigan was soaked through, her shoes wet and her tights ripped. She was hungry, tired and needed a toilet. In all, Pearl felt as horrible as she was certain she looked. Still, she waited, crouched on the balls of her feet, while she watched the guard inside the gates to Bletchley. Any minute now, his shift would end and a new guard would take over, hopefully one Pearl knew.

While she crouched, squeezing her toes inside her soggy shoes to keep them from going numb, she formulated a plan. It was a very loose one. It all depended on whether she could find Mum. If Mum was still there, maybe she could help somehow – she had contacts, and she knew Pearl wasn't a traitor. If Mum wasn't there . . .

well, she'd think of something.

Eventually, a tall balding fellow came down the path from the direction of the mansion. Reggie. It had to be Reggie. *Oh please, please let it be Reggie.* She caught sight of his face as he turned towards the lamp post – thank god, it was him! The other, stockier guard talked to Reggie for a while. Pearl heard laughing. Then the unknown guard left, walking the way Reggie had come. It was time.

It took a few steps for her legs to remember how to move again, her feet tingling with pins and needles as she loped along, trying to run. The key was to reach Reggie before he realized she had been banned from the Park. Which was why she needed her stupid short legs to move faster.

She got to the gatehouse, panting, just as Reggie sat down at the table and was flipping through the large book they kept. Pearl assumed the book was a record of who had passed by, but didn't really know. There could be warnings in there for all she knew, big black marks telling people not to let her in under any circumstances.

'Hello, Reggie!' she called out cheerfully. 'Horrible weather, eh?'

'Pearl, hiya.' Reggie's face fell when he caught sight of her. 'What happened to you?'

'Oh Reggie, it's been a night, I tell you. Silly me tripped and fell into a huge muddy puddle. It was quite a spill and I'm lucky I didn't break a bone, really. But I am cold and bruised and exhausted. Would like nothing more than a cup of tea and to see my mum if that's all right by you.'

'Pity, you just missed her,' he said, shaking his head. 'Two men took her down to the station – I saw them in the hall when I arrived earlier. Didn't say why or where they were going, but your mum looked right angry. Wouldn't want to be the bloke questioning her down at the station, if you catch my drift.'

'Ugh,' Pearl moaned, then added quickly, 'Mum hates these sorts of things. Happens all the time, really, when you work in such a sensitive area of the Park. They're asking her about all sorts. Top secret, you know. Maybe I'll just collect some of her things, warm up, and meet her down there. That's what she usually likes.'

Pearl bit the inside of her lip, hoping to not betray the immense sense of doom that had showered down on her like a bucket of icy water. This was all her fault. Her mum had never been arrested before. No one cared about an assistant, at least not enough to question them at the station. Whether it was because she'd escaped or because of the charges against her, Pearl had got her mother locked up.

'This happens a lot?' Reggie asked, crossing his arms over his bulky wool coat. 'I've never seen these fellows here before. Not the jokey local coppers I know from the pub. They were hardly friendly. Seemed serious, Pearl.'

Pearl made a show of nodding slowly as if she knew exactly what he was talking about. In truth, her mind was spinning, but she wanted Reggie to think what had happened was nothing abnormal, and that he shouldn't question letting Pearl in. 'I don't think it's their job to be nice, Reggie, but I know what you mean.' She shrugged and put her hands on her hips, sticking one hip out like she'd seen Miss Waincross do from time to time when talking to men. Pearl knew it was a bit silly in the dark, but she needed Reggie to move things along. 'Can I go in? I'd still murder for that cup of tea.'

'On with ya,' Reggie said with a sweep of his hand. 'I've paperwork to catch up on, don't you know. Piles of it. I don't know how they expect us to keep up on it all and keep this gate secure with all the changing rules and regulations they're piling on every single day. Ah well, good luck with it all. Give your mum my regards.'

'Will do,' Pearl said, spinning on her heel and taking off down the path at a brisk but what she hoped was normal pace, until Reggie disappeared into his little brick office. Then she ran.

Panting, she pulled open the huge wood doors and slid quietly into the front corridor. It was quiet save for the faint clacking of typewriters and, luckily, no one had noticed her come in. Pearl had expected a bit more chaos, perhaps with other officers holding those small flippy notebooks and asking questions. Instead, it was like any

302

normal quiet evening, with just the clacking of typewriters filling the still air. But her mum had been arrested. Which was not normal at all.

She would go to Mum's desk – perhaps she had left a note, clues, anything to help figure out what to do next. She had to stay hidden until she did – Pearl could *not* wind up back in jail.

In the hall, curtains and shades were pulled, and the soft light from wall sconces glowed, creating ominous shadows in the corners. Even though Pearl didn't have far to go, she kept looking over her shoulder and peering cautiously around the corners.

Mum's small office was just off the main hallway, beyond the staircase. Pearl peeked in the door before entering. Thankfully, it was empty. Another door, which opened on to the adjoining office, was closed. Tiptoeing across the room, she put her ear to it. She heard nothing.

Pearl scurried over to her mother's desk and lifted the wooden chair carefully away from the table – dragging it across the wood floor would be too loud. Then, sitting on the edge of the chair, she started to search the desk for clues.

Her mum's desk was very orderly, with only a typewriter, a folder containing documents to be typed, a blotter, and a notebook with pencil. In the drawer there was even less to go on. What must she do all day, Pearl puzzled. They never discussed what they did, though

303

Pearl got the impression her mother was more important than your average secretary. Then, her heart leapt when she saw a corner of paper peeking out from under Mum's blotter. Her eyes widened when she noticed that the letters were in Ellen's distinct swirly handwriting. Ellen had been here! And of course, it was in code.

She had just enough time to scan the page, her eyes leaping across the first, easiest decodes she could think of. Patterns, repeated letters, and finally – yes! – lined up letters revealing hidden words.

Then, Pearl caught a movement out of the corner of her eye. Hand still on the desk's surface, she crouched, trying to hide behind the desk. Only, she hadn't pulled the chair out far enough and bumped it with her leg, sending the chair crashing to the floor. So much for being sneaky.

The door to the hallway opened. Pearl raised her head, knowing hiding was useless.

'Pearl! What are you doing here?'

It was Mr St John.

36

ELLEN

The windscreen wipers clacked back and forth loudly, slapping and creaking with each ineffective swipe. They were nothing against the storm, barely clearing the window long enough to see the road, faintly illuminated in the dimmed headlights. Still, Miss Waincross tore down the lane from Bletchley Park, crashing through puddles as big as ponds and skidding as she took corners at what Ellen figured must be racing speeds. Ellen braced herself against the door of the car with one hand, the other flat against the leather seat to keep her from sliding. She didn't protest. Not until Miss Waincross turned away from the centre of town.

Ellen's neck snapped to the left as she watched the road that led to the police station retreat into the distance. 'Miss Waincross,' she said timidly, 'aren't we meant to go that way?'

Miss Waincross didn't reply, gripping the steering wheel tighter with her black leather gloves. She'd been quiet since they drove away from the mansion.

Maybe she knows another way, Ellen told herself, taking long, deep breaths in through her nose.

Now, Miss Waincross leant over the steering wheel as if willing the Wolseley Super Six to fly even faster along the waterlogged roads. It was only when Ellen spied the Waverlys' long, curving drive that Ellen spoke up again.

'This is not the way to the police station,' she said, still very polite, though she felt like screaming. Her breathing exercises went out the window as she clutched the door handle, wondering whether she should throw it open and jump out. Something about this seemed very, very wrong. 'Where are you taking me?'

Miss Waincross didn't answer, instead putting her foot to the floor, causing the car to lurch as it accelerated. *Well*, Ellen thought, *I am decidedly not going to jump out now.* She turned so she was facing the driver's seat. 'Where are you taking me?' she tried again, slower and louder this time. 'I can see we're not going to the police station, so you'd better tell me where we are headed. Or I'll . . . I'll . . .'

Miss Waincross reached down to her handbag at her feet and, in one swift movement, produced a gun. She pointed it at Ellen. 'You'll what, Miss Davies? What will you do?' Her voice was calm, and she appeared to have no trouble steering with one hand while pointing the gun with the other. 'Tell me, please.'

Ellen had never felt fear like this before, hitting her like the ground had given way. Suddenly, she was plummeting thousands of feet down below the earth, her heart in her throat and her stomach not far behind. How had she not seen this before? She'd blindly trusted this woman as her last chance, someone Pearl looked up to, not recognizing Miss Waincross as someone with the means and authority to access information, pass it on and frame her subordinates. And as a result, Ellen had foolishly walked into the arms of the Bletchley Park spy.

Richard had been duped just like Pearl had. Just like Ellen herself. She remembered Pearl saying how she'd confided in Miss Waincross about the worn envelopes Richard had been receiving. Miss Waincross had also seen Pearl at her most vulnerable, when she'd accidentally dumped the contents of a top-secret delivery on the hallway floor. Had it been a coincidence that the envelope wasn't properly sealed?

Ellen tried to swallow, her mouth dry, her tongue thick and heavy. Of course, Miss Waincross had been keen to steer Ellen towards Richard's supposed guilt and had been overly eager to help Pearl. They weren't going to the police. That was never an option. Ellen, like Richard, knew too much. And Ellen knew from her brother's mystery novels that any good spy disposed of their liabilities. Quickly. First Richard. Then Pearl. And now . . .

Her heartbeat rushed in her ears, and although the fields were flying by them, everything slowed for an instant. Then she realized that part of it wasn't simply the fear. Miss Waincross had changed gear, the gun somehow still in her hand. *Well*, Ellen thought, *that couldn't have been easy. She's clearly done that before.* The car slowed. Wherever they were headed, they were about to arrive.

Ellen's eyes frantically searched the floor and seats of the new, pristine car. Not only were there no weapons, but she was certain Miss Waincross was not about to shoot her in the vehicle. If she'd learnt anything about her, it was that she was tidy. Shooting someone at close range would be messy at the least. Ellen's stomach lurched at the thought, and she looked out the window. They were definitely slowing, and now she knew where they were heading.

Miss Waincross had turned down Mill Road.

37

PEARL

'I . . . uh . . .' Pearl stammered, then stopped.

'Pearl,' Mr St John said, putting his hand up to stop her protestation, 'are you not supposed to be in custody? What are you doing here?'

'I'm not guilty. I had to get out,' Pearl blurted, unable to think of any other reason why she needed to remain free. It was the truth and, based on how he was looking at her, he knew it. 'Look, we don't have time for this. People are going to get hurt.'

'You only have a few minutes to plead your case before I call the authorities.' He crossed his arms over his unbuttoned suit jacket and waited.

'I, uh, I've been framed. There's evidence . . . which I do not have now, but Ellen does! She'll be here soon. She can explain why someone framed me – and Richard – to steal sensitive information. Like the cribs. Why would I take the cribs? It's not logical and besides, I wasn't there to steal them.' In one last effort, she blurted, 'Besides, Mr St John, I loved Richard with all my heart and I begged him, in a letter, to be careful. People were using him, framing him too. It's why he died. I just know it.' Tears welled up and Pearl's shoulders sank. *Logic, not emotion, stupid.* Mr St John did not respond well to feelings.

Mr St John raked his fingers through his hair. It stuck on end as if he'd been struck by lightning. With his hands on the back of his head, he looked to the ceiling for what seemed to be for ever. While time slipped through her fingers faster than water out of a tap, Mr St John was lingering, pondering, and using up time Pearl simply did not have. She felt every muscle in her neck tense as she waited, wondering when he would grab her arm and usher her to the nearest guard.

Finally, after what seemed like an eternity, he dropped his hands and looked directly at her. 'I believe you, in spite of your rather spotty argument. I've questioned your guilt for a while – as you said, it did not add up. Yes, you're young and clever, but spies need a network to collect and distribute this information. Your mother is hardly the guilty type and when she vouched for you the morning that boy died, I started wondering how the pieces all fit together. And when I finally saw this, I realized they do not.' He pulled an envelope out of his coat pocket. 'Earlier today, the Don R's bag was found. It was abandoned in a field beyond your house.'

Pearl felt her breath catch. The bag. Of course it was found near her house. That wasn't good for her case. Then she realized the letter he held was hers. For Richard. *Good god.* Her heart pounded and she leant against her mum's desk, her knees suddenly weak. That would have to help her, right? She'd exposed everything – the envelopes in the hallway, Richard's tampered-with deliveries – and followed it up with a wildly jealous and untrue rant about Dennis. 'Mr St John, did you read it all? I mean, all of it?'

'Of course I did, Pearl. You knew I would. Even the bits I couldn't read at first, I worked those out,' he said. 'I'm still calling the police. Whoever stole the bag read your letter. They'll be after you, I'm afraid. You're in quite a bit of danger.'

'I'm aware,' she said, trying to sound braver than she felt. 'But first, I need to work this out. It's a message, I'm sure, from Ellen. She's helping me. I'm certain of it.'

She nabbed a pencil from her mum's desk drawer and worked out Ellen's secret message, taking more time than she wanted with the pressure of Mr St John's eyes on the back of her head.

'First letter!' Mr St John exclaimed and her eyes flew to the start of each stanza. She let out a sigh, relieved Ellen hadn't made things more complicated than necessary:

311

Where the birds fly
Against the wind
Never far
East or west
Exactly there.

'That's where she is!' Pearl blurted rather loudly. 'She's in Miss Waincross's office. "Wane Ex" with the "ex" like a cross. Waincross. Has to be. Ellen has the evidence I need – two coded messages from Richard. If nothing else, those will prove my innocence.'

'Right,' Mr St John said. 'I don't think it's safe, but—'

'I don't have time to worry about what's safe,' Pearl interrupted. 'I'll go to Miss Waincross's and you . . .'

'I'll find security. Ask if they've seen anything out of the ordinary.' He buttoned his jacket and nodded firmly. 'You go. Quickly. Report back here. I'll do the same.'

That was all Pearl needed to hear to take off running.

38

ELLEN

Miss Waincross carefully navigated the pitted, muddy drive, pulling the car into the barn. Ellen couldn't help but congratulate herself on identifying recent tyre tracks, indicating this was used as a garage, but the victory fell flat when she was ordered out of the vehicle. Her mouth went dry and her knees started to shake. She did not want to leave the car. If she got out, it would mean death. Their arrival had to indicate the house was abandoned, or Aunt Myra was elsewhere, but what about Dennis? Without a plan or hope of one, Ellen did the only thing she could think of – she started talking.

'I know where we are. Why have you taken me here? What are your intentions? No matter how sinister, I deserve to know,' she started, her voice wavering on the last sentence.

Miss Waincross opened the driver's door, keeping the

gun pointed at Ellen. 'You think you know where we are, but you do not. Step out, please. I will not ask twice.'

Ellen wanted to protest but did not see much point. The woman would get her out of the car one way or another, and she shuddered again at the image of Miss Waincross dragging her body from the passenger seat, limp and bloody. Ellen stepped out of the car, her shoes sinking into the soft mud in the leaky, dilapidated barn. She shut the door firmly and debated running. As she scanned her surroundings, panic rose in her like water in a boiling kettle. There was farmland as far as the eye could see, barren and muddy and flat. No neighbouring houses. No noises indicating cars on the road. She had to get out of this another way.

'Come with me,' Miss Waincross ordered, though she gave no option but to comply as she grabbed Ellen's wrist and dragged her across the muddy ground to the front door of the cottage. 'Open the postbox,' Miss Waincross told her, the gun still trained on Ellen's skull. Hands shaking, Ellen pulled open the metal door. Inside was a proper door key. 'Unlock the front door and walk inside. Put the key on the table next to the door, light the candle there with the matches, and sit in the chair facing the wall. Do not try anything.'

Knowing she had no other option, Ellen steadied her hands and unlatched the door. It swung open and Ellen fought back a flood of tears. It was just as Mr Waverly had

314

insisted – dirty, abandoned and not suitable for living. Dennis hadn't lived here. He had lied to her. But why?

Once inside, Miss Waincross pushed her through the only open door of the three off the small entryway. The place stank of mildew and decay. It took Ellen several tries to find a match dry enough to catch fire, but finally, she was able to illuminate the room just enough to see where she was. As instructed, she walked across the worn floorboards into what was once a sitting room, her shoes scuffing against the fine grit of dirt on the surface. There was an old chunky table in the centre of the rectangular room, a fireplace and two wooden chairs along the wall opposite the front windows. The windows were covered in heavy black curtains, which made the room incredibly dark, but also would keep any passers-by from seeing inside the house. The curtains were not the type to be removed during the day, but were nailed to the wall in their heavy frames. Ellen placed the candlestick on the rutted dining table and looked in vain around the dark room for a fireplace poker, logs, anything she could use for a weapon.

'Sit!' Miss Waincross ordered and so Ellen did, facing the fireplace. There were a few well-burnt logs in the hearth, resting on a sort of metal grate. It looked heavy enough, with iron spikes rising to cradle the spent wood and ash.

She heard the distinct sizzle of a match being struck

and feared for a moment that the place would soon be ablaze. Instead, more light flickered around the room, casting shadows that allowed her to track Miss Waincross's movements. Turning her head only slightly, she saw her captor lighting sconces on the far wall. Ellen wondered if she could grab the fireplace grate and swing it at her captor, knocking her to the ground before she had the chance to fire the gun. The room was so small – Miss Waincross was only a few paces away – but by the time Ellen had mustered her courage, her captor was standing at the table behind where Ellen sat. She'd have to wait until Miss Waincross left the room to grab the grate. Unless, of course, she just shot Ellen now. Ellen willed herself to act before thinking. The opposite of what she was comfortable with. But there was no time for comfort when your life was at stake.

There was no doubt – Miss Waincross *would* dispose of Ellen. Ellen wasn't foolish enough to believe she was more valuable than Richard. But she wondered if there was a reason why Miss Waincross had brought her here instead of, say, dumping her body in a well somewhere. If the place truly was abandoned, it was the perfect location for a murder – isolated, quiet, forgotten.

Ellen took two shuddering breaths and finally managed to speak. 'What is your plan, Miss Waincross? You won't get away with this. People are looking for me. They'll find you.'

'They are not,' Miss Waincross said confidently, her voice and shadow indicating she was still at the table just behind Ellen, not far enough for Ellen to get away with making any sudden moves. Slowly, Ellen shifted her weight on the chair, turning her body just slightly to catch sight of the opposite wall and, barely, Miss Waincross. 'Turn around!' her captor ordered, quickly covering up the papers she'd been reading. 'No more movements! You do what I say.'

'But the police will be here soon,' Ellen tried, though she was well aware no one was on their way.

'No one has phoned the police and no one has any reason to suspect anything. If I've learnt nothing else recently, it is to deflect all blame on to anyone else, especially if they're dead.'

'You preyed on poor Richard, didn't you? He didn't stand a chance,' Ellen said, hoping Miss Waincross would continue talking, explaining her motives. The longer she could keep this woman talking, the better chance she had of coming up with some sort of escape plan.

Miss Waincross chuckled casually, as if Ellen had made a quip over afternoon tea. 'No, dear, not really. He was effective for a bit but was not cut out for this line of work. And you know, there is not a brilliant future for flunkies, unfortunately. Not my decision, of course, but not a lot is. Not any more at least.'

The hair on the back of Ellen's neck pricked to

attention. Miss Waincross was bitter about something, a lack of power? 'You didn't want to kill Richard?' she asked tentatively, hoping her assertion was correct.

'He was floundering and had too many questions. The amount of effort wasn't paying off; a decision was made. It was designed to look like an accident, though there were too many mistakes – a stray branch in the road with no trees around? Please!' she exclaimed, clearly exasperated. 'I thought it messy and we both know the execution of everything was appalling. As usual, no one consulted me. If they had, I wouldn't have agreed to it.'

'You wouldn't have agreed to his death?' Ellen tried. She turned around at the sound of something hard hitting the table. Had Miss Waincross put the gun down? If she had, Ellen knew she had to make a run for it.

'Face the wall!' Miss Waincross yelled, picking the gun up and training it on Ellen once again. 'Do I need to tie you up? I thought I could trust you, Miss Davies. Don't make me do something neither of us want me to do.'

Heart pumping, Ellen faced the wall again. She would've done it. She would've grabbed the gun or run for the door or done anything to escape. Even though she wasn't in restraints, she was trapped. Miss Waincross wouldn't make the mistake of putting her weapon down again. 'Why are you doing this to me?' Ellen asked shakily.

'You know too much now, my dear. You and your side-kick nearly unravelled the whole thing in a matter of days.

It's hardly quality work if a couple of amateur girls can crack it.'

'We're hardly amateurs or girls,' Ellen asserted, though they were indeed both those things. 'But that tree branch was a bit less—'

'Enough! I don't want to talk about that blasted tree branch ever again!' Miss Waincross cut her off. Ellen tracked Miss Waincross's shadow as it moved closer. Should she make a run for the window? Try to break it open?

Then she heard it, a soft metallic click. Miss Waincross had the gun cocked and ready to fire.

'Do not move, or this will be worse,' Miss Waincross ordered, 'for both of us. I do hate a mess.'

Time slowed. Ellen could hear her own uneven breaths. Then Miss Waincross's, short and shaky. Tensing every muscle in her body, Ellen leapt from her seat.

The gun went off.

39

PEARL

She ran faster than ever, her footsteps thudding loudly down the familiar route to Miss Waincross's office. Ellen would save her. Ellen could end all of this. She just had to get to her. Fast.

Skidding to a stop in front of the office door, Pearl panted for a few seconds, trying to gather her wits. She leant her head against the cool wood of the door and just as she made contact, it creaked open. There was no noise. The room was empty.

Pearl ran behind the desk, checked behind the door. The room wasn't large enough for someone to hide for long. Nothing. No one. She scanned the orderly desk. Nothing out of place. She threw open the two desk drawers – paper, pencils, envelopes. New envelopes. Stacks of them. She groaned. There had to be one little clue. Otherwise, how would she find Ellen? Dropping to all fours, she peered under the desk.

And there it was. Hiding under the front of the desk. Just behind the bin. Folded.

'Thank you, Ellen,' she whispered, and sprawled out to reach the paper.

It was a letter. From Dennis to Ellen. On first glance, it seemed normal. He was calling into the Waverlys' at half seven to talk about putting Pearl back in jail. *The weasel!* she thought, seeing red. Well, if that was his plan, she'd show him. Surprise him and prove him wrong before he had a chance to phone the police. With one last look around the room, Pearl shut the door and sped down the hall. The old grandfather clock in the foyer read 7.15. She had no time to lose.

'Wait! Pearl!'

Pearl skidded to a stop just inside the foyer. Mr St John ran to her, putting his hand over his heart as he caught his breath.

'What? I have to go. It's already almost seven thirty. Dennis left a note for Ellen. He's going to meet her at her billet to convince her I need to be in jail. I have to stop him.'

'I saw Ellen.' Mr St John was red-faced and panting. Pearl realized she had never seen him move this quickly before. 'By the garages. She and Miss Waincross were getting into a car. I called out to them, but neither looked my way.' He coughed loudly and before she could consider how inappropriate it was, Pearl reached up as far as she could and clapped him on the back. She simply didn't have time for him to work through his exercise-induced hacking right now. 'Pearl, it was *not* right. Miss Waincross didn't sign the car out. A guard tried to stop her and she kept driving. I have a horrible feeling about all of this.'

'You have to call the police,' she said. 'Now. Or head to the station. The spy could still be here, watching, so you can't alert anyone to our plans. But perhaps they can help secure the Park. Find the spy. I'll head to Ellen's billet. It's possible she was just getting a lift back home. With luck I can convince Dennis not to call the authorities.'

As she stepped outside the front door to the mansion, the weight of the situation hit her. Mr St John was correct. It was all *not right*. What if Ellen was in trouble? What if she and Miss Waincross were fleeing someone? The spy? What if they were in danger?

Rain pelted her face as she tore down the path to the gate. Her breaths coming in heaving bursts, Pearl knew she couldn't keep this pace up all the way to Ellen's billet. As she ran towards the gate, Reggie came out of his little building and she nearly collided with his solid frame.

'Hey now!' he called. 'Slow down there. What's the rush, eh?'

Pearl bent over, hands on knees, panting. Finally catching her breath, she looked up.

'I have to get to the Waverlys' house. Any chance you

have a car, um, and a driver?' Pearl blurted.

'In this weather?' He paused. 'Pearl, you're not even supposed to be here. Why don't you come into the shelter and wait for me to call my supervisor and we can straighten this whole thing out?'

'No time, Reggie. I have to go. My life depends on it, maybe Ellen's, too.' Pearl had no intention of letting him detain her. Not after all of this. 'You didn't see me, Reggie. They'll never know. You won't be blamed for anything. But I have to go . . . now!'

'Wait, wait!' Reggie called uneasily as she started jogging towards the road. 'You can't run there in this weather. You'll never make it. Can you ride a bicycle?'

'They say you never forget, right?'

40

ELLEN

The bullet hit the wall, splintering the plaster just beyond where Ellen crouched.

Miss Waincross snarled like an angry cat and strode towards Ellen, gun pointed. Just as Ellen was scanning the room, hoping for an easy exit she'd missed previously, there was a loud knock on the door. Miss Waincross froze where she stood, then put a finger to her lips.

'Not a sound,' she purred. In two steps, she had Ellen by the arm. She yanked her to her feet and pulled her to the door before lifting the latch and opening the door a crack.

'Hello Dennis,' Miss Waincross said smoothly.

Ellen's heart sank. What was he doing here? He was walking right into the fire. Ellen wanted to scream out a warning, but she could still smell gunpowder. She hoped he'd be cautious, at least, and that he could outsmart Miss Waincross.

Dennis stepped inside and shut the door firmly. He caught sight of Ellen, and the gun, and the whites of his eyes gleamed bright.

'Jesus, Dot— Miss Waincross. What are you doing to poor Ellen? Ellen, are you all right? Has she hurt you?' Dennis's hat dripped water on to the floor and he pulled it off, putting it over the key on the small table beside the door. The motion looked natural enough, like a husband returning from work, and Ellen wondered why he was familiar with this abandoned cottage. Clearly, he did not live here with his aunt.

Suddenly, the black cloud that had hovered so near to her since the war started, warning of the potential for horrific, awful things, was upon her, exploding with flashes of the truth as severe as bolts of lightning. She had been duped. Played. Such a fool.

Ellen looked to her captor and did her best to puff out her chest confidently. 'She won't hurt me. She can't muster the courage to make a straight shot. She's hardly who she claims to be, but you must've known that, as neither are you.'

At that, Miss Waincross laughed. Her eyes were focused and her arm steady. Everything that had seemed so ordered about her was chaotic - hair falling from its twist, forehead glistening with sweat. Even her Union Jack neck scarf was askew.

'I knew you weren't as thick as the others. Tell your

dear Ellen, Dennis, who I am to you. And who *you* are.'

'I don't know what has come over you, Miss Waincross, but this is no way to treat one of our valuable cribsters. Let her go before this has gone too far,' Dennis said, his voice higher-pitched than normal. He had both his hands out in front of him, palms forward, as if he could calm Miss Waincross somehow. His gaze was intense, like he was trying to drill something into her head without saying it outright. Ellen looked from one to the other. She couldn't be positive, but there was a familiarity there. You didn't try to communicate to a stranger with merely a look. No, Dennis *knew* Miss Waincross.

'It's already out of hand,' Ellen said with a nod towards the lady with the gun, 'don't you think?'

Dennis looked at her sympathetically. 'Miss Waincross, I would say this *has* got out of hand. Why don't you let Ellen come with me and we'll leave you alone? No one has to know about this, and,' he paused, 'I can take care of it.'

A shudder ran down Ellen's spine. The way he said 'take care of it' wasn't implying he'd drop her home. There was an edge to it, another meaning. Then it made sense. *I loved. I was betrayed. Oh, poor Richard*, she thought. He'd been killed by the man he adored. Pearl had been right. That was why Dennis had been conveniently on the road that morning. *He* placed the branch that caused the accident. Then he watched the young man he'd seduced die. Ellen's eyes welled. What a mess.

Dragging Ellen behind her, Miss Waincross side-stepped her way back into the small sitting room, placing both Ellen and the sturdy table between herself and Dennis. Although she couldn't feel it or see it, Ellen was aware of the gun hovering just behind her head. 'I am not giving her to you,' Miss Waincross said through her teeth. 'I let you *handle* the last one and see where it got us? It's a mess.'

'If you release her to me, we will go without a fuss. I won't call the authorities. I will leave you alone. I promise.' Dennis walked towards them slowly, inching each foot forward like a big cat stalking its prey. He held his hands in front of him, fingers spread wide, as if trying to calm a barking dog. Ellen watched him cautiously. He certainly didn't want to spend any more time with Miss Waincross than necessary, but Ellen could hardly fault him for that.

Miss Waincross tightened her grip on Ellen's arm and pulled her closer. Her breath smelt sour, like cigarettes and the sharp, spent tea leaves at the bottom of a cold pot. 'None of this is my fault,' she said, as if Ellen had asked for an explanation. Her voice was unhinged, panicked and Ellen pulled at her arm, trying to put more distance between herself and the weapon. 'I went along with *his* plans – I knew there were holes in them and sure enough! How else can you explain how quickly this all crumbled? I was foolish. Brainwashed.'

'Betrayed?' Ellen said quietly. Then, surprising even herself, she turned slightly and put out a trembling hand, palm up, towards Miss Waincross. In the pictures, she would have surrendered the gun, bowing her head and agreeing that Ellen was right. They'd wait for the police after restraining Dennis, and 'Dot' would tell her story while Ellen told hers, freeing Pearl from any false charges.

Instead, Miss Waincross pointed her weapon again and let out a sad, pitiful moan. She, too, was trapped.

'Never attempt to reason with a rabid dog,' Dennis quipped with a snort.

'Damn you, Dennis,' Miss Waincross spat, pointing the gun in his direction now.

Ellen gulped. Surrounded on all sides by danger, she swallowed down her fear and thought of Pearl. What crazy, daring, spontaneous thing would her friend do? Whatever it was, Ellen had to do it. And fast.

With one swift movement, Ellen wrenched her arm from her captor's grip. She put her hands under the heavy table and flipped it over, sending it crashing to the ground in front of Dennis. With the reflexes of a cat, Dennis leapt backwards. Then, without skipping a beat, he jumped over the broken table, yelling loudly as he charged at Miss Waincross. Almost paralysed with both fear and astonishment, Ellen scampered towards the door slower than she should've, unable to take her eyes off the ugly scene before her. Dennis wrestled Miss Waincross for her weapon, pulling at her hair while being whacked in the ear by the woman's free hand. They both screamed profanities at each other as Dennis rammed Miss Waincross against the wall, jostling the still-lit sconces. Then, as she scurried towards the door, Ellen stupidly tripped over an upended chair and went careening into the window, grabbing the frame of the blackout curtain as she went down. It ripped slightly as she fell, her arm, shoulder and side slamming into the wall as a result. As she righted herself quickly, Ellen made a break for the door, but froze when another gunshot echoed through the tiny room.

'Do not move, Ellen,' Dennis ordered. Gone was the friendly, caring tone of earlier. This man was not going to rescue her. No, this was a man who had just attacked his partner in crime and would think nothing of doing away with her too. She was, perhaps, in more danger now than she had been with Miss Waincross. Ellen turned slowly to face the man she had been besotted with.

He stood over Miss Waincross, who was crumpled on the floor and moaning. The gun was, once again, pointed at Ellen.

'Oh Dennis,' she gasped, her eyes on the steady, focused barrel of the gun. His eyes narrowed, his mouth a thin line. Ellen's heart dropped. This was the face of a man who would not hesitate to pull the trigger again.

41

ELLEN

Miss Waincross lay crumpled on the ground, a dark stain of blood spreading across her midsection. The woman had her hands feebly on the wound, but her head rested against the floor, eyes closed. She looked grey, even in the flickering yellow candlelight.

Dennis stood, gun in hand, Miss Waincross behind him. The gun was pointed at Ellen. The room smelt of sulphur, metal and dust. Ellen blinked against the flood of angry tears in her eyes, hoping Dennis did not misinterpret them as a sign of fear. Instead of feeling petrified, rage surged through her veins like a swollen river after a rainstorm. How dare he? Ellen squared her shoulders and looked directly into his deceptive, gorgeous eyes. Now they appeared steely and uncaring.

'You are not going to shoot me, Dennis,' she said as she took a step towards Miss Waincross, getting close enough to see Dennis's nostrils flaring with each breath he took. The struggle for the gun had tired him, but he did not let his aim waver. Ellen tried to ignore it as she glanced down at Pearl's former supervisor. The woman was still alive. Her breath was uneven and, every once in a while, she gurgled like a baby learning to drink from a cup. 'I am going to assess Miss Waincross's injuries. And you are going to let me.'

Dennis sidestepped slightly in response, but kept the gun pointed at her. Ellen tried to pay no mind, even as her heart practically leapt out of her chest with each frantic beat. Kneeling down, she leant over Miss Waincross, gently unwound the patriotic scarf and tried to apply pressure to the wound.

'What were you thinking?' Ellen exclaimed, looking up at Dennis while feebly trying to stem the flow of blood. 'Why would you want to kill her? Or me, for that matter? I thought I knew you.' Ellen took in a long breath, steadying herself before she finished her thought. 'Who *are* you?'

Dennis cocked his head to one side. 'I haven't changed, Ellen. I've always been me, true to who I am and what I believe. That has never been an act.'

'But a lot of you *was* an act, how . . .' She trailed off as, like the final letter in a successful crib, everything clicked into place. She saw, with the clarity of a film, what had happened and how blind she'd been to the truth. She also knew she had to keep Dennis talking long enough for

Pearl to rescue her. Because the tiny coded message she'd left for her friend back at Bletchley was her only hope now.

Dennis scoffed loudly but motioned for her to continue.

'You appealed to Richard's tendencies; you quickly diagnosed both his political and romantic leanings and devised how you could use both to your advantage. He transported your messages. It now makes sense why all the notes you left at my billet were typed. You couldn't risk anyone recognizing your unique, slanted handwriting. But when Miss Waincross told you Richard had been questioning the things left in his bag, well, you couldn't let that continue.' Although Ellen's entire body trembled, she managed to keep her voice steady, as if reading from a textbook. She could not show him her fear. Not now. 'You did the same to Miss Waincross – she was your contact inside Bletchley Park and had clearly fallen for you at some point. She had access to top-secret decodes and perhaps that's also why you started wooing me? You wanted the cribs?' Ellen quaked as she talked, every bit of her from her knees to the top of her head shaking. The idea that Dennis had blinded her with his good looks and charm was enraging. How dare he? The last thing Ellen ever wanted to be mistaken for was stupid, and here she was, looking the fool.

The gun was still pointed at her head. Oddly, the fact that she was potentially facing the last few minutes of her life only made her bolder. She wanted to get the truth out of him so she could spout it to the police with her last breath if need be. Keeping her hands clamped firmly on the blood-soaked scarf, she continued, 'You had no affection for me at all, did you? You saw someone you thought was weak and malleable, like Miss Waincross, but I wasn't, was I? I'll have you know, Dennis, you never would've made me a Nazi.'

Dennis's eyes grew wide and he erupted in laughter. 'Nazi? Oh no, no, no. Those clowns are absolutely rubbish at intelligence. No, Ellen – I come from a highly skilled and select group of fascists. We not only know how to not get caught, but – look at me – we're growing a movement! Right under the noses of the lords and ladies of this sad little country.'

'Fascists?' Ellen managed to croak. 'Nazis *are* fascists, Dennis. You're not above them at all. You're just as authoritative and oppressive and racist and—'

'All right, all right,' he said as casually as if she were telling him a friendly joke. Then his tone changed, getting chilly and stern. 'You can stop now. Understand?! Shut your bloody mouth!'

When Ellen did, pressing her lips together against an angry retort, he continued. 'You're a fool if you think the way the Allies are handling this war will suffice in changing the world for the better. They're not building a stronger race of people who can prosper and thrive. Look at all those who are riddled by disease or driven by unnatural and immoral desires. The slums! No one can think those people will rise to the top and help our country, especially without the leadership of a strong, sensible, intelligent individual.'

'That is you, I'm assuming?' Ellen said.

'You see, Ellen, when I was back at Cambridge and all the other fascist leaders in this country were blabbing about, trying to grow a movement, I went quiet. I gained supporters while all the other fools were arrested. Then, when the police were preoccupied with the war and the bumbling Nazi spies, my power surged. My plan is simple: give power and leadership to the new elite; the young, intelligent chaps working like dogs in universities with no reward because everyone is at the mercy of the old guard – the lords and ladies running the show and making the idiotic choices that are throwing this country to the dogs. Unlike the Nazis you're equating me with, I pay no mind to your religion or romantic leanings. And I'm the one selling the Germans the secrets, not the other way around. I'm in control, leading the irresistible surge. You could've benefited from my success, too, if you hadn't stuck your nose in where it didn't belong.'

'I was trying to find out who had murdered Richard. I wouldn't say that's doing anything wrong at all.' Ellen's voice had started to wobble. Her entire body was shaking, so she stayed kneeling. She was afraid of what would happen if she stood – both to her and Miss Waincross, whose breath was unsettlingly slow and shaky.

'Oh, but you were. I'd been hoping to get you on my side – think of how powerful we could've been together, with your brains and my vision?' Dennis undid the top button of his shirt and loosened his tie. A sheen of sweat glistened on his forehead. Ellen had never seen him in such disarray. It was shocking how quickly he went from Hollywood to unhinged.

'That's what you wanted me for? My mind?' Ellen couldn't help but feel flattered, even if Dennis was a crazed fascist murderer. He *still* wanted her? She hoped Pearl arrived quickly, because she wanted the pleasure of refusing him to his face . . . and to see him arrested, and live through it all, of course. 'Nothing else?'

'Well,' Dennis laughed, 'you are far more attractive than that sad sack you're trying to revive. And I saw potential in you from the moment we met. Not only because of your mind, but because of your unique way of thinking. You have feelings, but they're separate from your logical side. It could've worked so well for us, growing a movement and gaining power. You could still join me, Ellen. We could change the world.' Ellen shook her head in disgust. A bitter smile flashed across his face as he gestured to Miss Waincross's motionless form. 'No? I should've figured you'd be like her in the end. Perhaps you're not jealous, vindictive like she was. But you both have to go one way or another. So there we are. And now it's your turn, wouldn't you say?'

Ellen opened her mouth to speak, but nothing came out. What does one say when faced with the moment of death? Preparing for the worst, Ellen squeezed her eyes shut and tried to think of an escape. Only, there wasn't one. She was trapped.

42

PEARL

Turns out you don't ever truly forget how to ride a bicycle, though the first mile was a bit rocky. The seat was far too tall, her feet barely reached the pedals and the brakes were stiff and hard to press. The lashing rain saturated her completely by the time she'd passed the last of the houses. Still, she rode like her legs were on fire and they certainly felt like it as she rode up a short hill beyond the town.

As she rode, Pearl tried to piece together bits of the puzzle – a welcome distraction from the pain in her legs and lungs. She'd known something was off the moment she met Dennis. He was sneaky, slick, like a well-dressed weasel. Especially when he came to release her from custody. She'd heard his posh, smooth voice talking to the officer and knew she would not let him take her anywhere. She didn't trust him; it was as plain as that.

As she pedalled to the Waverlys' house, the smell of woodsmoke reassured her somewhat, squashing the nervous feeling that Ellen might not be inside. There was safety in that house. Though the house was dark, Pearl could practically feel the warmth from inside as she approached the front door. She knocked confidently, loudly, and hoped it would be her friend who answered the door.

'Shh!' ordered Mr Waverly as the door opened. 'You'll wake the baby and that's the *last* thing we need tonight.'

The hall was dark behind him. And quiet. Ellen hadn't rushed to the door. Dennis wasn't at her heels pleading with her. Pearl's breath caught. Something was wrong.

'Sorry, Mr Waverly. I was trying to find Ellen. She—'

'You and everyone else. That lad stopped by just a few minutes ago asking the same thing.'

'And what did you tell him?' Pearl asked impatiently. It was taking everything she had not to grab him by the collar and shake him to make him talk faster. Did he not realize this was unusual? Suspicious?

'I didn't have to say anything. A car passed just as we were talking, heading up towards Mill Road. He excused himself and followed it. Odd, since it's a dead end. There's nothing down there but an abandoned cottage.'

A chill ran down Pearl's spine at the words. *Dead end.*

'I asked the farmhand to round up the authorities and send them to the cottage. I'll stay here in case Ellen returns,' he said, concern in his voice.

Pearl spun on her heel towards Reggie's bike, ignoring Mr Waverly calling after her as she hopped on. Wind and rain slapped her in the face like a cold reminder of what was ahead and she heard Mr Waverly call out, 'Be careful!'

Once she was on Mill Road, Pearl allowed herself to crumble just a little, feeling fear tear through her, every bit as sharp as when she'd been taken away by the police. She let out a silent, racking sob, dropped her head, and squeezed her eyes against the driving rain. When she looked up, she spied a tiny glimpse of light at Mill Cottage and wiped her eyes. That bit of insecurity was done with. Now she needed to be strong, stealthy and clever. She needed to outsmart Dennis like Ellen would, and be ready for whatever lay ahead.

Pearl leant Reggie's bike against a tree several paces from the house. She didn't want anyone to know she was outside. Sticking low to the ground, she crept up to the window, trying her best to peer past what looked like a torn blackout curtain.

The scene inside was terrifying – Ellen on the floor next to an overturned table and what looked like Miss Waincross, only with blood everywhere. Ellen had blood on her hands, her skirt, and standing above both girls was Dennis – the creep – with a gun. *Figures*, Pearl thought, anger bursting through her like a surge of lightning. Clenching her teeth, she stepped back from the window, surveying the garden frantically. She saw a bicycle and car, both shiny and new, in the old barn and nothing much else of use.

'I just need a stick, a rock – anything!' she whispered to herself as she ran about like a crazed animal. Dashing into the barn, she saw it – a broken umbrella. It was long, the fabric was torn, but at the end of the handle was a shiny metal ball. Pearl nearly squealed, imagining it could do quite a bit of damage if swung just the right way.

With the umbrella in tow, Pearl ran around the back of the tiny cottage, looking for another way in. Though the back door looked solid, she had no choice but to hope it was unlocked. Biting her lip, she wiped rain from her forehead and gripped the top of the umbrella in one hand. With the other, she quietly turned the knob and, with a wave of great relief, swung the door open.

43

PEARL

The tiny kitchen stank of mildew and likely a dead mouse or two. There were bottles in the sink and clustered in a corner, as if someone had made an attempt to tidy up. But the room was, thankfully, dark. A trickle of light flickered down the short hall from the sitting room. The door to the one bedroom was shut, so Pearl made the decision to leave it for now. It was a gamble, but she'd seen Ellen and Dennis only a moment earlier. She needed to get Ellen away from that snake.

It was hard to walk on the creaky floorboards without making a sound, but somehow Pearl did, walking on her toes at the edges of the worn hall. Finally, umbrella in both hands like an upside-down cricket bat, she edged into the doorway of the sitting room. Dennis, thankfully, had his back to her. And although Ellen's expression remained mostly the same, Pearl could tell her friend had noticed her. Ellen's lip had twitched. Just once. But that was enough.

Tables and chairs were strewn about as if a herd of cattle had trampled through the place. Dust hung in the yellow lamplight, which flickered and cast eerie shadows on the dirty plaster walls. Miss Waincross was motionless at Ellen's side, with Dennis a few paces away, closer to the door. He had the gun in one hand while he talked. She hardly recognized him – his perfect hair ruffled, his suit jacket dusty and torn at the elbows. He was rattling on about something – what a pity it was that Ellen had gone against him – when Pearl heard a clicking noise. The gun was cocked. With Miss Waincross already wounded, possibly dead, the bullet was meant for Ellen.

Without a second thought, Pearl ran forward, bringing the heavy metal ball at the end of the broken umbrella down on to Dennis's skull with a rather loud crack. Surprised at herself, she stood back and watched while he fell.

'Hit him again!' yelled Ellen.

'What? Are you mad?' Pearl responded. She despised the man, but she didn't want to kill him.

'Don't let him get up!' Ellen screamed. She was frantic, her eyes wide with fear.

Pearl dropped the umbrella and snatched up the gun, which had fallen from his hand. It was surprisingly heavy, but easy enough to keep aimed at his stunned body.

44

ELLEN

She thought she heard wheels on gravel outside but didn't take her eyes off Dennis until a loud crash came from the front door. Within seconds, it had been reduced to splinters and uniformed men flooded the tiny cottage, weapons drawn. Ellen put her hands up innocently, but one of the officers had to physically remove the gun from Pearl's shaking hands. Once Dennis was in handcuffs, Pearl ran to Miss Waincross and pressed something – oh god, her favourite cardigan! – into the wound in her stomach. A wave of nausea and fatigue and emotion came over Ellen. It was too late. Miss Waincross was dead. Ellen leant against the wall, placing her palms flat against the cool plaster to try to steady herself.

No one put restraints on her. Once they assessed her and confirmed she was all right, they ushered the two girls into the hallway. Pearl wiped her bloody hands on a rag, scrubbing obsessively. Ellen looked at her own stained hands. The blood, Ellen feared, would never come out. *Out damned spot*, she thought, but she didn't dare say that to her friend. Ellen's heart rate gradually returned to something one might consider normal. Finally, one quiet policeman drove them back to Bletchley Park.

The two sat on the bottom step of the grand staircase while Mr St John and others talked to the officer who had returned them. Ellen took in a shuddering breath and tears sprang to her eyes. Wiping them quickly on her bloodied shirt cuff, she watched her friend jump up as Mrs Patterson walked through the door. While Pearl embraced her mother, Mr St John approached the staircase.

'You did it,' he said. He was smiling, the first time she had ever seen him smile so broadly. He pointed at the chaos around them with the mouthpiece of his pipe. 'When I got to the police station, they informed me Mr Waverly had called about suspicious activity on the road to Mill Cottage. I rode along, filling them in as we drove. I wasn't sure what we would find, but I heard you stood your ground and never crumbled.' He blinked at Ellen for a moment, his eyes more awake than she'd ever seen them. 'I am sorry for being so giddy. I know finding not one but two spies in a highly secret and secure war office is not cause for amusement, but Ellen, I cannot remember a time I have been so proud of the efforts of any one person at the Park, let alone two! I am gobsmacked. You and

Pearl outwitted the enemy!'

'How did you know to trust Pearl, sir? After all, she had been arrested and you believed she was guilty,' Ellen said weakly.

'Her message to Richard. She told me about it.'

'The letter? I thought it was in his bag.' Again, Ellen leant her back against the wall.

'It was.' Mr St John beamed. 'They found the bag in the field behind Pearl's house. Apparently, they'd searched her home, to no avail, but when the bag was found beyond their cottage, they brought Mrs Patterson in for questioning. Luckily, I intervened before they left the gates and took the letter,' Mr St John said, thrusting an envelope in her face. 'Here. Do you see why I doubted her guilt?'

Ellen unfolded the letter.

Richard,

I have done what I said I would. All seems well.

I am glad you trust me to handle this. I worry about you, though I know you'd tell me not to. You see, I thought there was something more between us, something that would make it all right for me to worry. Perhaps I was reading into what I saw at the pub. We need to talk.

I want you to know you can trust me, more than anyone else, with your secrets. If they're bad or good.

Our friendship is stronger than this.

Sincerely,

Pearl

PS – IS yOur Mother hOme? Never mind. Ant & your brother found something I need. Gladly I'll drop your notes on Sunday when Ellen & I leave the park to meet some girls.

Ellen brought the note closer to her nose. The letters in the postscript were so oddly spaced it was hard to read them. Also, it did not make much sense with the strange capitalization at the start, but then something clicked into place.

'Hang on,' she said. 'I'm assuming you have a ruler?'

'I thought you'd never ask,' Mr St John said giddily. He produced a small steel rule from his breast pocket.

Ellen placed the paper on the wall, lining the ruler up with the first letter, then the second, and then the message cleared up. The squished letters in between were fillers. She only cared about the letters that fell on the inch marks.

Someone may be using you to deliver msgs

'I doubt the poor sap ever realized what she was saying,' Mr St John said sadly.

'No,' Ellen said. 'He did.' She dug in her pocket for Richard's last message, the one he'd handed to Antony.

346

'Here. He was apologizing to someone that day he was killed. Maybe even Pearl. He probably knew his time was up. It was just a matter of when. The other message was not in his handwriting, but used the same code and' – Ellen dug in her pockets for the message she'd found hidden in Richard's room – 'was likely one he was meant to pass along. See?'

She pulled out the note, on which she'd written lightly below each word 'CASTLE BROMWICH AERO N TWENTY EIGHT'.

'It's good this never got delivered,' she said with a sigh.

Mr St John nodded, taking the note. 'If this had reached the Nazis, they would've had the coordinates needed to bomb one of our critical aircraft factories. Fine work today, Ellen. You have changed the course of history. Remember that always, even if this remains a secret for ever.' Then, Mr St John took the decoded paper, asked if he could take it to the police, and disappeared down the hall, closely followed by Mrs Patterson. Ellen couldn't take her eyes off Pearl, who was slumped on the same hard bench they'd sat on the first night Ellen had arrived at Bletchley. Ellen pushed off the wall and walked as steadily as she could over to her. Sitting down, she timidly put her arm around her friend. For once, it felt completely right. Pearl melted into her arm a bit and sniffled loudly. Finally, she looked up.

'You didn't kill her, did you?'

'Lord, no,' Ellen said.

'I didn't think so.' Pearl's nose was red and her eyes watery. She let out a loud sob and then crumbled again. 'Tell me what happened,' she mumbled into her skirt.

'I came to look for her, thinking she'd be able to help you, but saw the police arresting your mother instead. I stumbled out and there Miss Waincross was, waiting outside. I told her I'd come looking for her and didn't think anything of it when she suggested we talk in her office. Still, I left you a note. Just in case.'

'I got it,' Pearl said, looking up. 'Thank you for making it easy, for once.'

Ellen couldn't help but smile. 'I thought you might need something you could decode on the run.'

'I did.' Pearl sat silently for a bit, which Ellen appreciated. After a few moments, Pearl nudged Ellen with her shoulder. 'Go on.'

Ellen told Pearl everything from the time she was arrested – from getting kidnapped by Miss Waincross to when Dennis appeared and shot her former supervisor. 'They were both guilty, Pearl, both spies. Even Dennis.' She hesitated slightly. 'You were right about him.'

'Ugh,' Pearl said. 'I'm sorry I was.'

'They'd been working together. Dennis killed Richard. But Miss Waincross was behind a lot of bad things, too.'

'She framed me, didn't she?'

'You and Antony. They are fascists – Dennis and Miss

Waincross. Selling secrets to the Germans. Oh Pearl, I've never ever been so frightened.' Ellen started shaking again just thinking of it all.

'It's *all over*,' Pearl said, and Ellen felt the warmth of her friend's body against hers. It was comforting. 'Are you all right, Ellen? And, erm, do you forgive me?'

Ellen sighed deeply and wiped her face with her cuff. While she desperately wanted a couple of heavy blankets, an empty room and a cup of tea, she realized that for once she wanted to be with her friend rather than be alone. This was the first time ever she hadn't needed solitude to regroup from a stressful event, which was surprising because there were likely few things more stressful than what they'd both been through. Perhaps it was because she'd gone through this with Pearl, that they'd faced every challenge together. 'Silly Pearl. Of course I do! Do you forgive me? I never meant to hurt you and I'll never make eyes at another man if it ruins our friendship. I couldn't cope with it. You're my first true friend and that's the most valuable thing I have.'

Pearl let out a long breath. 'Thank you. I get so angry. Jealous. It's silly. But I feel the same. Mum is right; I need to think before I react. I was so worried you'd hate me for ever.'

'You really saved me, Pearl,' Ellen said, her body slumping into her friend even more. 'When things got really scary after Dennis shot Miss Waincross and I wanted to roll into a little ball and cry, I thought about what you'd do, how you'd act quickly before thinking of every possible outcome. It worked.'

Pearl's cheeks flushed. 'This is going to sound silly, but even though we were quarrelling and I was unsure whether you were going to forgive me at the end of it all, it still felt like you were right alongside me, telling me what to do.'

'It does not sound silly,' Ellen answered. 'After all, once I found out you'd been freed, I knew you'd come looking for me.'

'Dennis came to free me after I'd been arrested . . .' Pearl said slowly.

'I sent him,' Ellen interrupted. 'He has – had – more status than me. I knew they'd listen to a smart man with a posh accent.'

'That's how he got to where he is today, eh?' Pearl said with a laugh. 'He used his good looks and his education to convince people to spy for him?'

'Precisely,' Ellen agreed, then buried her face in her hands. 'Pearl, he pulled the wool over my eyes so easily. How could I not see him for what he is?'

Pearl patted Ellen's back lightly. 'It's all right. You figured it out eventually.'

'I was so enamoured of Dennis and kept ignoring all the warning signs. He knew just what to say . . .' Ellen felt so foolish. So ashamed. 'Feelings. I'm so embarrassed I let them take over the logic of everything.' She felt warmth rush up her neck to her cheeks. 'I am usually so good at assessing people. I have a system, you know . . .'

'I know, you goose. It's fabulous. Why do you think I trust your first impressions so much? It's a talent,' Pearl said with a smile.

Ellen couldn't help but return her friend's smile, proud for once of the strange quirks that she'd been told for so long to suppress. Perhaps her mum didn't know everything about social interactions. Then she remembered Dennis. 'But the system didn't work. Not with Dennis, anyway.'

'Your system wasn't broken. Dennis seduced Richard too. Likely others,' Pearl said softly. 'In spite of his bravado, Richard wanted love, just like the rest of us.'

'I'm sorry,' Ellen said haltingly. She was sorry she'd allowed her process to break down, but even more sorry that her friend was hurting. That alone made her wonder how necessary her system was any more. She'd trusted her gut with Pearl, after all, and that hadn't turned out half bad.

'It's all right, I suppose,' Pearl said, waving away Ellen's apology with her hand, not wanting to delve into the details. Richard's inclination one way or another would die with him.

Ellen continued, holding up her hand: 'Richard may have made a mistake, but he was trying to fix it all at the end. I decoded the messages. Pearl, Richard was sorry. He was aware of his mistake.'

Pearl gulped. 'He knew he was going to die?'

Ellen sighed. 'He knew he'd been betrayed.'

'Perhaps he felt loved for a while. Maybe not when he died, but for a time. That would make me happy at least, that he was happy,' Pearl said, which surprised Ellen. Pearl had always been one to curse her emotions. Ellen wondered what had brought about this change of heart. Perhaps losing one friend and seeing a gun turned on another had softened her a bit.

'He did well, Pearl. In the end, his clues helped us solve this and I feel awful having doubted him,' Ellen reassured her friend. 'Besides, he did feel love from you. It was a different kind of love than you intended, but it was love nonetheless.'

Pearl nodded. 'You know, it's nice to feel understood and loved, especially now when everything is so uncertain and scary. It's not the same, but I'd feel lost without my friendships – with you, with Fran, even with Ant . . .'

Ellen thought it curious Fran was on the list, but nodded all the same because she felt the same way. 'I suppose that'll be the best thing that comes out of this time, won't it? The friends we come to know.'

Pearl gave Ellen's shoulder a gentle squeeze and they sat quietly for a bit. Uniformed officers walked briskly by, oblivious of two girls on the bench who had, together, outwitted two very dangerous spies. Ellen rubbed her eyes, which were dry and tired. 'I have so many questions,' she said finally.

'We may never know the full story of what happened tonight, and no one will know what we did, either. Ever. Does that bother you, Ellen?'

Ellen shrugged. 'Of course. In a mystery novel, we'd go into the sitting room with everyone involved and go through the murders minute by minute. That will never happen here, just as I'll never know what is happening in the next hut over, let alone the details of the espionage that took place here. But I suppose eventually Bletchley will be a secret we swept into the back of the wardrobe, when the war is over. It will all disappear, because of the Secrets Act. We will have to forget it all, whether we truly understand what we've done or not.'

'I'll never forget you,' Pearl said quietly, and squeezed Ellen's shoulder.

Ellen's eyes flooded with tears. 'Nor I you. I don't expect they'll make us give up our friendships.'

'I won't, even if they try.'

'Agreed. We will always be friends,' Ellen said solemnly. Ellen leant forward to look her friend in the eye. 'You know what Mr St John said? He said we changed history today. For ever. Is that not amazing?'

Pearl shrugged. 'We have so much more to do.'

'Yes! Of course. No matter what happened here, there

is still a war on. But we need to be proud of this one moment. No one can know of it except us. No one ever will, but it is our moment. Right now. Let's be proud for now, all right?'

Pearl blinked rapidly, then smiled slightly. 'All right. We did it. We solved a great mystery.'

'Part of one. But yes, I suppose we did.'

They sat on the bench for a while until a police officer came to collect them for questioning. Then they went home to their beds and set the dials on their alarm clocks for seven, knowing they had to be back at the Park for an early shift.

The war went on and things got worse and work continued to be exhausting and challenging. People died – people they knew – and they simply worked harder, knowing they were somehow making an impact. There was also something else driving them: the knowledge they had done something extraordinary together. They'd keep doing it as long as it was asked of them, because they knew they could change history.

Eventually, Ellen was transferred to another posting, near enough that she and Pearl still met up when they had the same days off, but far enough that they often sent letters. In code, of course. Ellen missed her friend terribly but was so busy at Beaumanor Hall that the time between letters and visits flew by quickly. There was a long period where they did not see each other – the last, tense months of the war, where their schedules simply did not allow – but they were able to meet up on 8 May 1945, VE Day, which marked the end of the horrible war in Europe. When they finally saw each other across the crowded street in Bletchley, Ellen smiled so hard her cheeks hurt as she watched Pearl weave through the masses, surprisingly dragging Fran Farland behind her.

They hugged and didn't talk of anything important – certainly not Dennis and nothing about poor Fran, beyond Pearl whispering, 'If you say something about him, I'll clobber you. I don't understand it either, but he is so good' – but that was all right. Nothing that happened during those months at Bletchley Park was as important as the friendship that had grown between them. A friendship they would most certainly have for the rest of their lives.

HISTORICAL NOTE

I was inspired to write this book after visiting Bletchley Park with my family as a mostly ignorant tourist. I was shocked to learn that about three quarters of the workers at Bletchley were women. Most returned to their normal lives after the war, never mentioning a lick of what they'd done until the government declassified wartime information in the mid-1970s. After doing more research, I learnt that these highly intelligent women were often young adults, frequently working horrible hours without ever knowing whether their efforts amounted to anything. These girls were fiercely proud of their work. After hearing stories about the fun they had, the friends they made and the rich memories they kept secret, I knew I needed to write about this amazing place.

While Ellen and Pearl were inspired by actual young women who worked at Bletchley Park, they have been, like many events, places and details in the book, changed for the sake of the novel. Hut locations were changed to facilitate their promotion under Mr St John, distances were adjusted and entire streets were created. Ellen and Pearl are younger than most employees at Bletchley Park, but not by a lot. While most workers were over eighteen, I read about a fourteen-year-old messenger working there, and figured it was all right to take some liberties with their ages. Also, the spies. While there was some espionage at Bletchley, I definitely enjoyed expanding that quite a bit. That said, I did my best to stay loyal to the history where possible, and I take responsibility for any historical inconsistencies, intended or not.

I'd like to thank the historians at Bletchley Park for answering my endless emails about details of everything from the huts to the furniture and am grateful for the wealth of information found in the museum and on their website. I'm completely indebted to Jane Rosen, a librarian at the Imperial War Museum, who generously reviewed an early draft of this novel for historical accuracy. I spent the most amazing day in the museum's research rooms, reading letters and personal accounts of men and women who were called to serve their country.

Finally, some of you may have had questions about Ellen's personality, her assessment process and difficulty forming friendships. While I created Ellen as Ellen, if she were alive today her neurodivergence might be considered autistic. However, because there was no such diagnosis or language in 1941, she is never defined by her quirks or behaviour. Thank you to Lizzie Huxley-Jones for providing the sensitivity read that helped make Ellen as rich and real on the page as she always has been in my mind.

ACKNOWLEDGEMENTS

At some point in early 2020, I submitted *The Secrets Act* during the Chicken House Open Coop submissions window. Then, the world fell apart and I forgot about it. Which made it even more astounding when they chose me as a writer to be mentored. Thank you to the amazing Chickens – Barry, Rachel L, Rachel H, Laura, Jazz, Esther, Elinor, Olivia, Sarah and Laura Smythe – for seeing the potential in this book. I'm forever grateful to Kesia for being the most patient, insightful and encouraging editor imaginable; I cannot thank you enough for challenging me as a writer even when I told you it was too hard. You were always right.

Thank you to my wonderful agent, Lucy, who understood this book from day one. I am so lucky to have your support, advice and outstanding editorial eye and I'm thrilled to be a part of the PFD family.

There are two people who probably should have their names alongside mine on the cover. Brenda and Kevin, my invaluable 5 a.m. critique group. This book is as much yours as it is mine. You are the *best* literary midwives. I couldn't have done it without you.

To all my writer friends who have read drafts, offered advice and kept me on track: Kelly, Michelle, Karen and Beth. Thank you for listening to me complain, nodding understandingly when I told you it sucked and encouraging me to keep writing.

Thank you to my Dublin crew for the walks, coffee, cocktails and sanity breaks: Sarah, Kristen, Phill, Anna, Abby. And to my remote support team: Colleen, Jesse, Staci, David, Renee, Tory. Your texts and Zoom calls have kept me mostly sane through this whole process.

Thank you to my parents for always encouraging my passion for reading and introducing me to the books I still love today. To my sister and best friend, to my gorgeous nephew and fabulous brother-in-law; thank you for believing in me even when I did not.

Ryan, you've gotten me through the many downs of my publishing journey and are still here, reading my drafts and insisting they're good even when we both know they're rubbish. Thank you for never letting me quit.

Finally, thank you to my girls. When I first visited Bletchley Park ages ago, I knew I had to tell the story of the strong young women who worked there. I wanted to make sure that you, and girls everywhere, knew that you have the power and intelligence to change history, just like the real Ellens and Pearls of Bletchley Park.